THE CELL BLOCK PRESENTS…

UNDERWORLD ZILLA

Published by: The Cell Block™

The Cell Block
PO BOX 1025
RANCHO CODOVA, CA 95741

IG @mikeenemigo
Facebook /thecellblockofficial
Website: thecellblock.net

Send comments, reviews, interview and business inquiries
to: info@thecellblock.net

CONTENTS

DEDICATION

This book is for Norma Iris Rivera and Sandra Faye Williams for believing in me when no one else did.

Also...

I thank God, the Orishas, spirits, and fallen soldiers. To every ghetto, from Oak Park, to Alton Park, to Campo Rico, to Green Wood. Thank you for molding me into the man I am today.

This is for Stephanie-Lorraine (my heart) and Yomara (my strength).

Brody, thanks for the typewriter... I had a nine and my nigga had a forty-five...

To Mike Enemigo and the rest of the team at The Cell Block. Thanks for giving me the opportunity to share myself with the rest of the world.

To all my baby mammas: I love you! I know it's hard raising them kids by yourself, but keep at it, they're our future.

Jose, Alize-Marie, Jomarita, Dante, Dezy, you my Angels! Don't ever forget that!

Much love and respect, Guru

DEVILS & DEMONS PLAYLIST

Sleep Walking, Mozzy

Momma We Made It, Mozzy

Beautiful Struggle, Mozzy

Finding Myself, Mozzy

Catch the Sun, Lil Baby

Real Nigga Shit, Celly Ru

Gold Roses, Rick Ross

One of Mines, Mozzy

OMG, RJMr.LA

Revenge is Promissed, Philthy Rich

Roller Coaster Ride, Boosie

One Thing, Kevin Gates

Too Long, Yella Beezy

Up 1, Yella Beezy

Woah, Lil Baby

CHAPTER ONE

Friday... January...

Alize's knuckles turned white as she squeezed the steering wheel of her 2016 Chevy Malibu. She was speeding twenty miles over the seventy-five mile-per-hour speed limit, all trying to make it to another custody hearing at the Orlando District of Family Courts.

All the hard work she put in over the last four years was on the verge of unraveling. The painful frustration she felt was only surpassed by the blinding rage that she harbored for the system. Specifically, the people in it who were responsible for separating her from her son.

Almost half a decade had passed, and she could still hear Shawn's pleas echoing through her mind; "No, Mommy! Nooo!" Please, Mommy... nooo! The memories of that day burned her soul. If only she would've listened to her baby. Why hadn't she listened to her own intuition? It was a question that had plagued her conscience every day for the last four years.

Up until that point, Shawn's father hadn't wanted

anything to do with the boy. Then, after eighteen months of single-parenting, Alize's ex started showing up wanting to take his son on the weekends. Everyone told her that boys needed their father, so she had no qualms when it came to allowing her baby to spend quality time with his daddy. Yet, that last visit would forever haunt her thoughts; her baby had begged her not to let him go, but she refused to listen.

Even though that specific day stayed permanently etched in her memory, the rest became a blur. A series of restraining orders, court hearings, lawyers, and judges. All subsequent to the ultimate loss of her eighteen-month-old son...

As she sped along the highway, her thoughts were disrupted by her vibrating cell phone. She searched her rear-view mirror for highway patrol before reaching into the center console for her phone.

In truth, she was too stressed out to speak to anyone. She was already fifteen minutes late for her court hearing. Alize didn't have a choice, though. She was a business woman on a mission.

In order for her to accomplish this mission, she needed a lot of money. And the only way she'd be able to obtain that type of revenue was by answering her calls.

After picking up her phone and looking into its screen, Alize immediately recognized the picture that popped up. Nirobi. A regular customer. She activated the call, then put the iPhone to her ear. "What's up, dude?"

"Hey, Red, what's crackin'? I know it's early, but I need you right now."

"I ain't doin' nothin'," answered Ze, while

dangerously cutting off another driver. "I'm in traffic, on my way outta town."

"What?! You're killin' me, Red. I'm losing money every minute I don't got work–"

"For real, Nirobi! You're really sweatin' me like this? Nine times outta ten, all you want is a pound. And, chances are, you're probably short on the cash! So, stop sweatin' me! I'll be there when I get there!"

"Man, Red, what's wrong wit' you?" asked Nirobi, sounding as if his ego was hurt more than anything else. "You're trippin'."

"Nothing's wrong. Listen, I'm just a lil busy right now. I got a lot going on. I got you, alright? Just hold on to the money, I'll call you when I get back to Clearwater."

Alize tossed her phone on the passenger seat. She knew she shouldn't have snapped like that, but she couldn't help it. Then she heard a siren chirp. The sound came from a highway patrol car she had sped past while talking to Nirobi. Her thoughts quickly went towards the trunk... she suddenly remembered the pound of marijuana she had put back there the day before.

"Damn it!" she yelled at her windshield as she slammed her fist into the steering wheel. A felony possession charge was the last thing she needed. On top of that, she was definitely going to miss her court hearing.

Alize pulled over and went through the motions of a routine traffic stop. It took all of her self-control not to break down when the officer handed her the hundred- and seventy-five-dollar speeding ticket. But the moment he stepped away and her window was safely rolled up, she let the tears flow. The tough exterior of a woman in control was gone. The war she was fighting had become too much for her. For a woman who had matured in the streets, Alize thought she had seen it all, done it all, and felt it all. Yet, the agony of losing her only child ate at her soul to no end.

It was nine-thirty on a Friday morning. The custody hearing had been set for nine a.m. and Alize was parked on the side of the highway, forty-five minutes outside of Orlando. To all the other commuters travelling along Interstate 4, the tinted-out Chevy on the side of the road was just another example of what happens when you disregard the speed limit. However, on the inside, behind the safety of darkened glass, sat a broken-hearted woman crying over broken dreams that were caused by a broken system...

CHAPTER TWO

Talton lifted his arm to look at his big-faced timepiece. Realizing how late it was getting, he picked up the pace. Strip clubs in Clearwater closed at two in the morning. It was already fifteen past eleven. He was in the bathroom of the two- bedroom duplex that he shared with his pregnant girlfriend. The fights between the two had become more intense over the last several weeks. Talton refused to stop going to strip clubs, and Cita was tired of being left alone at night.

He double checked the lock on the door before stepping into the bathtub and opening the window. The screen didn't want to come off, so Talton punched a hole just big enough for a shopping bag filled with clothes to fit through it. He had already showered, and Cita braided his hair earlier in the day. So, now that his clothes were safely outside, all he needed to do was come up with a plausible excuse to leave the house.

Talton, or Gangsta, as he preferred to be called, had been religiously frequenting strip clubs for the last three months. Not necessarily spending a lot of money, yet definitely investing too much time. The drama he was forced to deal with after a night at the clubs wasn't worth the few hours of down time he'd get, but he didn't care. It was almost as if he was searching for something.

He couldn't explain what enticed him to leave his pregnant girl at home every night. It certainly wasn't the need for sex, or companionship. Talton was an attractive, light-skinned brother with long hair and a muscular build. He made his money in the dope game, and he was good at his profession. Therefore, he stayed in new clothes and expensive jewelry. Finding willing participants for his sexual endeavors had never been a problem.

Talton only had two friends in the whole state of Florida. At the moment, they were both in his living room watching the Boston Celtics play the Los Angeles Lakers on his sixty-inch flat screen. It probably would've been easier for him to make his exit if his comrades weren't parked on his cream-colored couches, looking like they were ready for a music-video shoot. The whole scene was just too obvious, but there was no way around it.

Cita was also in the living room; silently perched on one of the love seats, puffing on a Newport. It was hard to imagine that she had been carrying Talton's baby for the last eight months. Her figure didn't show it, and she was as sexy as ever.

She was an exotic specimen of a woman. Her long black hair was a beautiful contrast against her porcelain skin. She had deep blue eyes and a mouth filled with diamonds and gold. She looked Arabian, and her stare had a hypnotic effect on men just as well as women. Knowing this, she never failed to utilize her God-given assets.

Cita wasn't accustomed to dealing with men like Talton. For as long as she could remember, she had been able to manipulate every man she ever came into contact with. Cita used men as tools, never allowing herself to fall in love. What threw her off about Talton was that he was unpredictable. She knew that she had a strong hold over him, yet there was something inside of him that she couldn't tame.

In her short time with him she had exercised all of her tactics. From psychological manipulations to sex. Nevertheless, there had always been a large part of him that she couldn't seem to capture. This vexed her, but it also motivated her to stay with him. To Cita, it was a game. A game where she had finally met a worthy opponent. Ergo, her main objective was to conquer this man. The rest was collateral damage.

Cita was just as smart as she was sexy. But she did have her weaknesses. One was that she loved sex, and the other was that she was a control freak. Sex with Gangsta was outstanding. However, the fact that she couldn't domesticate him rained on her proverbial parade.

She even though the pregnancy would give her the upper hand that she longed for. Yet, the closer she got to her due date, the more distant he became. She knew he adored children by the way he fawned over his niece and nephew. But lately, she had started fearing that she had miscalculated when she had decided to stop taking her birth control pills.

Cita was sure of one thing, though. She wasn't going to end up like her twin sister, living in a trailer park with three kids and no baby daddy. Before she let that happen, she'd break Talton for everything he had. But then again, that was the plan anyway.

Talton stepped out the bathroom wearing a pair of jean shorts and a white tank top. On his chest sat a platinum medallion with the letters OP hanging from a diamond-studded chain. Only one other necklace like it existed. Gangsta never took it off. It was a gift from his older brother, Anthony, who owned the only other replica.

When he entered the living room, Talton gave his friends a look that said, "Get up! Let's go!" But out loud he said, "What's good, y'all? You ready to go?"

Both Mike and B.A. jumped up, but not fast enough to dodge Cita's reaction.

"Where the hell you think you're going?!"

"We're gonna go get some beer and cigarettes," replied Talton. "Is that cool wit' you?"

Cita stood up and stepped towards Talton, who was on his way to the front door behind his friends. "You must really think I'm stupid! I know you got something planned, and I'm tired of this shit! I've been left here way too many times to fall for this bullshit."

Knowing that another domestic dispute would stall their escape, B.A. decided to step in. "Come on, ma. Look at what this nigga's wearing. You got me fucked up if you think I'm going anywhere with this cat dressed like that. Stop being so paranoid, we're only going to the–"

"I don't wanna hear it, B.A.! He does this type of shit every night, and I'm tired of it!"

Then Mike stepped in; "Yeah, Cita, stop trippin'. We'll have your daddy back in less than fifteen minutes."

White Mike was the most level-headed one out of the trio. Cita knew this, yet he only seemed to anger her even more. "Both of y'all need to stay out of this. Talton, I'm not playing with you. If you walk out that door, and don't come back in fifteen minutes, there's gonna be problems! I'm tired of sitting in this house, night after night, while you're out there trickin' with stripper hoes! I'm not playing with you, Talton!"

"I got you, baby. I'll be right back," Talton lied, while ushering his crew outdoors. Even after he was outside and the door was shut, he could still hear Cita's tirade.

"...I'm not playing with you, Talton! When I have this baby, you'll be the one watching him while I run the streets..."

A few minutes later, Talton was in the back seat of B.A.'s box Chevy, changing into his new Gucci outfit while his associates sat in the front, laughing at his situation. Someone lit a blunt, quickly filling the cabin with weed smoke as they headed to the strip club.

CHAPTER THREE

The outside of Show Girls was a spectacle of sorts. It was hard to miss the brightest lit club on the busiest street in Clearwater. All of the windows to this house of iniquity were tinted and bordered with the same pink neon lights that illuminated the large billboard at the top of the building.

To some, the bright neon sign depicting one dancer spanking another was the promise of a good time; an invitation to come in, and escape their dreary lives. For others, it was an eye sore, an abomination. Nevertheless, to the women who worked within the walls of this establishment, it was the source of revenue that paid for their livelihood.

For Talton and his crew, Show Girls was a place to relax after a long day of hustling. The walls were lined with open booths so partygoers could sit with their group and enjoy the atmosphere. The stage sat against the back wall, with the bar next to it. And, off to the side, across from the bar were secluded booths for the private lap dances. Black lights provided just enough light to enhance the average pair of beer goggles, making the experience slightly surreal. All in all, Show Girls was a place to relax at. Exactly what Gangsta and his friends had set out to do that night.

The thugged-out trio were in their usual booth; smelling like expensive weed and brand-new clothes. They were in the process of enjoying their Friday night when the DJ decided to change the whole vibe. He changed the music from a Pit Bull club banger to a 1970's AC/DC rock song. All of a sudden, the lights throughout the club started flashing. "Highway to Hell" was blaring through the speaker system, and the DJ started yelling over the microphone:

"Ohhh yeaaah! Show Girls is on fire tonight, boys! We've got a very special lady for all you hard-working pervs. So, I want you guys to pull out your tens and twenties for Show Girl's very own, Red Devil! Get ready to taste the ultimate experience of dominance! This lady ain't playing, boys. Say hello to Red Devil!"

For a split second, the club went completely dark; the music stopped, and the lights went out. Then, someone turned on the spotlight, centering it on the most alluring woman Talton had ever laid eyes on. Red Devil was dressed in all black, from head to toe. She had on stiletto boots, and an extremely tight dominatrix outfit, whip and all, and small devil horns atop her head.

Despite the stage smoke that was engulfing the stage, everyone could see that she had the smoothest legs in the club. She also had the derriere of a black woman, but her skin was milky. Her eyes were apple green, and her hair was an uncontrollable bushel of fire.

Talton was awestruck by the scene that was playing out. Getting up from his table, unnoticed by his partners who were currently flirting with two other dancers, Talton made it to the stage just in time to catch the leather vest Red had thrown into the crowd, causing her to advert her attention towards him. They both made eye contact, and in that exact moment in both of their lives, everyone else ceased to exist. All time had frozen. Red was taking in what she thought was either a light-skinned brother, or a tanned Puerto Rican. And Talton was staring at the vision of a seductive demon.

In that moment, their souls connected as one. All of Alize's unbearable problems retired, and Talton had the unshakable feeling that he had finally found what he'd been searching for. Nevertheless, their conjugated peace only lasted a few seconds before Red had to succumb to the crowd.

Talton saw all that he needed to see. He wanted the one with the whip, and he knew enough about strippers to realize that if he wanted the attention of the belle of the party, he'd have to make it rain. So that's exactly what he did. Pulling out a thick wad of bills, Talton started throwing them on stage, not caring that they were mostly tens and twenties.

At that point, White Mike noticed his friend throwing money from the foot of the stage. He lightly elbowed B.A., cutting him off in mid-sentence, and pointed towards Gangsta. The scene made them curious so they decided to take a closer look at what was causing their comrade to throw so much money in the air. Once they realized there was a dime on the stage, it didn't take long for them to fall in line. By the end of the song they were all making their dollars precipitate.

Alize heard all about Talton and his crew of drug-dealing friends the moment they entered the club. It seemed as if he had a fan club of sorts. When word hit the locker room that he was there, all the girls got riled up, talking about him and his gang. Since her whole mission revolved around stacking lawyer money, she jumped at the chance to seduce the infamous hustler. However, she wasn't prepared for the feelings that flooded her chest when she made eye contact with the one they called "Gangsta."

Talton was in love with the atmosphere. The whole club was alive, with rock music blasting from the speakers, and the crowd cheering for the woman on stage. But he didn't seem to be part of the chaos surrounding him. All his concentration was trained on what was happening in front of him. Even though Red Devil was performing for a whole club filled with inebriated men, she somehow made him feel like he was the only other person in the room.

At one point, she seductively danced her way across the stage to where Talton and his boys were posted up at. Then she proceeded to give them the most illicit show they had ever seen within the walls of that strip club. The seductress got down on her hands and knees, giving them a full view of her nether regions. Having secretly slipped her G-string to the side, she revealed a red-haired pussy that radiated power.

Someone in the background yelled, "Make dat booty clap!", and the dominatrix never missed a beat. Her butt started clapping just as hard as anyone could've done with their own hands during the most passionate standing ovation. All of this excited Talton even more, making him additionally animated. He started spanking Red's bottom with a stack of bills, all while the rest of the crowd showered her with money and cheers.

By the end of her second set the crowd thinned, and she was graciously picking up the money that was strewn across the stage when she heard someone call out, "Hey, Red." She knew who it was, yet she purposely looked around as if she didn't know where the voice was coming from.

When she finally rested her eyes on Talton, he said, "Say, ma, why don't you come by my table after you freshen up."

Alize walked over to where Talton was standing and squatted down in front of him. Then she softly grabbed the back of his neck, pulled him closer, and gave him a warm kiss on the lips. When she pulled away, still holding the back of his neck she whispered, "Is that all you want me to do?"

The rest of the night was filled with a series of lap dances given by Alize to Talton. Other than the times when she had to go back on stage, they were inseparable. The rules on lap dances were strict and simple. The patrons couldn't touch the dancers. Knowing that tonight it would only work in her favor, Alize honored that rule. With every dance, Gangsta was building a tension that made him long to taste what she had to offer. Yet, she steadily pushed his hands away every time he tried to test his limits.

Then came the dreaded... last call for liquor.

Talton didn't want to leave, and he really didn't want to go home. He'd gotten the vibe that Red was feeling him just as much as he was her, but, then again, they hadn't done much talking throughout the night. Nevertheless, he decided to try and seal the deal.

Alize was finishing Talton's last lap dance when he looked up and asked, "So, Red... we gonna get a room, or what?"

"Why we gotta get a room? You live with your mother?" Alize already knew the answer to her teasing inquiry, yet she was curious as to how he would answer.

"You know what," replied Gangsta, "you're a cold piece of work. I know that you can't, for one second, believe that I live at home wit' my moms. You're a slick one. But since you asked, I gotta keep it gutta wit'cha. The fact is, I got a girl at home. But, for real, I'm feeling you. I can't stand the thought of this night ever ending. If you're not with the idea of going back to a hotel room, let's go back to your place. I don't care what we do, and it don't gotta be about sex, either. It doesn't matter to me as long as I'm with you."

Talton was campaigning extra hard. Partly because he really didn't want to go home to deal with his hostile baby mamma. But another part of him just wanted to ride off into the sunrise with the red-haired dominatrix.

"I'm not gonna play with you, Gangsta. I really like you, but it's not gonna happen. At least, not tonight. You should get home to the wifey. If she's half the woman that I think she is, she's probably at home waiting on you right now. If you still wanna see me after waking up next to her then come to my day job."

"Where's that at?"

"I work at the Wachovia on 49th Street. If you're serious, I'll see you there." The last song ended, signaling the end of the night. Realizing this, Alize leaned in and gave Talton a soft kiss on the lips. "Hope to see you soon."

$$$$$

A little while later Talton stuck his key into the front door of his duplex, fully prepared to be met by full-on verbal attack. But it wasn't going to happen. The pregnancy had gotten the best of Cita; she had fallen asleep on the couch.

Cita looked so peaceful in her sleep. She was so beautiful that Talton briefly forgot about their problems. After quietly shutting the door, he walked towards her and whispered in her ear, "Get up, baby. Let's go to bed."

That night didn't end until dawn. Talton spent it making love to the woman who carried his seed. When it was all over, Cita couldn't believe how tender he'd been. For the first time in a long time she felt as if they had become one entity.

But they hadn't. If they truly had become one, Cita would've seen into the depths of his soul. And there... she would've met a redheaded dominatrix...

CHAPTER FOUR

The next morning Alize woke up in her king-sized bed. She was still groggy from only getting a few hours of sleep. But, nonetheless, she had to get up; she had to go to the bank for a half day of work.

Alize had first applied for the teller position when she moved to Clearwater from Orlando two years earlier. She didn't want the job for the money; the salary was only nineteen thousand dollars a year. She had more lucrative ways of coming up with the money to pay her bills. She needed the job to establish the fact that she was a responsible adult, worthy enough to raise a child on her own.

The only way she could hope to get her baby back was by maintaining the appearance of a model citizen. She also chose to live in a three-bedroom house instead of a small apartment, because the judge wouldn't allow Shawn to stay overnight unless he had his own room. So, every time she woke up feeling tired or depressed, she let her maternal instinct drive her to get up.

Alize gave birth to her healthy baby boy six years earlier. His father refused to have anything to do with them for the first year and a half; forcing her to do the best she could with what she had. Then, well into the second year, Rick came back into the picture with a heavy conscience. The damage to their relationship was unmendable, yet Alize wanted her son to have a father, so she let Rick take him on the weekends; an aberration that would open the door to the darkest mistake of her life.

Rick was a handsome dark-skinned brother in his mid-thirties when he first courted the seventeen-year-old Alize. As far as she was concerned, he was a single man living in an apartment above the studio that he owned and operated. She had no idea that he was married and had three children. She quickly fell in love with him, and before long, she became pregnant. That was about the time when Rick decided that his relationship with the young white girl was becoming too complicated. So, he started looking for a way out.

Alize was alone when she gave birth to her son. Rick had been too busy mixing beats to come to the hospital. Scared and alone, she named the baby herself. She christened the child Shawn Patten, after her brother who had committed suicide over a decade beforehand. Rick didn't see his spawn until the morning Alize showed up at his music studio with the infant bundled up in hospital blankets. And, the moment he laid eyes on the baby, he found his exit.

Shawn was obviously a mixed child, yet Alize's Irish roots run deep. Therefore, most of his physical attributes were those of a Caucasian baby. He came into the world with a head full of curly red hair and soft white skin. This gave Rick the perfect alibi. He took the road of least resistance; which was claiming that Shawn wasn't his.

Ze cried herself to sleep for too many nights after she brought her baby home from the hospital. It got to the point where the memories she had of that day seemed to have come from an out-of-body experience. Over and over, she would see it play out from the aspect of a spectator. She saw herself standing at the front door of the studio with her baby in her arms, while Rick yelled at her as if she were an animal.

"… I already told you, bitch! That ain't my motherfucking kid! You gotta be crazy if you think I'm gonna claim the next man's baby!

"How can you do this?" pleaded Ze.

"Easy, bitch! Get the fuck away from my studio before I call the police!"

"He's your baby–"

"He's your baby, cracker! Get the fuck outta here!"

Alize would never forget the sounds of laughter that surrounded her that day. There had to have been at least twenty people in that parking lot. And every single one of them found the most devastating experience of her life humorous.

At first she was lost; a runaway with no one to turn to. The only family she had was a younger sister who was currently bouncing from foster home to foster home. It would've been easy to give up at that point. She knew that she could've gone to any church or fire department and leave her baby in safe hands. But that wasn't an option. This was her child and she was his mother. She would die before she would let him go.

From that day forward, Alize had a reason to strive. She had to; for her baby's sake. She knew other teenage mothers in her same predicament, and the outcome was always the same: the baby was taken by CPS, and the mother becomes a drug addicted street walker. Knowing how these things played out, Alize vowed not to fall victim to the system. Someone would die before she lost her baby.

$$$$$

"Talton... Talton, baby, your brother's here," said Cita, while lightly tugging on her man's shoulder.

"Tell blood to come back later. I'll call 'em when I get up." Talton turned away from her, not realizing his brother was already in the room.

Cita knew Anthony would wake him, so she left them alone and went back to the kitchen to finish cooking breakfast.

Anthony immediately started trying to find his brother an outfit to put on. When he found one, he tossed the matching T-shirt and jeans on his brother's torso. "Time to get up, fam. Snoop's in Jacksonville waiting on us. Come on... all he has left is a half a key, and he's holding it for us. Hurry up, blood. We're the only thing holding playboy from leaving state."

Talton slowly started waking up. "Damn, nigga. Why we gotta drive all the way out there? That's a three-hour drive, ain't it? Plus, I still got coke... man, you're trippin'."

"I already told you, Snoop's leaving Florida. We might not see 'em for the next few weeks. And, unlike you, I'm out of work. If we don't catch him now, we'll end up losing money when we can't find no more work. So get up!"

Talton sat up and started putting on his pants one leg at a time.

Anthony was rushing but it wasn't because of his connect. He knew that Big Snoop wouldn't leave the state without their ten thousand dollars. Anthony was rushing his brother because he didn't want to get caught in the middle of another domestic dispute. He knew, from experience, that it didn't take much to trigger a verbal firestorm between his brother and Cita. Right now, he was trying to avoid that at all cost.

Anthony pulled a pair of socks from the drawer and tossed them on the bed. "So, how much money you got? He's gonna want ten for the half. I got close to seven."

"I told you, I still got work left." Putting on his socks, he said, "I think I got about five in cash."

"That's cool, we'll just go sixty-forty, and you'll still end up fat after we rerock it."

"Does blood got any smackers?" asked Talton, after getting up and heading to the bathroom.

"You know what, I don't know if he got any ecstasy. I'll call 'em when we're on the road, though."

Anthony wanted to get out the house fast. Right now, Cita was on some Rachel Ray trip, but he knew she could switch up at the sound of a bell. He'd already been through the whole baby mamma drama

22

with the mother of his two children. Therefore, Ant knew that some relationships weren't meant to be. Yet, the situation with his brother bothered him deeply. He knew everything his brother was capable of. But Cita didn't, and this is what worried him the most.

Cita didn't know that she was living with a certified serial killer. She would entice him into loud arguments, not knowing that with every dispute, her life came closer to its final demise. Anthony knew that it was only a matter of time before he received a late-night phone call from his brother asking him to help dispose of Cita's lifeless body. It wouldn't be the first time he got a call like that. And he had his brother's back, but this wasn't California. They were out of state, in a city where disappearances and violent murders weren't the norm.

Talton was brushing his teeth when Anthony decided to wait in the car. On his way out, he saw Cita and said, "Alright then, lil sis. I'll be in the car, so make sure he doesn't take too long."

"I got you, Ant." Cita watched Anthony walk out the door. She liked Talton's brother; he never turned her down for anything, and she respected the fact that he truly loved Talton. Yet, she also knew that if it weren't for her relationship with his brother, Anthony wouldn't have anything to do with her.

Talton came out of the bathroom a few minutes later. She hated how handsome he was; it was hard to stay mad at someone she was so physically attracted to.

"Alright, ma. We gotta take a road trip to

Jacksonville, and I won't be back until tonight." Talton reached into the cupboard, retrieved a plate, and started scooping eggs and bacon onto it.

"Why didn't you tell me you had plans?"

With a mouthful of food, he said, "To tell you the truth, I really didn't know. Ant's connect just got to Florida, and he'll be leaving soon, so we gotta catch 'em while we can." Talton picked up a glass of orange juice that Cita had been drinking from and gulped down its contents. "Why? What's the problem now?

"There is no problem, I'm just tired of being left alone all the time. You got me over here selling all your dope while you're out there trickin' the money off on strippers. I keep telling you it bothers me, and you don't listen."

Talton stuffed a large fork full of eggs into his mouth, set the plate down and grabbed a few slices of bacon. Then he headed for the door.

"You ain't gonna say anything?"

"I'm not trying to fight with you, Cita."

"You think I'm some type of joke, huh! You stay out all night, getting your dick rubbed by stripper bitches, then come home and give me the dirty dick!" Suddenly Cita went from Rachel Ray to an insane homeless woman in a blink of an eye. "It doesn't work like that, motherfucker! I'm tired of this shit! Hey, look at me when I talk to you!"

"Gotta go, ma."

"Whatever, Talton! Just mark my words, after I have this baby, I'ma make you cry! You're gonna beg me to stay home, and I'm not gonna listen!"

Talton rushed out the front door, shutting it behind him.

CHAPTER FIVE

Anthony was waiting for Talton as he sat behind the steering wheel of his girlfriend's Mazda 6. He usually drove around in his 2015 Thunderbird, but today, he left it at home. He was about to traffic a large amount of cocaine from one part of the state to another, and the flashy 24-inch rims were the last things he needed.

The car was idling when Talton walked up and opened the passenger side door. Before getting in, he pulled out a chrome fifty caliber Desert Eagle from the small of his back and placed it underneath the seat. Once the door was shut and they were on their way, Talton started scrolling through his phone.

"I don't understand why you always wanna bring that cannon with you every time we do a business transaction."

"Old habits die hard," replied Talton without looking up. "And this particular habit saved our asses on several occasions, so I don't know why you're trippin."

Ignoring the comment, Anthony asked, "What're you looking for?"

"Man, I met this breezy at Show Girls last night.

I'm trying to find her number, but I don't think I got it. I could've sworn I put it in my phone... but I can't find it."

"Who you talking about?"

"You don't know her, she's new."

"All you gotta do is call Alexus, she'll know how to get ahold of her."

"I don't think so. This one's new. She seemed like a loner. She's got this wild red hair, and she carries a whip."

"Bruh... you're talking about that dominatrix from Orlando? Lil' titties, big ol' booty?"

Talton put his phone down and gave Anthony his full attention. "Yeah, that's her. You know her?"

Anthony switched lanes, checking his rear-view for anything out of place. "I don't really know her, per-se. But I know of her. I met her a couple of weeks ago when I was up there with Snoop. I know that she is originally from Orlando, and that she sells pounds of dro."

"Pounds of hydro, huh... she told me she worked at a bank. She didn't say shit about sellin' work."

"She probably does both. You hit them cheeks?"

"Naw, bruh... she wouldn't leave with me."

"I didn't think that she was your type," commented Anthony, as a smile crept across his face.

"Why you say that?" asked Talton, sensing a trap.

"Well, she carries a whip, for one. She's probably gonna want you to act like a dog, or something. I never figured you for the kind of guy that likes to get tied up and shit." Anthony started laughing, "I can

27

see you now... dog collar'd up!"

"Man, fuck you, blood! Ain't nobody gonna have me wearin' a dog collar, and I'll be damned if I ever let a bitch tie me up." Talton smiled as he thought of the sexy dominatrix.

The brothers rode in silence for a while. They made it to the highway and Anthony navigated through traffic at a conservative speed. He had something on his mind, though. A subject that he needed to get off his chest, and he decided that this was as good a time as ever to hit his brother with it.

"Talton."

Staring out the window, he answered, "What's up, bruh?"

"What you plan on doing once this baby's born?"

Talton turned away from the glass to face his brother. "What kind of question is that? I'm taking care of it."

"That's not what I mean, and you know it. That baby's gonna slow you down. Cita ain't gonna help, either. Talton, we just got in the game out here, and we're about to start coppin' bricks.

"That's not all of it, either. All that hustlin' you're doing out the spot where you lay your head at is dead wrong. And, what I can't understand is that you've been through all this before. You've already done all this in Cali and Tennessee and you're still acting like a rookie. I can't understand it."

"Man, come on, Ant. I know this already. You think I'm stupid or something?"

"Then why you keep doing this shit?"

"I've been on Craig's List and Apartment Finders

looking for spot to put Cita and the baby. I'm gonna keep the duplex for a trap house, just like I did in Chattanooga with Melody and Dezire."

"Talton, this isn't Chattanooga, and Cita ain't Melody. You can't trust this bitch, and you know it. What part of everything she's been screaming don't you understand? You're about to become a single father, nigga!"

"Look, blood, I'm not trying to go through all this right now. It's way too early for all this bullshit."

"All I'm saying is you need to start lookin' at the bigger picture. I'm just trying to open your eyes, bruh. We're on the verge of hittin' the next level of our hustle. I need you on top of your game. That whole set-up you got at home is way too sketchy. Once that baby gets dropped in your lap, which is exactly what's gonna happen, it's gonna slow us both down. Talton, we can't afford any loose ends right now."

Anthony looked at Talton. Talton stared out the window.

"I'm just worried about you, bro," continued Anthony. "Go ahead and light up that 'gar I left in the ashtray. You look like you need it."

Talton didn't move, so Anthony reached into the ashtray, grabbed the half-smoked blunt, lit it, then passed it to his brother. It didn't take long for the smoke to overtake the cabin. Talton plugged his phone into the dash and played some music through the Mazda's stereo system. Both men then rode into their own worlds.

Gangsta was lost in thought. He knew his brother

was right. Everything he said was real... so real that he couldn't argue. What frustrated him the most was that all of his problems were self-inflicted. And now, they were beginning to metastasize. Talton thought about it until the weed suffocated his problems.

$$$$$

That evening, Cita was in the kitchen pouring herself a glass of Mt. Dew. She was trying to rush back to the living room to catch the beginning of her favorite show, Atlanta Housewives. The microwave read 8:27, she only had three minutes. Talton had called her earlier, letting her know he was on his way back home. She was trying to enjoy the last bit of peace and quiet before he got there. Knowing that, once he got back, Talton and his brother would be up most of the night, smoking and drinking while remixing their cocaine.

Cita had barely stepped into the living room when she heard her bedroom window shatter. A few seconds later, she was knocked off her feet by a loud explosion. She was still conscious, but she couldn't hear a thing. Then she saw something, small and round, fly over her head, landing a few feet from where she had fallen. Moments later the object suddenly exploded, leaving Cita blinded by the flash.

That second blast had knocked the air from her lungs, causing her to become disorientated in her own home. She lost all sense of time and place. Next came a bombardment of movement. She could tell there was something going on, but she couldn't see a thing because of the smoke from the flash grenades.

After a while, the smoke cleared, and she started regaining her senses. Sight first, which allowed her to see images of men wearing black uniforms with yellow lettering across the front. Then she felt something heavy on her back. She had the distinct feeling that she was being yelled at. *Could that be a boot on my back?* she asked herself. Someone was demanding something of her, but she couldn't understand what the heavy-footed person was saying.

Suddenly, her view of the world changed. Someone lifted Cita to her feet and was now guiding her to the bedroom. The voices were becoming clearer. She was now able to read the yellow writing on the men's shirts. Nevertheless, it took her a moment before she connected the word "SWAT" with what was taking place. Then, she figured it out ... cops!

Cita was sat down at the edge of her bed. A few minutes passed before a man wearing a ski mask entered, carrying one of her dining room chairs. He set the chair directly in front of her then sat down facing her. The breeze coming through the broken bedroom window was a godsend, helping Cita gather her senses. Then, the man in the ski mask started talking.

"I'm gonna get straight to the point. If you don't wanna go to jail, you need to tell me what I wanna hear. My first question is where the hell your boyfriend is?"

Then, just as the detective finished asking the

question, a member of the SWAT team entered the room. He was holding Talton's Gucci bag in one hand and a large resealable freezer bag in the other.

"Excuse me, sir. Looks like we found four or five ounces of cocaine."

"Alright, bag it and put it in evidence. There's some bags in my car." After sending his colleague away, Detective Krasinski turned back to Cita. "You see that? That was a trafficking charge. Since you're the only one in the house, I have to assume that it's your contraband. This means that you're going to jail. If you don't want to have that baby in a prison hospital, you need to hurry up and tell me where your boyfriend's at."

Cita was beginning to grasp the magnitude of the situation. Her crotch felt wet, and when she took a whiff of herself, she realized that somewhere between the first explosion and that moment she had urinated on herself. Then she saw her reflection in the mirror, and was immediately shocked. She looked terrible.

Suddenly, Cita couldn't make up her mind to which was worse; the fact that she pissed all over herself, or the way her hair and make-up looked around all these men. That was all the motivation that she needed.

"He went to Jacksonville."

CHAPTER SIX

Anthony glanced at the dashboard, checking the time as he turned into the subdivision where his brother lived. The night was still young, it was nine-thirty. He was proud of himself for making such good time without breaking the speed limit. He looked at Talton, who had dozed off, and said, "We made it, bruh. Time to get up."

Talton slowly started coming to, "What time is it?"

"It's only half past nine. I figure we'll be finished cutting this shit by midnight. Then we can get a few hours sleep before we start working the phones." Anthony was feeling upbeat until he turned onto his brother's street. The whole block was lit up like a Christmas tree; red and blue lights everywhere.

Talton shot up in his seat, "Stop the car! That's my house!" He then pulled out his phone, scrolling as quickly as possible to Cita's number. A few seconds later he told his brother, "She's not answering. Just back the car up, get off the block ASAP! Don't even turn around, just back up."

Anthony slapped the gear shifter in reverse. A wasted attempt based on the fact that his path was blocked. In his rear-view mirror he saw two unmarked cars blocking the street. He recognized the set-up, and quickly put the car in first gear. He was prepared for a high-speed chase until his plans were thwarted when two more cars pulled out of adjacent driveways and blocked the street in front of him.

All of a sudden, they were surrounded by police in SWAT gear. All of them were masked up and carrying automatic assault rifles that were menacingly pointed at the brothers.

Then something happened that confused both siblings past the point of apprehension. The passenger-side window was suddenly smashed in, causing glass to fly all over the inside of the car's cabin. In a split second, Talton's door was snatched open and he was violently dragged from the car. Talton didn't have a chance; he was thrown into the back seat of one of the unmarked police vehicles before he knew what hit him.

Anthony was stunned. In less than one minute they were surrounded, accosted, and now Talton was detained. He couldn't do anything except watch as his brother was taken away. It was obvious that something wasn't koshure about the arrest. Anthony wanted to do something, but then he remembered he was in the car with an unregistered firearm and over a half kilo of cocaine.

Anthony put the Mazda in reverse and slowly backed out, leaving the neighborhood before the cops decided to come back to arrest him as well.

$$$$$

Detective Krasinski sat in the same chair that he was in while interrogating the girl. His ski mask was still pulled over his face as he admired the comforters on the room's king-sized bed. He recognized the satin sheets and silk throw pillows. Once upon a time, he had wanted to purchase a set for his ex-wife, but was never able to afford them. He knew he could rape the house for all of its expensive accessories, yet that wasn't his thing. He didn't want to set a bad example for his team. He was in charge of a special task force dedicated to arresting mid-level drug dealers, and he loved his job.

He should've been ecstatic over his last conquest; they successfully raided a drug house, finding a pistol and drugs. The girl immediately turned into an informant and her boyfriend was minutes away from being brought in. On the surface, all seemed in order. However, from experience, the detective knew that taking the suspect off the street was only a third of the job. The other two thirds consisted of turning the suspect into a snitch, and making the case stick. Knowing all of this is what made Krasinski such a good detective. And his experience told him that he was in big trouble. They hadn't even arrested the suspect yet, and the case was already falling apart.

The frustrated detective couldn't help but ask himself how he managed to allow this case to slip through his fingers. It all started a few weeks earlier. He had received an anonymous tip informing him that there was a drug house operating in a small Clearwater neighborhood. So he placed a surveillance detail on the residence, and it didn't take long to recognize the presence of drug activity.

It was obvious that the drug dealer whom the detective later found out through DMV records was named Talton D. Robinson, hadn't been at it for long. Mr. Robinson owned a late-model Suburban and an early-model Delta 88, all on expensive rims with shiny paint. But Detective Krasinski knew that if he would have been a high-level drug dealer, Mr. Robinson would've owned something foreign.

Upon entering the home, the detective was surprised that his suspect had invested so much money on the interior of his home. The living room was laid out in authentic Italian leather sofas, and they sat on top of brand new, snow white carpeting. Not to mention the five-thousand-dollar sixty-inch flat screen that he personally ripped off the wall.

Since the case hadn't been flagged as high priority, Krasinski hadn't requested a wiretap, nor did he assign around-the-clock surveillance. His team was in the process of wrapping up several other investigations, so they had only watched the house in the evenings. Up to that point, all of their intel had been spot on. There were only two adults living at the residence; Myriam "Cita" Wilford, and Talton D. Robinson. The surveillance had uncovered Robinson's taste for local strippers, as well as his girlfriend's audacious sexual appetite which included one of Talton's closest associates.

From the outside, the investigation could be viewed as a simple act of going through the motions. Isolate the suspect, make an arrest, and apply pressure. Then use that newly discovered information to arrest the suspect's associates and supplier. That's how Krasinski's team went about it every time. So far, it had given their squad a hundred percent conviction rate. But that wasn't how this particular investigation was turning out.

The obstacles started materializing when the team began sending in confidential informants. Most of the time Talton wouldn't be at the house. And, in those rare instances when he was at the residence, he would refuse to deal with someone he didn't already know.

That was in the beginning of this problematic investigation. So, the detective decided to take the next option straight from the police academememy's playbook. He arranged to have one of Mr. Robinson's regular customers picked up. It was a simple mission that was accomplished almost immediately.

There was an ex-prostitute who lived in the same neighborhood as their suspect. She was picked up one evening, after leaving the drug house. Krasinski made the arrest himself; finding a fifty-dollar-slab of crack cocaine in her possession. The detective then threatened to expose her past form of employment to her current benefactor, which happened to be a decorated army veteran, and she reluctantly agreed to do what was asked of her.

For the past two weeks Detective Krasinski had sent her into the home wearing a wire. The goal was for her to get their suspect on a recording device making a transaction, but it never happened. That's when the team came to the conclusion that Talton must have been operating his enterprise strictly over the phone. So, they followed him. Night after night, they tailed their suspect, only to end up at one of the several strip clubs in the area where the only crime he would commit was a precursor to DUI.

Krasinski had gotten fed up with waiting on Talton to make a mistake. He decided to use another tactic. He would send in his confidential informant to make a buy. It wouldn't matter who made the sale, as long as there was a transaction made, then he and his team would have the right to ransack the home. That usually worked in most cases, but this time, the detective had to admit that he rushed the play.

This evening, he sent in the ex-prostitute and she successfully made a buy while wearing a recording device. So, he sent in his team without confirming the presence of their main target assuming that, since both of his vehicles were parked in the driveway, Talton would also be inside of the apartment. That mistake would ultimately cost them the case. Not only was their suspect's pregnant girlfriend the only person inside when they raided, she was also the sole voice on the recording.

During the search, officers located a nine-millimeter Berretta, three ounces of powder cocaine and one and a half ounces of crack cocaine. The only cash in the home was a few hundred dollars that their female suspect had accumulated throughout the day.

While Cita was giving her song and dance about not having anything to do with the drugs that were being sold from the home, Detective Krasinski was doing the mathematics in his head, and he was beginning to fume over the possibility that he wasn't going to be able to legally arrest the man for whom they had come for. While she was droning on and on about Talton's drug enterprise, Krasinski was trying to figure out a way to write up the arrest report to justify the actual imprisonment of the elusive Robinson character. He knew that he was going to have to embellish the report to either show that Robinson was in the home during the raid, or that he was apprehended while trying to flee. This was precisely why he ordered his team to stake out the front of the cul-de-sac, and bring him back to the scene the moment he showed his face. Krasinski didn't want to compromise the situation any more than it had already been. That's why he gave his officers specific instructions to bring Talton back to the scene alone. He had no way of knowing that this decision would end up blowing up in his face, while also triggering a string of homicides in the weeks to come. In retrospect, it was the worst mistake of his career.

CHAPTER SEVEN

Talton was furious! His house had been raided and he'd just been snatched out the car like a terrorist. He knew he was dealing with dirty cops the moment they let his brother go without as much as asking his name. This told him that he needed to get to the county jail as fast as possible; before they resorted to their more violent tactics of getting what they wanted.

The second he stepped inside of his living room, Talton was taken aback by the destruction. If there was one thing he prided himself in, it was the inside of his home. He had spent thousands of dollars on furniture and fixtures. Just for these marauders to come in and vandalize everything. The entertainment center was in pieces, the bathroom was flooded, glass was everywhere and they had tracked mud all over his new rug.

The blatant disrespect they showed towards his rug caused his blood to boil. But the ultimate slap to the face was the way his most prized possession hung from the wall. His 3-D TV was dangerously hanging from one screw, and its screen was shattered. His flat screen was dead, and one of these K-9's had killed it.

Talton was told to sit down, so he found a spot in the love seat closest to the kitchen. Cita was seated a few feet away, at the dinner table. She looked horrible, her hair was a mess and mascara stained her face. Talton had never seen her like this. No matter how upset she had ever gotten, Cita always managed to keep her appearance up. Talton couldn't help but take it as a bad omen.

Not long after he got there he tried to get Cita's attention. Yet, for some reason, she kept looking away every time they made eye contact. He needed to know if she was able to flush the drugs before the cops came in. Talton had security cameras all around the duplex that were hooked up through wifi to his television. If she was watching it when the police showed up, they might be in the clear.

"Cita...Cita," whispered Talton.

"What?!" replied Cita, loudly.

He then mouthed the words, "What happened?" to his girlfriend, and was caught off guard by her response.

"What the fuck you think happened?! They found your shit! That's what happened!"

In that moment, Talton realized that Cita was less friend than foe. In his book, what she had just done was called dry snitchin'; from that point on, he made no other attempt to communicate with her.

A few seconds later Talton was ordered to get up and was led to the back of the apartment. From the hallway he saw a plain-clothes detective in his bedroom, hiding under a ski mask. He had never cared about cops either way; to him they had a job to do, and so did he. But, right off the bat, Talton really hated this one.

The detective motioned for Talton to sit down at the edge of the bed. It was still moist from when Cita had been stationed there.

"Sit down, Mr. Robinson. I trust that one of my officers already read you your Miranda rights. So now I have a few questions that should help us speed up the process. We wanna get you out of this predicament as soon as possible."

Gangsta was fire hot at the fact that he was in handcuffs, that his house was in shambles, and at the way Cita reacted towards him only moments earlier. He knew that it was in his best interest to stay calm and cordial with this officer, but that wasn't going to happen. "First of all, you got me fucked up if you think I'm gonna talk to a man wearing a mask. Second, the only possible way I see us speeding this process up, is by us bypassing all this talking, and you taking me straight to the county jail. We might as well start on that process and everything else'll run smoothly, ya dig?"

"Do you realize that I found a handgun with several ounces of narcotics? I can charge you with armed trafficking... that's a decade in prison. Ten years of your life down the drain."

Krasinski paused and stared at his prisoner for a moment before starting again, "So, you're a wise ass, huh? You're not afraid of the county jail. Have you ever been to prison, Mr. Robinson?"

"Man, you're the cop. Shouldn't you know this shit already? Check this out, I need you to stall out all this bullshit and take me to the county so I can bond out, homey. If we ain't talking about putting me in the back of one of those police cars, and taking me downtown, I ain't got nothing else to say."

By now Krasinski had the feeling that he wasn't dealing with an amateur. The accent sounded like it was from the West Coast, and the longer he stared into Talton's eyes, the more he recognized the coolness of a seasoned criminal. That's when the detective started to wonder if maybe Talton Robinson was deeper in the game than he had first assumed. "Where you from, Mr. Robinson?"

"Man, I'm from Florida, homey. The good ol' Dirty South. And, no, I've never done time. But I'm ready to go do some right now."

"Yeah, I see that. But, I gotta be honest with you. We found a lot of drugs in here, not to mention the loaded firearm. I can understand why you may not want to help me further this investigation, some guys just don't snitch. And, I can respect that. However, if you don't go on record, taking full responsibility for the contraband we found, your girlfriend's gonna have that baby in prison."

For a second, the ultimatum caught Talton off guard. That baby meant a lot to him. Yet, the way Cita had gotten at him in the living room weighed heavy on his decision-making process.

"Mr. Robinson... do you understand what I'm telling you?" The detective thought he hit pay dirt. If he could somehow get the suspect to make a written confession saying the drugs were in fact his, they'd be able to work around the other mishaps and wrap up the case. But then he watched Talton's eyes turn cold.

"Let me tell you something, Mr. K9; I have no idea what you found in this house, cuz I don't live here. I don't deal in drugs, and I don't know anyone who does. So, from this point on, I have nothing else to say. With all due respect, I am formally requesting that you either take these cuffs off me and let me leave, or take me to jail."

Detective Krasinski wanted to hit Talton so bad, he could taste it. "You know what, you piece of shit! I know damn well all these drugs are yours! I've been watching your punk-ass for weeks, and now, I'm telling you I'm gonna send this poor girl to prison with your baby inside of her. And you're gonna sit there and "formally request" some bullshit! You're a real son-of-a-bitch! Krasinski had to turn away from Talton just so he wouldn't attack him. Then he yelled, "Get this piece of shit out of my face, *now!*"

CHAPTER EIGHT

Both Talton and Cita had to spend the night at the Pinellas county jail. They were booked on armed trafficking and sales of cocaine charges. Cita's bond had been set at fifty-thousand dollars; she called her parents and they immediately posted the five-thousand that it took to get her out. Talton, on the other hand, had to stay put. His bond had been set at a hundred thousand. Since he and his brother had spent most of their cash earlier that day, he'd have to wait awhile to see the streets.

Anthony was on the case from the moment he got home. He wasn't worried about the money; he'd get his brother out. Nor was he stressing off the fact that Talton would have to spend a few days in jail. His brother had basically spent his whole adolescence in one jail or another. What really bothered Anthony was that they had just barely opened up shop and Talton was already in jail. After a few months of accumulating clientele, blowing money on cars, clothes, and jewels, they were finally ready to step up their game. And then this happened.

Anthony moved to Clearwater with his wife and three children a few years earlier. Then, the accident happened. His youngest had drowned in the bathtub on his wife's watch. He never blamed her, yet their relationship soon deteriorated. Not unlike what was now happening with his brother and Cita. Eventually, he and his wife separated, but he stayed in Florida to be close to the kids.

Then his brother got out. Talton was released from a Tennessee prison earlier that year and Anthony invited him to Florida. Their union was like a clip to a gun... it didn't take long for them to set up shop. Anthony was an experienced drug dealer. So was Talton. Except, Talton was a cold-blooded killer. Anthony knew this, and intended to use it. It would come in handy with the starting and maintaining of a drug empire.

Anthony was no pushover whatsoever. He had experienced his share of gunplay, but he was more of a businessman who could manipulate numbers easily, whereas Talton had a natural flair for violence. Their contrast made them a perfect team, and Anthony knew this, so he went ahead and set out to do whatever it would take to get his brother out.

$$\$\$\$\$\$$

It had been eight minutes since Alize last tried callin' her son. Part of her court appointed privileges included nightly phone calls with him. However, the sad truth of the matter was that she rarely ever got to speak to him. Most of the time, the phone would only ring; other times, she'd get the answering service. Whenever she brought it up in court, Rick would be ready with a scripted excuse as to why no one was home at the time she had called. And the judge would tell her to keep trying.

After thirty minutes of unsuccessfully calling her son, Alize was emotionally exhausted. For the last several years, she had been constantly depressed. So much so, that she felt as if she had forgotten what it felt like to be happy. It seemed as if she had been separated from everyone she had ever loved. Other than her younger sister, she had no one else. What made things worse was that she couldn't even remember what she had done to deserve such a sad existence.

Alize got up from the stool at her breakfast bar and walked into her living room, finding a spot on the sectional couch. She knew that she shouldn't drown herself in self-pity, she had to stay focused and control her emotions. As she settled in to watch television, her bookshelf caught her attention, causing her to remember another time in her life. Alize owned hundreds of books. She had read them all when she first lost her son. Shortly after he had been taken, she fell into a deep depression. Her only escape was through the fictional worlds that her urban books offered her. Her favorites were those by Mike Enemigo, Dutch, and King Guru.

For months, reading her books was how she dealt with her problems. Until one morning, she woke up and had an epiphany. She suddenly realized that she couldn't keep running from her problems. If she ever wanted her baby back, she'd have to fight. That's when she decided to start bleeding the streets for cash. At first, she started out dancing, and the money was good. But then she met a group of girls who were taking weekend flights to Las Vegas. They were making twice the amount of cash in half the amount of time that it was taking in Orlando. So, she gave it a whirl. It worked; she stuck to it, all the while, saving her money for lawyer fees.

That's how she met her marijuana connection. She wound up befriending the drug dealer and pretty soon she was bringing back pounds of hydroponic weed from the West Coast. In the beginning she was only buying one or two pounds at a time. Then, one day, her supplier called and asked her about Orlando. He wanted to leave Vegas for the Dirty South, but he needed a place to live so Alize set out on a mission to find him a house, a feat that proved to be simple since her connect seemed to have an unending amount of cash flow.

Once Mark Sanders, her weed connect, moved to Florida, things changed for her. He started giving her twenty, sometimes thirty pounds at a time. Everything on consignment, and she suddenly didn't have time to fly out West anymore. Things started moving so fast that she decided to move away from Orlando. The last thing she needed was for her ex to find out how she was making the money to pay for her lawyer. But then her money slowed down.

She didn't know as many people in Clearwater as she did in Orlando. And the people she did manage to hook up with were all small-time hustlers, only able to afford one or two pounds at a time.

Alize leaned back, TV remote in her hand. She

was channel surfing for something to watch, when like a plume of smoke, the thought of the man she had met at Show Girls entered her mind. Talton was a hustler. A real one, too. Maybe he was her key to success. She let her thoughts linger for a moment, suddenly feeling a surge of longing. The color of his skin, and the sound of his voice haunted her. If only he'd call...

CHAPTER NINE

Talton was released from the Pinellas County jail on Tuesday morning. It took Anthony nine days to come up with the money, and now, Gangsta was walking out the gates into the open arms of his pregnant girlfriend. To the casual observer, the couple that embraced in the county jail parking lot was the epitome of an expecting couple who were young and in love.

It would've been impossible to know that Talton's heart wasn't in the embrace. That during another time in his life, he probably would've greeted Cita with a swift slap to the face. However, over the years he had learned the art of concealing his emotions. A skill that saved his life, as well as the lives of others, on several occasions.

The last week and a half was hectic for Talton. His first few days were spent dipped in anxiety. He assumed that his felony warrants from California and Tennessee would come up on the National Crime Information Center's computer system. It was common practice for a jail's intake process to include a fingerprint scan through the system's computer log. Yet, after a week passed and he hadn't been called out for a surprise extradition hearing, he started to think that he'd probably see the streets again.

Every day Talton would call Anthony, just to be reassured that he was doing everything in his power to come up with the bond money. But that did nothing to ease the stress. Whenever breakfast trays came around, he expected to see his name on the court docket list that was posted on the pod's window, but it never happened.

What Talton didn't realize was that the booking officer who filled out his intake paperwork was going through an avalanche of personal problems at home. His wife had a pill addiction, and his daughter was strung out on crystal meth. For the last four days, they had been missing; most likely on a joint drug binge. He was worried sick, hoping they wouldn't show up at his workplace in handcuffs. All of that, plus the fact that weekends were so busy that the booking area in the county jail was like a mad house, put the deputy in a daze. Talton's NCIC paperwork was never filed.

Another thought that constantly raced through his mind during his imprisonment was how Cita had answered him when he tried to find out what happened. After they were taken downtown, they sat next to one another in the booking area, but Talton didn't say anything. Cita was a sociopathic liar, Talton knew that any accusation he made towards her would only be denied vehemently. Therefore, he decided to keep his mouth shut, realizing that he had more pressing issues at hand.

The couple stepped into Gangsta's Delta 88; Cita

in the driver's seat, Talton in the passenger's. The morning was cool, so the leather was still cold to the touch, but Talton loved his show car so much that he welcomed the feeling. He allowed the familiar smell and comfort of the brand-new leather to erase the rancid memories of jail.

Cita glanced at Talton as she pulled into traffic and said, "Your brother's at the Denny's on U.S. 19. He's waiting for us to meet him there. I figure we can have some breakfast while you guys talk business. But, Talton... there's something I need to tell you. I felt bad about it before, so I didn't say anything while you were in jail."

Talton looked at Cita, wondering if she would really admit that she talked to the police about his business.

"I had all the furniture moved into a storage unit. I had to; the police destroyed the bathroom, and the whole duplex was flooded. I could've called a plumber, but I didn't think you'd want to stay there with the carpet like that. And, now that the cops know you sell drugs, they'll be watching the house. I hope you're not mad that I didn't tell you before."

Talton made a mental note of the fact that she said, "...the cops know you sell drugs." He knew that this was gonna be a problem in the future, because his mind wouldn't let it go. He was sure that she had forsaken him, and he knew he'd eventually have an outburst if he didn't find a way to deal with it soon.

Nevertheless, he bit his tongue and replied, "Naw, it's cool, you're right. It was time to move, but you didn't give the bondsman the new address, right?"

"No. They think I'm staying at my mom's house and that you're living with your brother's baby mamma."

Talton felt like he was missing something, then it came to him, "Where are we staying then?"

"I put some of our clothes at my sister's house."

"Damn, Cita! Not Shannon. Man, that house stays nasty and her kids –"

"Talton, that's my sister, and it'll only be for a lil' while."

"You know what; we'll talk about this later. But, first, I need you to stop somewhere on the way to Denny's. I met a guy in the county that told me he had a plug on security deposit boxes at the Wachovia on 49th Street. I wanna check it out real quick. I think it'll be a cool spot to stash my dope in the future...

$$\$\$\$\$\$$$

"Just listen, cuz, this ain't no false alarm. I've been coppin' from this girl for a couple months now. She's got pounds, so there has to be a stash of cash in the mix. She ain't got no man, and she's from outta town. It'll be the easiest mulah you ever made." Nirobi was sitting at a dirty kitchen table with his phone against his ear. His nieces and nephews were running around the house, so he had to talk loudly for his cousin to hear what he was saying. "I'm telling you, she's a punk-ass white bitch... I cop from her all the time."

"The last time you came up with one of your million-dollar plans, we got all set up and you flaked on me. What makes you think I'ma let you pump me up again?" Yada was sitting behind the wheel of his parked Buick Lasabre, across town, splitting a cigar so he could fill it with some cheap weed.

"Man, fuck that, cuz! That was before you went to prison. I grew up since then. This is the real deal. I already told the bitch I got a homey that wants ten pounds, and she didn't even blink. She acted like it wasn't shit! She's gotta be sittin' on at least fifty pounds! It'll be easy. We can't pass this up."

"I'ma give you the benefit of the doubt on this one, cuz. This better not be some bullshit! I'll meet you at the park on Greenwood in about an hour. Robi, don't tell nobody else, cuz." Yàda put his phone down then lifted the blunt to his mouth so he could lick the leaves and seal it shut. He was already plotting on what he would buy with Alize's money.

$$$$$

Mondays were usually slow at the bank where Alize worked. Most of the traffic came from local businesses that dropped off their weekend deposits. Ordinarily, her idle time would be spent worrying about her pending court issues. However, over the last week, Alize had spent most of her days with her seat slightly positioned towards the front entrance of the bank's lobby. From her spot behind the teller's counter, she waited for the young hustler she had met at the strip club a week and a half earlier.

Every day she'd tell herself to forget about him. Yet, time after time, whenever she heard the bell that signaled the bank's door being opened or closed, she'd look up, hoping it was him, only to be let down every time it wasn't him. Then, the one time the bell sounded and she hadn't looked up, she was surprised by a familiar voice.

"Bet you didn't think you'd ever see me again, huh?" When Ze looked up, Talton stared into the eyes of the woman who had danced her way into his heart. For a moment, he saw a sparkle in her eyes, but then it was quickly followed by a stoned-faced glare.

"Excuse me, sir. You must have me confused with someone else. I don't believe we've ever met before."

Talton felt as if he had been slapped. "Are you serious? You don't remember me? Man, Red, stop playin' with me. You know exactly who the fuck I am." For a moment, Talton wondered if she had really forgotten who he was.

Then she smiled, "I'm just playing with you. You should see your face right now. I remember you; I just didn't think you'd ever show up."

"You kidding me? I haven't stopped thinking about you since the night we met. You told me to come here if I was serious, so here I am; and this time, I ain't leaving without your number, either." Talton had his composer back, and he wasn't about to let it go. "You might as well pull out some of that Wachovia stationary and get to writing cuz I ain't playin."

Alize stared at the man standing before her. She couldn't imagine anyone more handsome. And he reeked of self-confidence, yet it wasn't the obnoxious kind that came from years of having everything handed to a person. No, she thought to herself, his self-worth came from being a self-made man. "OK, I'll give you my number, but you gotta promise to stop calling me Red. My name is Alize Marie." Ze grabbed a post-it and started scribbling her contact information. "Here's my number, but you can't expect me to take you serious when you take two weeks to get at me, and when you do finally come in, you walk in here with your clothes wrinkled and your hair all frizzy."

"Damn," replied Talton, suddenly aware of his shabby appearance. "I didn't even think about all that. The truth is, I just got out the county jail a few minutes ago."

"That's crazy," said Ze. "What was the case?"

"A trafficking charge. It's good though. I'll beat it. But check this out, I got some business I gotta handle right now. I'ma call you at five, is there anywhere you wanna meet at?"

"What makes you think I wanna go anywhere with you?" replied Ze with a grin.

"Man, I've been waiting my whole life for this. Trust me, we're gonna meet up."

"Call me at five, I'll tell you where to go. But make sure you call, because I've got a proposition for you."

"You know, I'm not into all that S&M shit."

"Come again," replied Alize.

"All that gettin' tied up and shit–"

"I'm talkin about getting money, crazy man! Get

your mind out the gutter.

"Ah, man, I thought–"

"I know what you thought. It ain't that type of party... unless you want it to be," added Ze, playfully.

Talton started laughing; "I'll call you in a few hours."

"Alright," replied Alize as Talton turned and walked away. She watched him leave through the glass doors and saw when he stepped into the passenger seat of an older vehicle with big rims. Its driver was a dark-haired female, probably the baby mamma. *This guy's got nerve*, thought Alize as she repositioned herself on her seat suddenly realizing how slippery her inner thighs had become.

She couldn't wait till five...

CHAPTER TEN

Talton had a smile on his face when he stepped out the bank. He had to admit, Alize was just as beautiful in the day as she was at night. He hadn't given it much thought, but there had been a chance that the club's black lights could've fooled him. However, after seeing Red again, he was, once again, captivated by her beauty.

As he approached the car, he looked at Cita. With her pregnancy in full bloom, she had a particular glow about herself. She was pretty, too, yet hers was a different kind of beauty. Cita had an exotic ambiance that felt fast and dangerous just like her attitude, where Alize had more of a sophisticated aura. It would be impossible to compare the two, since they were of two different breeds. Nonetheless, the dominatrix had his attention, and he was curious as to where it would take him.

Talton opened the passenger door, stepped in the Delta and said, "Alright, let's go see Ant." After shutting the door, he flipped open the sun visor and looked in the mirror. When he saw his reflection he said, "Damn, Cita, why didn't you tell me I was looking like this?"

"What are you talking about?"

"My hair is all fucked up!"

"What did you expect? You didn't just come home from a health spa. So, what happened? Did you get the safety deposit box?" Cita pulled into the street, upset with herself for not going inside the bank with Talton. If he had a secret bank account, she just missed out on the chance to find out.

"Naw... dude was full of shit. I should've known better than to have listened to a nigga in jail. I remember meeting another nigga in jail, and he did the same shit."

"I didn't know you've been to jail before," Cita commented, while navigating through traffic.

"I've been to jail a few times. I just don't like talking about it. But, anyways, I met this guy in jail, in Georgia, and he was always flossin' on niggas. He was the type of nigga that barely went to commissary, but talked about how much money he had on the streets. I still ended up gettin' pretty tight with blood. I knew he was really doing something on the streets, because I saw his flicks, and he was in there on trafficking charges. Dude had an old-school Impala, a Benz, and a Durango. So, anyways, one night, he tells me he's got 15 G's in a jar buried underneath some rims in his back yard. At the time, I didn't think nothin' of it. We were both in jail, so that money wasn't doing anybody any good. Plus, I had my own issues to deal with.

"See, this was when I had caught a weed case on my way through Georgia. I was going to South

Carolina with some weed, when the police pulled me over in the middle of nowhere."

"Damn, Talton, I didn't know you knew people in the Carolinas."

"Yeah, well, that was then, this is now. So, in Georgia, there's counties that only hold court every six months. On petty cases you either pay the fine and get out, or you sit in jail until you go to court. I sat out there about a week before I found out I could pay a fine to have my case disappear. As soon as they told me, I called my baby mamma and had her drive out there with the forty-five hundred they wanted for the case. The next morning, they called me over the loud speaker and told me to pack my shit. Everyone in the pod was surprised; most of those cats had sat in there for months on some petty-ass cases."

Cita handed Talton a blunt that she had rolled while he was in the bank. He paused to take a hit, and then continued with his story.

"So, I'm rushing to pack my shit and the dude I was telling you 'bout came up to me and handed me a piece of paper with his information on it. I guess he wanted me to write him, or something. After that, I went through the whole release process, not thinking anything about the paper he gave me. Then, when I got out, and got in my car, something hit me. Something in my mind told me to check that paper he gave me. When I looked at it, I realized he had wrote his information down on a money receipt."

"What was so special about that?"

Talton took another hit from the blunt, then passed it back to Cita before answering. "Well, his girl was the person who put that money on his books. It had her address on it. She lived in a lil' town called Boston, right outside of Thomasville. So, instead of heading back to Tennessee, I told my baby mamma to follow me to Thomasville. When we got there, I got a motel room, then I went to a supply store and bought a shovel. After that, I waited 'til nightfall –"

"You mean you fucked your bitch 'til nightfall!" commented Cita, while abruptly changing lanes.

"Man, stop cutting me off, and slow your roll! You scratch my rims, we're gonna have problems."

"Whatever! Keep going... tell the damn story."

"So, the address was out in the sticks. The only reason I found it was because I had GPS. It was out in the woods, surrounded by trees. So, I parked my car a half-mile away and walked up from the back of the property. That's when I saw the cars. The Durango, the Benz, and the old school. I couldn't believe it, everything blood had said was true. All the way down to the stack of rims next to the shed. I went over there, moved the rims and started diggin'. Cita, I dug for hours!"

Without taking her eyes off the traffic, she asked, "Did you get the money?"

"Hell, naw! The dude was full of shit."

Cita finally arrived at the Denny's where Talton's brother was waiting. As she pulled into the parking lot she asked,"What'd you do?"

"Nothing. I left, telling myself I'd never trust another jail-house nigga again. But I obviously didn't learn my lesson, cuz I just wasted our time back there."

"Don't trip, baby. It was on the way. Now, let's hurry up and get inside, I gotta pee."

Talton didn't dare tell Cita what really happened on that warm, summer evening in Georgia.

After two hours of digging, Talton was livid. Still hoping there was a chance that he could find the money, he broke into the house and forced his way into the wife's bedroom. He asked her about the money, but when she said she didn't know anything about it, Talton lost it. He started beating her like she had stolen something from him. Next thing he knew, her teenaged son had barged in the room, toting a twelve-gauge shotgun. Before the boy could get a shot off, Talton wrestled the gun away from him and shot them both.

After the murders, Talton ran back to his car and drove back to the motel where Melody was waiting. They left the room that night and drove straight back to Chattanooga. On the trip back, as he followed his wife, Talton suddenly remembered something about the guy saying he had an eighteen-month-old daughter, also. Talton told himself that God must've been watchin over the little girl, because if he would've seen her, he would've killed her, too.

CHAPTER ELEVEN

The moment Talton and Cita stepped inside the restaurant, Anthony's daughter, Fanny, ran towards her uncle and jumped into his arms. "Uncle Talton!"

Picking her up, Talton said, "What's up, baby? What're you doing here? Shouldn't you be in school?"

"Yeah, but I got in trouble," answered Talton's niece.

Anthony took Fanny from Talton and said, "She got suspended for throwing a chair at the teacher."

"It was an accident, Uncle Talton!" cut in Fanny.

"I know it was, baby," said Talton.

Anthony put his daughter back down and told Cita, "Go ahead and order us some steak and eggs. I got something I need to talk to my brother about, and then we'll be right back."

"Alright," replied Cita before looking at Fanny. "Come on, Fanny, let's go powder our noses. After that, we might start breakfast with some ice cream, what do you think about that?" Cita then took ahold of the little girl's hand and took her to the restroom.

Anthony and Talton walked outside, heading towards Ant's Thunderbird. The black car was in pristine condition; wet paint, and brand-new 24-inch Asanti rims. It was Anthony's most prized possession, next to his OP chain. Once both of them were inside the Thunderbird, Anthony reached under his seat and pulled out his brother's Desert Eagle. "Here, take this big motherfucker," he said while handing the gun to his brother.

Talton took the weapon, dropped it on his lap and said, "Look, Ant, I already know what you're gonna say."

"Your bitch talked, blood. Now, I'ma ask you one last time; what're you gonna do when this kid comes?"

"Man, the way you're acting, you're starting to make me feel like there's something you're not tellin' me.

"Man, dismiss me with the theatrics. The bitch snitched! Any bitch that'll tell on the father of her kid ain't 'bout shit!"

"And you know this. The bottom line is that she's gotta go. Whether it's in a body bag, or on her own accord, she's gotta go. And, with that being said, you need to figure out what you're gonna do, cuz being a single father isn't an option."

"Ant –"

"No! Let me talk! We're on the verge of making some big moves. At some point, we're gonna run this city. And we both know we're gonna have to bump heads with them Miami niggas. How we gonna do that when you've got a newborn on your hip?"

"I got three babies, by three different women, in three different states!" replied Talton angrily. "Not one of my kids even knows my name! This is my one chance to finally be a father, and I can't give that up. Ant, I love the game, I respect your foresight, but this may be the only chance I'll ever have to raise one of my pups. You of all people should respect that. Cita's a sqaure bitch; she's young and never seen shit. Of course, she talked. But this is just a petty dope charge —"

"A petty dope charge! You call a hundred-thousand dollar bond a petty dope charge? We damn near gotta start all over!"

"It ain't shit, bruh. I'll hire a mouth-piece and get probation. After the baby's born, I'll let her go and I'll cover my son. Even if it takes hiring someone. Or I'll just pull another bitch. So, let's talk numbers. What are we working with?"

"After you got locked up, I turned that half into a whole thang and dumped it for twenty-thousand, plus a couple G's on the side. I also gave Mike and B.A. some weed so they'll have a couple racks, too."

"We got enough for another half, then."

"Yeah, but Snoop's back in Cali. And, you know how that is. We might not hear from him for a couple of weeks. I got bills; by the time he comes back, we'll be down to quarter brick money."

"I holla'd at Red earlier, maybe we can get some trees from her. You said she sells pounds, right?"

"Who?"

"The stripper from Orlando."

"How'd you talk to her? I thought you didn't have her number?"

"All that doesn't matter. I'm supposed to meet up

with her when she gets off work. She said she has a 'proposition' for me–"

"I bet she does."

"It ain't like that, nigga. I think she wants to talk business. If she really got it like you say she does, we might be able to add her to the portfolio."

"She's got it, bruh. I asked around while you were gone and niggas know her. She got it big."

"Alright, so, other than that, I guess we wait on Snoop."

"Maybe not," said Ant. "Why don't you call Black and get us a half a brick from the Miami niggas?"

Talton gave his brother a surprised look. The dope boys from Miami were their competition.

"Shit, why not?" said Ant. "It's our money, and it'll keep them trusting us. You never know how far that'll go. It might work to our favor when it's time to make the checkmate on them niggas."

Talton smiled, clearly impressed. "Alright, let's do it."

Gangsta made the call, ordering half a kilo from his connection. His connect had to go through someone else to get it, so he, in turn, told Talton that he would call him back. After that, the brothers went back inside the restaurant and ate a festive breakfast with the girls.

When they were finished they went back to Anthony's house. Anthony lived in a two-bedroom cottage on Clearwater beach. He took pride in his place, investing in all high-end electronics and furniture. It was a glorified bachelor pad with an array of man toys in its driveway. Not only did he own the T-bird on 24's, Anthony also had a Jeep Wrangler, two Harley Davidsons and a pair of Kawasaki jet skis. The only visible sign that he was a family man were the bunk beds in the spare bedroom.

Shortly after arriving at the beach house, Talton received the call he'd been waiting for. The deal was a go. All they had to do was show up with the money and they'd have the drugs they ordered. Fanny was left with Cita while the brothers went to pick up the contraband. When they got back, a cab was called and the girls went to the movies, leaving the men alone to handle business.

Gangsta and his brother spent the rest of the afternoon mixing and pressing their newly acquired product. The whole process took several hours. They had to put the half kilo of pure cocaine in a dry blender, a few ounces at a time, then blend the blocks into dust. After all the coke was broken down into powder form, they mixed it together with another half kilo of cut. Then they sprayed it with acetone and put it all inside the press. The final product was a hard block that weighed one thousand grams. Just as white and just as hard as the original package they bought only a few hours beforehand. The only difference was the weight and the potency.

Talton loved this part of the business. It gave him time to bond with his older brother. In the years since Talton left Sacramento, he had always felt alone, isolated from his real friends and family. But, now that he was running the streets with an actual relative, he felt as if a piece of him that had been missing all along was finally there.

Every time Talton and Anthony got together, Gangata made the best of it. While rerocking their investment, the siblings would spend their time smoking and drinking. All the while, playfully arguing over how much cut to put on the cocaine. Ant would always try and push the limit, while Talton tried to stop him. What Talton didn't know was that Anthony always snuck in a few extra ounces.

On this day, the scenario played out as usual. Despite the pending criminal charges, both of them seemed lighthearted. They had the house to themselves so they turned the music up and went to work. Neither one of them had the slightest idea that this would be the last batch of cocaine they would ever rerock together.

CHAPTER TWELVE

Nirobi was sitting in the passenger seat of his cousin's Buick. They were parked at a Sonics, waiting for the girl on skates to deliver their meal. Nirobi was contemplating whether or not he should ask the waitress for her number. He had long dreadlocks, along with a mouth full of gold teeth. Most of the time, all he had to do was smile and women would throw their number his way. The Sonics waitress was looking real good to him in the short shorts she was wearing, so Nirobi was about to make his move when she came back with their food.

"What's up wit' you, cuz?" asked Yada from the driver's seat. "Tell me some more about the redhead bitch."

"Like I said, she's got weight. When I mentioned the ten-pound deal, she didn't even blink. It seems like she does numbers like that on a regular basis. I figure we can order the ten P's, then hit her with a rushed transaction. Give her a stack of fake bills like we did that dude a couple years back."

"Robi, you think too small!" The Sonics waitress skated up to the driver's side and connected the tray to the door. Yada handed her some bills before

Nirobi had a chance to say anything, and she skated away. "Do you know where she lives?"

"No. But I'm on that. I tried following her home from Show Girls the other night."

"What was she doing up there?"

"She works there. Well, actually, she only goes in once or twice a week. Cuz, pass the food."

Yada handed Nirobi a burger, taking some of his cousin's fries before passing them as well.

"So...yeah, I haven't been able to find her spot. I figure we can just call her to a Wal-Mart, or something, and do a rush deal with some fake bills. After that, I just change my number and it's a dun-da-da."

Yada didn't say anything. He needed the money in a bad way. He didn't feel right riding around in a car that had its back window busted out. He was used to having money. But ever since he came home from prison, he couldn't seem to bounce back. This lick could bring him back, though. Yet, ten pounds split two ways wasn't going to be enough. If this girl was sitting on fifty pounds, like his cousin was saying, he'd have to go all the way with it.

"How often do you cop from her?"

"Shit... probably once a week, I'll buy a pound for thirty-five hundred."

"OK, then. This is what we'll do: the next time you call her, you'll order your pound. Then, after you pay for it and she leaves, you're gonna call her back. That's when you'll tell her that your homey needs one too. I'll be following her to see where she goes to pick it up. That's how we'll find out where her stash is at.

You said she's got at least fifty pounds, right?"

"I said I *think* she should be sittin' on that much. I don't really know what the bitch got."

"So when's the soonest you can call her without raising suspicion?"

"Shit... I can call her tonight."

"That's what's up!" said Yada, while taking a bite out of his burger. He couldn't remember a better tasting meal...

$$$$$

Five o'clock took forever to come. Alize spent the better part of her day stalking the clock. She thought she had it all planned out. So that she wouldn't seem thirsty, she told herself that she wouldn't answer the phone the first time Talton called. Her plan didn't work, though.

The moment she got in her car, her phone vibrated and she answered it immediately. It was Talton, so she told him to meet her at the McDonald's up the street from Show Girls. She told him she'd be there at six, giving herself an hour to get ready.

When she got home, she barely got through the front door before she started stripping down. Dropping clothes everywhere, she was completely naked by the time she reached the bathroom. Then, as she went to turn on the water, she caught a glimpse of herself in the mirror that hung from the door. Her bushy, red pubic hair stared back at her defiantly. In the last several months she had neglected to shave her private areas because she didn't have anyone to impress. Things had changed, though. It was time to clean up the yard.

When the water hit the right temperature, she stepped in letting the warm stream run down her body. After a few moments she reached for a bar of soap and started soaping up her pubic region; getting it ready for the razor. As she was doing this, she accidently rubbed her fingers across her clitoris. This triggered an avalanche of erotic stimuli. Her whole day had been spent thinking of a man whom she was extremely attracted to. Unable to ease the sexual tension, she settled for a passive massage triggered by rocking her thighs back and forth.

But, right now, in the shower, with her finger between her thighs, she could no longer help herself. After that initial brush with her love button, the rest was a wrap. She quickly began masturbating, fast and hard. Since she was in a rush she treated herself roughly, feverishly attacking her silky folds with her soapy fingers. At one point, she almost lost her footing, so she placed her free hand on the wall to steady herself as she violently penetrated her nether regions.

Alize's heart was beating wildly, her breath became short and her knees started to shake. An orgasm was mounting; this made Ze switch gears. With the tips of three fingers, she stroked her swollen clitoris as fast as humanly possible. Then, she felt it coming. With her eyes closed, she visualized the man of her dreams. At the moment when the waves of ecstasy overcame her body, she made the conscious decision to make Talton the father of her next child.

CHAPTER THIRTEEN

The time was 5:58 and Talton was at the McDonald's where he was supposed to meet Alize at. He had taken his braids out, opting to put his hair in a ponytail earlier in the day. It was the only attempt he had made to clean up. He hadn't even taken a shower yet. Usually, this wouldn't bother him; he was on his grind, and sometimes, as a hustler, he'd go several days wearing the same clothes. But today was different. He liked Alize, and he wanted to make a good impression. He just hadn't had the chance to get situated.

He was studying his reflection in the rear-view mirror when his phone vibrated. Cita's picture popped up on the screen, so he activated the speaker function; "What's good, baby mama?"

"Nothing much. Just sitting here wondering why you aren't here with me."

"You still got Fanny wit' you?"

"No... I dropped her off at her mom's house, then I rode back to my sister's. You need to get here; I feel stupid sitting here all by myself."

"You know... I'm not too sure we should be staying with your sister. She doesn't even like me, and she's got a house-full already. And, I got way too much shit going on to be putting myself in a situation like that."

"You should've thought about all that before you got our house raided," said Cita, clearly preparing for war.

That's when Talton spotted a familiar looking car pulling into the lot. The burgundy Malibu looked just like a car he had seen at the bank earlier in the day. When it pulled into the spot next to his, he knew it was her.

Talton had backed his Delta into the parking space so he could see who was coming and going. Alize slid her car into the space adjacent to his, stoppin' close enough for their windows to be aligned. If his car hadn't been sitting so high, they would've been face to face.

"...Talton, you fucking hear me? What are you doing?!"

Talton brought the phone closer to his mouth, "I gotta go... this nigga just pulled up... gotta handle some business. I'll get at you when I'm done." After dropping the phone onto the passenger seat, Talton directed his attention towards Alize. "So, that's how you do me? Keep me waiting for two hours?"

"Shut up," she said, playfully. "It's not even six o'clock yet. Besides, I had to go home and shower, unlike some people I know." Ze gave Talton a look of mock disgust. "How come you don't got no tint on your car? It looks like a big-ass fish bowl. I can't ride like that; can't have cops being able to see in my shit."

"That's how I ride in my Suburban. Sittin' high, limo-tinted out the game. It's like my office on wheels, but this the Delta, baby. When I'm in this one, I want the whole world to see me." Talton winked, "But, seriously, this is my flossin' ride. I really don't push it like that."

"Yeah, but your wifey does."

"What you mean by that?"

"I saw the girl that drove you to the bank. I'm half expecting her to show up at any time, with some baby mamma drama."

"That ain't gonna happen. I got my end under control." Talton was beginning to feel more comfortable with Ze.

"Anyways... you ready to talk numbers?"

"Now you talking, ma. You know what?"

"What?"

"I'm a firm believer that there's only one thing more important than money."

"What's that?"

"More money!"

"So I got a philosopher on my hands. Follow me; let's see if we can come up with a way to make 'more money'."

Talton pulled into traffic behind Alize, wondering how long he'd have to drive to reach her house. In the end, it wasn't far at all. She made a few turns, and they were in a residential area. When they finally arrived, Talton was surprised. She had a big house. *This'll be interesting*, he thought, fully expecting to walk into a house full of people.

Alize waited for Talton to get out of his car, then

she walked him inside. His first impression was that the house was dark... almost too dark. In the living room, there was a large sectional facing a wood-grain entertainment center. He was surprised to see that she only had a fifteen-inch flat screen for a television. The living room was connected to the kitchen, separated by a breakfast bar. So far, nothing too spectacular.

Alize got a call just as they were entering the house. She told Talton that she had to take it, then she stepped in the kitchen with the phone to her ear. Talton tried to make himself comfortable, but something wasn't right. Ever since he met Ze, she had given him an air of self-confidence. Yet, her house was a total contrast.

Then, it came to him that she probably lived with a grandmother, or another older person. There were pictures all over the living room, so he decided to check them out... maybe they'd shed some light on the situation. But, as he looked around, he noticed that all of the pictures were of a little kid. A baby boy with curly red hair. By the looks of the photos, Alize was obviously the mother of a toddler.

After that, Talton set out to take a better look at the house. Alize was still on the phone, so he called out, "I'm finna use your bathroom, a'ight?"

"Yeah, it's in the hallway," she said from the kitchen.

On the way to the restroom, Talton looked inside of one of the bedrooms. He saw a crib and a changing table. The room was also filled with boxes upon boxes of unwrapped toys. Remote control cars, water guns, even a Big Wheel. Talton didn't really have to use the toilet; he wanted to count the toothbrushes. It was the easiest way to figure out how many people lived in a house. Anytime he went to a new female's house, the first thing he did was check out the bathroom; that's how he'd find out if there was another alpha male in the picture.

Alize's bathroom was just as dark as the rest of the house. The first thing he noticed after turning on the light was that the shower curtain, toilet seat covers, and floor rug were all black. That's when he figured out what bothered him about Alize's house. It was too dark. All the windows throughout the home were covered and the lights were dim.

Talton didn't have a college degree, but he had read a lot of books in prison. And he remembered reading one that said a person's living quarters usually represented their mind. The way a person takes care, decorates, or even neglects an area where they spend most of their time at is a representation of their inner self.

If someone keeps his office, car, house or prison cell cluttered, their thoughts are usually cluttered as well. Alize's house was dark and glum. All the writing on the wall spelled "Depression," but why? For what?

There were two toothbrushes next to the sink. Not a good sign for Talton, so he took a closer look. He opened the medicine cabinet, finding femine shaving cream, midol, and dental floss. *Nothing too masculine*, he thought to himself. Under the sink, he found more female hygiene products. He was beginning to think that Ze really did live with her grandmother. By the time he finished in the bathroom, Talton was convinced that two adult females lived in the house.

Alize was waiting for Talton in the living room. She was sitting on the couch with two glasses and a bottle of Johnnie Walker Black Label on the coffee table. Talton sat next to her and they started conversing. The topic started out as business.

It was uncharacteristic for either one of them to discuss their finances with strangers, yet they both opened up.

She told him how she would pick up twenty to thirty pounds of weed from her connection, in Orlando, for twenty-five-hundred dollars a pound. Then, how she would turn around and sell each unit at a thousand-dollar profit. In turn, Talton explained how he and his brother put their money together to buy cocaine from different suppliers and how they turned one into two with their press. He also told Alize about the case he caught, and how it affected him both financially as well as emotionally, when he found out that Cita couldn't be trusted.

Alize was slightly surprised by Talton's conversational skills. Most men didn't know how to shut up and listen. Talton was different, though. He wasn't stuck on himself; on the contrary, he seemed more interested in hearing about her than talking about himself. So, she opened up, not just about finances, but also telling him why she hustled. When he asked about the bedroom with the gifts, she told him that that was where Shawn slept on the weekends. Shawn would spend so much time bonding with her that he never played with his toys.

Then Talton surprised her again by asking about the extra toothbrush. That's when she told him about Brittany. Alize lived with her younger sister. She was never around because she worked at a convalescence home and her schedule was hectic. And, when she was off from work, she'd run the streets.

When she explained the reason for the extra toothbrush, Talton couldn't believe his luck. The opportunities were limitless. Alize was a beautiful, single mother who only had her kid on the weekends. She also had a three-bedroom house, her own car, and a federal hustle. She was a dime! He suddenly wished he would've met her before Cita; he would've been ahead of the game by now. That's when he finally realized what his brother had been trying to tell him this whole time. Talton had been double hustling, and this meeting with Alize made him realize it.

By the time he looked at his watch he saw that they had been talking for almost three hours. A lot had been discussed during that time. They agreed to put their money together for joint investments and Talton planned on introducing her to his brother as soon as possible. By the end of their conversation, it was hard not to feel optimistic.

Then Talton got up, not wanting to leave. "Alright then, Ze."

"Where you going?" asked Alize, at the risk of sounding too anxious.

"Man, I gotta get home... take a shower. You

already made that clear. I'ma call you when you get off work, though."

Alize stared at Talton's mouth, wanting to put her lips against his, but she held back. The timing wasn't right. Nonetheless, she knew he was the one. Throughout the last several hours, Alize was able to ascertain that Talton was a man of his word. She recognized his eyes as those of a predator, but she also saw a man with morals. She wanted him in a bad way. This was the man she wanted to have a child with. He was so different than all the other men she had met along the way. He had wisdom beyond his years, and his eyes harbored scars from experience. She could tell that he would make a dangerous enemy, yet, at the same time she felt that she could trust him with her life.

Alize decided to test her assumptions. "Alright, I can see that your mind is made up about leaving. But, before you go, I need you to give me a hand with something. Come on." Alize led Talton to the hallway, between the bathroom and the bedrooms. "See that door up there?" asked Alize, signaling towards the attic door. "There's three duffle bags holding ten pounds apiece." Pulling the stairs down. "Go ahead and grab one. Take it with you. If we're gonna be serious about this business arrangement, we might as well start now."

Talton climbed up the ladder and saw the duffle bags off to the right of the entrance. He grabbed one and brought it down the stairs. At the bottom, he opened the clothes bag and marveled at the Christmas-tree shaped buds. The cannabis was inside of a clear garbage bag, yet he could still smell the scent from the high-grade marijuana.

"I'm giving you this because I'm at work most of the time. It'd be crazy to make you wait for me to get off of work every time you need to make a sale. Just shoot me the twenty-five G's that I'm supposed to pay my connect, and it's all good. I do wanna tell you something, though. If you run off with this weed, I'm not gonna blow up your phone, or come looking for you. I'll take the loss, but you'll be losing the opportunity of a lifetime."

Talton looked at her, knowing that what she was saying was true. If he wanted to, he could take it all, but why? She was handing it to him at her price. He'd have to be a certified idiot to forfeit a relationship like this.

"I got you," replied Talton. "Don't worry about nothing. You know... it doesn't seem like you'd do this for just anybody. For that alone, I would never play you. Trust that."

"I know. Now, hurry up and get back to the wifey. I don't want you getting grounded."

"What you finna do?"

"I gotta go sell a pound to one of my people."

"It's already late; you always do business this late at night?"

"Yeah... it's just a pound. I got this, Talton."

Talton left a few minutes later. Alize was about to leave behind him when she remembered that she hadn't called Shawn that evening. In four years, she had never missed a call. This was unacceptable, and she had no one to blame except herself. The thought of the missed call bothered her so much, she totally forgot about the sale she had waiting for her.

CHAPTER FOURTEEN

"Man, call that bitch again, cuz!" Yada started getting mad at Nirobi when Alize wouldn't answer her phone. He was starting to think that she didn't have it like his cousin had led on. It wouldn't have been the first time Nirobi had had him on a bunk mission. That's why he never really associated with him back when he was ballin'; he didn't have time for fake niggas.

It was already ten p.m. and Alize wasn't answering any of Nirobi's calls. It made him look bad in front of his cousin, but there was nothing he could do. So, he called it a night. "She's not picking up," he told Yada. "We might as well wait till tomorrow. I'll call her in the evening–"

"Evening?! Is you crazy? We're callin' that bitch early in the morning!"

"Naw... that ain't gonna work. I think she's gotta job."

"What you mean, you *think*? She either got a job, or not." Realizing the night was a waste, Yada started driving towards Nirobi's house. He was going to drop him off; he couldn't stand being around him any longer than he had to. "Man, this bitch is all over the board, huh? She dances, sells pounds, and has a day job. What the fuck does she do with all the money?"

"I don't know, but I know she got a lot of it."

"Alright, this is what we're gonna do. I'ma call you in the morning and we're gonna go by all the strip clubs in the city. You do know what kinda car she drives, right?"

"Yeah, a burgundy four-door."

"OK, we'll look for her car. If we find it, we'll follow her home and do a home invasion. A simple jux, nothing to it."

A while later, after dropping his cousin off, Yada stopped at a Chevron station on his way home. While he was pumping gas a black Thunderbird pulled up to the pump next to his. A Puerto Rican guy was driving and a caramel skinned princess was in the passenger seat. She was bouncing her shoulders to the tremendous beat that was coming from the car's trunk. The shiny rims glimmered under the gas station lights. Then the driver hopped out and went inside.

Yada was envious. That was exactly how he wanted to ride. He was tired of being broke. At that point, he would do just about anything to climb out of his rut. Then he remembered the gun underneath his seat. And that's when it came to him. If he wanted to get back on his feet, he'd have to take what he wanted... Why not start now?

A few minutes later, Anthony came out of the gas station with a bag in his hand. He and his girlfriend had taken several ecstasy pills before leaving the house, so they were high. So high that neither one of them paid any attention to the shady looking Buick that just pulled away. On any other night, Anthony would've been more aware of his surroundings. However, tonight he was busy enjoying life.

A few yards away, in the car with its back window busted out, Yada was taking a pistol out from underneath the seat. It was an old thirty-eight revolver, wrapped in a black ski mask. He put it there before he left the house that morning. And now, he would put it to use.

When the Thunderbird pulled out, he followed.

CHAPTER FIFTEEN

Morning came, finding Talton in a dead sleep. The night before had ended better than he expected. When he arrived at the trailer, all the kids were in bed and the inside was surprisingly clean. He was accustomed to being two feet deep in children and dirty clothes whenever he stepped inside of Cita's sister's double-wide trailer. But this night was different.

Cita answered the door wearing Victoria's Secret, and there was a candle light dinner waiting on the kitchen table. After their meal, Cita gave Talton a bubble bath. Afterwards, she led him into their bedroom. It was small, yet cozy. Talton prided himself in being able to satisfy his lover's every need, but this night it was Cita's turn. She catered to his darkest sexual desires; putting Gangsta to sleep without a care in the world.

Before they knew it, morning came. Talton was sleeping in late, but the uncomfortable heat was starting to wake him. He knew he had to get up and start moving, yet he wasn't ready to give up the comfort of complete solitude.

Then, suddenly the bedroom's door flew open,

startling him out of his sleep. The light flicked on just as Talton opened his eyes. Cita was standing in the doorway with red-rimmed eyes.

Gangsta sat up, grabbing his phone from the night stand; he saw that it was ten a.m. "What's wrong?"

"It's your brother!" Cita started sobbing. She fell on the bed, and put her arms around Talton.

"Oh my God, Talton, I'm sorry."

"What're you talkin' 'bout? What's going on?"

"Anthony's dead!"

Talton was stunned, unable to speak. His chest suddenly felt constricted, the room was beginning to spin. He searched her eyes for an ounce of doubt, but found none. This was real.

"Did you hear me?" asked Cita. "Why are you looking at me like that?"

"How you know he's dead?"

"His girlfriend, she's at the hospital. Whoever it was, beat her pretty bad." Cita couldn't hold it in any longer, she broke down crying. She had never experienced the loss of a loved one. In some ways, this affected her more than Talton. Where he would release his frustrations through violence, she would internalize it. Talton had already lost a multitude to the streets; she hadn't.

"Cita," said Talton, sounding uncharacteristically cold. "I need you to get a handle on your emotions right now. What hospital is Angelique at?" Talton stepped out of bed and started getting dressed.

"She's at John Hopkins, I told her we'd come get

her. I think she has something for you, but I can't be sure. I was crying too hard when she was on the phone."

Talton slipped his feet into his Jordans. "It's OK, baby, just get dressed."

They were outside within minutes. Gangsta made sure his fifty caliber Desert Eagle was loaded before tucking it in his waistband. On the surface he seemed calm, but Talton was an emotional wreck. They took the Suburban. On the way to the hospital, Talton called his boys and set up a meeting at B.A.'s apartment.

Talton's thoughts were blurred. He kept replaying the last hours he had spent with his brother. They drank liquor, smoked weed and cut cocaine. He didn't want to believe that his brother was really dead. But it was true, that's how the game went sometimes. Talton knew that he'd have to come to terms with it, yet that didn't mean he'd let it go. Someone had murdered his brother, and that same brother would watch from heaven as Talton murdered his killer.

$$$$$

At the hospital they found Angelique on the third floor, sitting on a bed in a hospital gown. The whole right side of her face was swollen and bruised. She could have been in a car accident. Cita ran straight in and gave her a hug. Angelique barely squeezed back. The whole time, her eyes were locked on Talton's.

Gangsta didn't enter the room; he hated hospitals

second to prison. "What happened?" he asked from the doorway.

"He's dead. That motherfucker shot 'em. He killed him, Talton. Anthony's dead!" Angelique covered her face as she started to cry uncontrollably.

Cita started crying too. Both women started sobbing within each other's arms. The whole scene was heart wrenching, something Talton had witnessed way too many times.

"Hey!" announced Talton, loudly. "I know it hurts, but I need y'all to stay strong. Cita, help her get dressed. Angelique, you're coming with us. I'ma need you to tell me everything. First things first, did you talk to the police?"

"No... I mean, yeah, they were here. They gave me a card." She handed the card to Cita. Cita handed it to Talton.

"I'll be in the truck," said Talton. Then he turned away and left.

The hospital staff wouldn't let Angelique walk out of the hospital herself, so she was pushed out in a wheelchair. Talton was standing next to his truck when the girls came out. He helped her into the back seat, not wanting her in the front. He needed her off the radar. She had a nasty gash on the side of her face, but that wasn't why he wanted her out of sight. She was his only source of information; he needed her safe and out the way. In other words, she was now officially placed in Gangsta's version of protective custody.

Once they were inside the Suburban, Talton drove away from the hospital in silence. He was mentally preparing himself for the murders he would soon commit. At that moment, he had no idea who killed his brother, or why. But he was sure that after he sat down and really grilled Angelique, he would at least know in what direction to head. It always worked that way. He just hoped he could catch the killer before the police did. Talton didn't have the connections in the Florida prison system like he did in California. Therefore, he had no choice, he'd have to handle it in the streets.

Over the years he had lost a lot of loved ones to the game. He knew how to handle a situation such as this. An eye for an eye, pretty simple. Yet, this time it was different. Anthony was his older brother; even though they had different fathers, they were raised together and they loved one another.

Anthony was the only connection to his past. This was killing Talton, and the thought of having to tell the kids that their father was dead made him tear up. Another generation of fatherless children would come of this. It seemed as if no matter how hard they tried, the cycle refused to be broken. All the children in their family were destined to grow up without fathers.

The silence was finally broken by Angelique; "Talton."

Looking at her through the reflection in the rear-view, Talton asked, "What's up, ma?"

"I know about you. Anthony told me things. When I said I talked to the police, it's because I did. But I didn't tell them the truth. I told 'em it was a white guy. And, I didn't tell them I was raped so they

wouldn't get his DNA. I also didn't give them this."
Angelique handed Talton her phone.

When Angelique reached over his seat and handed Talton her cell phone, he instinctively knew it would contain the information he would need to track down Anthony's killer. Yet, nothing prepared him for what he would actually see. Gangsta pulled the truck over and pressed the play sign on the phone's touch screen. Cita, who was watching everything play out, leaned in from her seat to get a better view.

As the video started, they heard Angelique's laughter and Anthony's stereo system playing music. At first, the picture was grainy, but then it focused on Talton's brother. Anthony was obviously high; he must've been having fun. He was playfully throwing up gang signs and popping his collar, clearly feeling himself. Then, there was some sort of crash. Anthony's attention was diverted and the camera suddenly went out of focus.

Next, they heard the screams and the video showed a struggle. Anthony was wrestling someone wearing a ski mask. It reminded Talton of the cop at his house the night the house was raided. The picture on the screen was moving around too much for anyone to see anything, especially with Angelique trying to help fight off the attack.

Then... they heard the gunshots. One after the other. Five murderous shots in all. All of a sudden the music stopped and the video went quiet. The phone must have fell from Angelique's hand because now the picture showed the ceiling of the car. A few seconds went by, then in the corner of the screen they saw the man in the mask slowly taking it off. He reached for Angelique and another fight ensued. However, this time the goon didn't waste any time. He lifted his gun and started hammering away at Angelique's head and face. Within moments the fight was over.

Talton let the phone drop to his lap. Cita had tears streaming down her face. They both knew the rest of the video was of Angelique being raped.

"Talton," said Angelique. "You need to keep watching."

He recognized the tone in her voice. He'd heard it many times from his dead homeboy's mothers, sisters, and baby mammas. He didn't want to watch anymore, he was about to break down. But he knew that he had to stay focused; he needed to control his emotions.

So he picked up the phone and continued to watch. He couldn't see much, but then he heard a voice. It was the killer talking to someone. The killer was giving someone named "Nirobi" directions to where he was at. Then everything went silent.

"We were on our way to Chico's house," began Angelique. "Anthony was on his way to make a sale and we had just stopped to get gas at the Chevron on Eastbay Road. After we pulled out I noticed an older car following us but I didn't think much of it. Then, when we turned into Chico's neighborhood, the guy rammed us.

The rest, you saw. I don't remember much except for his gold teeth. The police said Anthony didn't have any money or jewelry on 'em, so I guess that guy took it all "

Cita listened in awe. This was too much for her. She felt like she was watching a movie. "Why didn't you give this video to the police?"

Angelique stared at Cita with an emotionless mask of contempt, yet said nothing. Instead, she looked at Talton.

"You did the right thing, ma." Talton knew that if his brother had really laced Angelique with pieces of their past then she could be trusted. She had been smart by not giving the police her phone. Now it was totally safe to murder this man. The only loose end was Cita. As he got back in route to B.A.'s apartment, he began to realize that he was out of pocket by bringing her along. She had already proven her disloyalty. Nonetheless, she was there, and he was in a hurry. He just had to make sure he didn't say anything important in front of her once they got there.

CHAPTER SIXTEEN

Nirobi was sitting at the table inside the Days Inn room where he and Yada went to celebrate their latest caper. He was rolling a blunt with the weed his cousin had taken from the chico he killed. There was also a pile of cocaine next to the weed, but that was for snorting. If it were up to him he'd put it inside the weed and smoke it, but Yada didn't get down like that.

Yada was in the bathroom, staring at his reflection in the mirror. He was feeling real good about himself now that he had real money in his pocket. Not to mention the diamond necklace hanging from his neck and the gold Rolex dangling from his wrist. He hadn't had time to get the rims off the car, but he still came up. It was just the type of lick that he needed to get the ball rolling; several thousand in cash, a few ounces of cocaine and a half pound of trees. And he wasn't done yet. If the redhead thing was real, he could kiss being broke good-bye forever.

After making sure his waves were in order, Yada stepped out the bathroom. He saw his cousin at the table and said, "This is how a gangsta's 'posed to live, cuz."

"Damn right," called out Nirobi, while sealing the blunt.

Yada walked across the room and sat at the table with his cousin. The sliding glass door was only a few feet away, giving them a view of the pool. The sun was out, making the chlorinated water glisten, but the calming backdrop was ignored. Both Yada and Nirobi had other things on their mind.

Nirobi lit the blunt, took a few puffs and then handed it to Yada.

"I told you it's real wit' me, Robi. I make shit happen. Now, what's up wit' the white bitch?"

"I'm on it. I already called and left a message."

"She better not pull no more bullshit. That janky-ass shit she pulled last night was bullshit. The way I'm feeling right now, anybody can get it." Yada took another hit from the blunt before passing it back to Nirobi. "This ain't no game, cousin. I'm knockin' niggas down."

"Why you think the news said that a cracker murked that chico last night?"

"Shit... I don't even know, fam. I know the bitch saw me, cuz I took the mask off before I knocked her ass out. But, for real, though. I think she wanted to get in the car wit' me from the gate. I just didn't have no time, that's why I just gave her a two piece and bounced."

"You shoulda brought that bitch wit' you, cuz." Nirobi reached below the table and squeezed himself. "At least we'd have a lil' pussy right now."

"Don't trip off that bitch, cuz. Get the redhead

lined up and we'll get ours."

CHAPTER SEVENTEEN

Alize was on break, standing outside the bank smoking a Newport. She wanted to call Talton but didn't want to look so anxious. After handing over all that weed to a man she barely knew, she was beginning to have second thoughts. Especially since she still owed her connect seventy-five thousand dollars. Another reason for her hesitation to call Gangsta was that she didn't want to give him the opportunity to give her a sob story. In the back of her mind, she expected him to give her some nonsense about somehow losing the work she had given him.

Then, just as she was about to snuff out her cigarette in the sand-filled ashtray, her phone vibrated. It was Talton. "Here we go," she said to herself as she answered the phone. "What's up, partner?"

"Hey, Ze. Man, I just wanted to call and let you know I woke up to some fuck-shit this morning–"

"Let me guess; you left the weed in your trunk, and it got stolen. You know... You had me fooled. I thought you were a real hustler. But, ten pounds ain't shit, bigshot." Alize was upset. She didn't want to sound weak, but she was hurt. And she hoped he didn't hear her voice crack towards the end of her last statement. She didn't know what hurt more, a twenty-five-thousand-dollar loss, or that the potential relationship she was cultivating was over before it started.

"What da fuck is you talking 'bout?" asked Talton. "You're trippin', blood. I still got the trees you gave me. Listen, I know you don't know me like that, but I'm not a petty-ass nigga. Stealing your shit is the last thing on my mind. I called to tell you that my brother was killed last night. I just wanted to keep you in the loop since you gave me all that work last night."

"Oh, shit! I'm sorry. I feel like an idiot. Did the cops catch the killer?"

"Naw, but it's good. I got it taken care of. I just wanted to let you know, so you don't start worrying if it takes me a minute to flip the weed."

"I'm glad you called. Damn, this is crazy. Take your time, Talton. Handle your business. If you need someone to talk to, I'm here. All you gotta do is call, or come over."

"I'm good, I just need to take care of a few things."

"Alright then..."

After ending the call, Ze leaned against the wall, and looked up at the cloudless sky. The day was so beautiful, yet it was filled with death. But, wasn't that what life was like sometimes? Beautiful days turned ugly...

At B.A.'s apartment, Talton and his boys were crowded around Mike's laptop. The girls were in the bedroom, so Gangsta felt safe discussing business. Mike had downloaded the video from Angelique's phone. And now, they were watching the crime play out on a thirteen-inch screen.

Talton studied his associate's facial expressions as they watched the video. He was trying to read their thoughts. In all actuality, he didn't know them as well as he wished he did. He had only known them both for about a year. Meeting them separately at the same telemarketing job.

Talton met Mike one afternoon after they pulled into adjacent parking spaces. Mike walked away from his car, absent-mindedly leaving a quarter pound of marijuana on the passenger seat. When Talton saw it, he flagged Mike down to let him know he was slipping. A thankful Mike offered to buy him a drink during their lunch break and Talton accepted. The two men quickly hit it off, and ever since that day the two unlikely associates became close friends.

Mike was a tall white guy who always wore button-up Polo shirts. From just looking at him, one would never guess that he had just finished serving eight and a half years in state prison. He wasn't overly muscular, nor did he have an excess amount of tatooes. Yet, he was a convict, and that gave him a connection to Talton that made them click.

B.A. was a dark-skinned brother, fresh out of prison as well. He'd done close to a decade behind the wall for attempted murder on a confidential informant who wore a wire on him. He had swagger. He was always draped in new clothes, even before he was able to afford it.

When Talton first got his job at the telemarketing company he was single, so he spent most of his down time flirting with his female coworkers. B.A. saw this and figured Talton would make a good wingman. So, he approached him and a friendship ensued.

It didn't take long before they became a trio; partying and hustling together. After a few months, they started making enough money to quit their jobs. All of this had taken place in the last year.

Now, as Talton presented them with this video, he silently wondered if he could trust them with murder. Yeah, he had counted money and fucked bitches with them, but he was stuck on whether or not they could be trusted with this type of thing.

As he contemplated his next move, Talton thought of his teenage years. At any given time, while growing up, he could look around any car he was in and he'd be surrounded by killers. Everyone he knew had at least one murder under their belt. That's how it was growing up on the darker side of the tracks.

Right now, he couldn't have been further from his old turf. He was three thousand miles away from home; about to plot a murder with some guys he really didn't know that well. Of course they would listen to him He had a track record of making things happen. Ever since entering their lives, Talton had Mike and B.A. making more money than they ever thought possible. But that wasn't the point. The question was whether or not they could be trusted with murder.

As soon as the video ended, B.A. looked at

Talton and said, "This is some wild shit. I don't recognize dude, but that name he said sounds familiar. Maybe we can freeze a frame and Instagram this nigga's mug. We'll eventually find someone that knows 'em. But, Talton, we can't stop getting money, bruh. I know it's too soon, but do you know your brother's connect?"

"Man, I ain't worried about Ant's connect right now! My motherfuckin' brother just got killed, B.A.! That's all I'm worried about."

"Bruh, don't get me wrong," replied B.A. "I know what the main objective is. But we need money if we plan on going to war. We can't just let everything go because of some haters."

"The connect isn't an issue. Don't worry about all that. It'll be there when we need it. Right now, I need to find my brother's killer. What about you, Mike? You got any ideas?"

"Actually, I think B.A. might be on to something with the Instagram thing. But, we need to clarify what the main objective actually is. Yeah, he killed Ant. An eye for an eye sounds about right. But once we post his flick on the Internet, everybody's gonna know it was us when his body gets found floating in the bay. So, the question is, what are we gonna do once we find 'em?"

Talton stared at Mike for several seconds before answering his question. "I want this nigga dead. We can put a caption under his picture making it look like some females that met him at a club are looking for him. But, truthfully, I really don't give a fuck. This dude killed my brother; I don't care if I have to kill 'em in front of the D.A., in a packed court room."

Talton paused to see if his comrades weren't up for the job. Detecting no weakness, he continued, "And, yeah, B.A., you're right about the money. We're gonna need more money than ever. That also means less spending, more hustling. You can both start by getting on your phones and letting people know that we got pounds of dro for sale. You can sell 'em for thirty-five a piece, and you'll get five-hundred a unit."

"Where'd you get the trees at?" asked Mike.

"That stripper I met at Show Girls the night before I went to jail. I hooked up with her as soon as I got out."

"That's what's up!" said B.A., as he started tapping out a mass text to all of his contacts.

"How much you got?" asked Mike.

"About ten P's."

"Damn, Gangsta!" exclaimed B.A. "That bitch got it like that?'

Before Talton could respond, Cita and Angelique came out of the bedroom. Angelique sat down at the table in the kitchen, Cita came into the living room.

"You alright?" asked Talton.

"Yeah, but I'm tired," replied Cita. "This baby's kickin' my ass. There's something I wanna ask you."

"What's up?" asked Talton, hoping Cita wasn't about to ask about anything regarding his brother.

Cita sat down next to him and said, "Me and Angelique were talking, and we realized Ant's house is empty. You and I need a place to stay and Angelique doesn't need to be alone, so we were thinking about staying at the beach. It'll be better than staying at my sister's house. What do you think?"

Talton thought about it for a moment before answering, "You're right. Let's do it. But, first, there's somewhere I need to go...

CHAPTER EIGHTEEN

When Alize came home from work, she found her sister in the kitchen warming up a pizza pocket. Brittany was nineteen years old and didn't look anything like her sister. Where Ze was tall and slim, Brit-Brit was short and thick. The only physical attributes they shared were the same green colored eyes and their extra-large derrieres. After losing Shawn, the only family Alize had was her younger sister. However, Brittany was only thirteen at the time, so it wasn't like she was able to offer anything more than moral support. But that didn't matter. They both struggled, eventually overcoming the odds that were against two runaway teens. This made their already unique bond unbreakable.

Alize was still bothered by the news Talton had shared with her earlier in the day. Even though she had never met his brother, she still felt bad for Talton. She knew what it was like to lose a sibling.

After shutting the front door, Ze plopped onto the couch. Nonetheless, she barely had enough time to get comfortable before her phone started vibrating. When she looked at its screen, she saw Nirobi. This time, she was glad he called. She missed his sale the night before and she was desperately hoping he hadn't spent his money with anyone else. Alize activated the speaker button and spoke into the phone, "Hello."

"Ze! Man, what's up, girl? What happened last night? You left me hangin'." Nirobi covered his phone's mouthpiece and waved at Yada. When he got his attention, Nirobi whispered, "I got her on the phone, cuz!"

"I'm sorry about that," said Ze. "I ran into some problems last night. I got sidetracked, but everything's good now. So, what's up?"

"You got a pound?"

"Come on, Nirobi, you know I got a pound. I got pounds on top of pounds, just waiting for you to step up your game. Where you at? I can meet you right now."

"I'm at the Days Inn on U.S. 19, in room 112. You really comin' this time, right?"

"Hell yeah, I'll be there in twenty minutes."

"A'ight."

Ze put her phone down and called out to her sister who was sitting at the breakfast bar eating her pizza pocket. "You wanna take a ride, sis?"

"Where to?"

"I gotta meet this guy at the Days Inn. He wants to spend a few G's."

"Is he cute?"

Alize thought about it for a second, then said, "Yeah, he's kinda cute..."

$$$$$

When Talton pulled his Suburban into his brother's ex-wife's driveway, Cita didn't even make an effort to try and look as if she wanted to go in with him. Telling Anthony's children that their father had been killed was a mountain she didn't want to climb. It was obvious that Talton didn't want her to come in anyway. So, she sat in the truck and watched as he approached the house.

As always, Fanny was the first one to greet her uncle by jumping into his arms. Then Alicia came to the door. Moments later, as if sensing something was wrong, her facial expression changed and she made way for Talton to enter. They went to the living room; joined by Anthony's son, Jr. The curtains to the picture window were open; therefore, Cita was able to watch as Talton spoke with Alicia and the kids. She couldn't hear what they were saying, but she could tell that Alicia had started yelling at Talton. At one point, she attacked him, hitting him wildly as the stoic children watched in silence. Then he grabbed her and held her tight. That's when they all began sobbing, including Talton, who had finally allowed his emotions to run freely.

Cita never saw him cry before. The scene was surreal, almost like watching a movie. In the last two weeks, her whole life had seemed like a movie. Including the next chapter, in which they would move into the beach house. A move she had deliberately orchestrated herself. The thought of moving into the cottage first occurred to her on the way to the hospital after realizing that no one would be living there. She didn't want to seem like she was being opportunistic, so she made it sound as if the idea had came from a joint conversation between her and Angelique. But the truth of the matter was that it had been from her own manipulations.

The scheming didn't stop there, either. As she sat in the truck, watching the depressing scene play out in front of her, she started thinking about other things. Anthony had cars, jewelry, clothes, and money. Yes, Angelique was his girlfriend, but she couldn't lay claim to any of his things. It would all go to Talton. They were bringing Angelique with them, but there was no way in hell Cita would let another woman live in the same house with her and her man. So, after a few days, Angelique would have to go, leaving everything in the house to her and Talton.

The coup-de-grace would be getting rid of Talton and keeping everything for herself, which would be easy. She came up with a whole plan on the way to B.A.'s apartment from the hospital. As soon as the baby was born, she'd push Talton over the edge. He had never laid a hand on her before, but she was sure that she could bait him into hitting her. Then, she'd call the police and get a restraining order put on him. Since she'd have the baby, she knew Talton wouldn't allow them to be homeless. Therefore, he'd have to pay the bills and she'd have her own house on the beach.

Through the rear-view mirror, Cita saw Angelique staring out the window. Angelique had been quiet ever since they left B.A.'s apartment. While looking at her, Cita thought of the statement she had made when they were leaving the hospital; "I know about you..." What the hell could Angelique know about her baby daddy? There was nothing to know; he was from Tennessee, he had a crazy mother, a few brothers and a sister in prison. A family of crazy people and convicts.

She was probably talking about all of his bastard children. Talton couldn't keep his dick in his pants, that's for sure. It made Cita think that she may have to get rid of Angelique sooner than planned. The more she thought about it, the clearer she saw past the damsel in distress routine. If she didn't know better, she'd think Angelique was trying to move in on Talton. Even though Cita didn't love Talton, she'd be damned if she let another woman have him. The thought of it made her seethe with anger. By the time Talton came out of the house, she was already itching for a fight.

Talton got in the truck without saying a word. He immediately pulled out his phone and started texting. He was trying to get ahold of Alize, figuring he'd gain more ground if he could utilize her network of people to help find Ant's killer. If Talton would've been any less of a man, the emotions he had just experienced would've broke him. His nephew hadn't said much, but then again, Jr. had always been a quiet kid. His niece ended up running from the room where he heard her cries resonating through the walls. And Alicia... he knew the death had hit her the hardest. Throughout all of their struggles, Talton knew that she loved Anthony with all of her heart. It became obvious when she grabbed his arm as he was leaving and said, "Make sure you kill whoever did this." Talton hadn't replied, yet they both knew that he would.

Inside the Suburban, Cita asked, "Who're you texting?"

"Nobody."

"Well, I told you I was tired. So, where we going now?"

Talton put his phone in his pocket and started the truck. "We might as well go to your sister's house and pick up our shit, then head to Ant's house."

"You know, it's not really Ant's house anymore. You do realize that all of his cars, clothes, and even his clientele is all yours now, right? I know he just died, but you gotta realize–"

"He was killed, Cita! He didn't just die, he was killed!" He couldn't believe her. His brother had just been murdered and she was thinking about his cars and clothes.

Angelique sat in the back seat listening to the pregnant bitch. Cita thought she was so smart, but her game was elementary. Angelique had watched as Cita's thoughts went from shock to greed, all in a matter of minutes. Back at B.A.'s apartment, all she kept asking about was what Anthony had at the house. She was completely blind to the fact that her man was on the verge of snapping. Anthony had just been murdered, and all that bitch could think about was his money. If only half the stuff he had told Angelique about Talton was true, it wouldn't be long before he ended up killing Cita. Anyone with a half a mind could see that it was only a matter of time before she crossed the line.

Talton turned away from Cita and continued to text as he pulled out of the driveway. However, Cita wouldn't let up...

"Is that why you got this attitude? You think you're a big-time baller now, so you think you're the shit? Don't forget, I'm the one with your baby inside me, Talton. You can't treat me any way you want to."

Talton fought the urge to lash out towards the vociferous tramp. But his mind was beginning to fog like it usually did when he was about to lose control. Talton stopped the Suburban in the middle of the street and turned to face his thoughtless girlfriend. Then as calm and precise as he could, he said, "Everything you're saying right now is bullshit, Cita. I can give a flying fuck about what Ant left behind. None of that shit means anything to me. My brother was all I had left. The pain I just felt when I told his kids was the worst feeling I've ever had. And now, I got you in my motherfucking ear talking about cars and clothes! Cita, that nigga came outta my mamma's pussy! How you think I feel knowing that I have to call my mom to tell her that her first-born son is dead? Can you honestly, for one second, really believe that any of that bullshit you just mentioned means a goddamn thing to me? If you do, then you really don't know me. Since you obviously don't know what you're saying right now, I'm gonna give you the benefit of the doubt by begging you to please, shut the fuck up! Right now, I'm looking at you in the eyes, and asking you, please stop talking to me."

For the next twenty minutes, the inside of

Talton's Suburban was completely silent.

CHAPTER NINTEEN

Yada was sitting low in the driver's seat of his car. It was parked next to a trash bin, in the back of the parking lot, across from room 112. He was waiting for Alize to show up with the weed so he could follow her back to her place of residence. As he sat there, alone, he thought about how he would take his Buick straight to the paint shop after robbing Ze for everything she had. He was tired of riding around in a bucket with its back window busted out. He couldn't even open his trunk without the help of a screwdriver. Now that he had money, it was time to upgrade. He was in the process of fantasizing about trips to Miami when he saw the burgundy Malibu pull into the parking space directly in front of room 112.

A tall redhead in a business suit stepped out of the driver's side. Then the passenger side opened and another female got out. This one was shorter, but just as sexy. She was wearing a white button-up and a pair of capris. They both had on stilettoes and large sunglasses. They weren't the normal tennis-shoe-wearing females that Yada was used to dealing with. This intrigued him so he decided to take a closer look. After Nirobi opened the door and let them inside the room, Yada switched game plans.

When the girls stepped inside the motel room they were welcomed by the aroma of expensive weed and liquor. It was obvious that Nirobi had rented the room to party. That was cool with the girls; free weed and drinks were always part of the program.

Nirobi led them to the couch, and after they sat down he said, "Man, Ze, I didn't know you was bringing a friend."

"This is my sister, Brittany. Brit-Brit, this is Nirobi."

Brittany purposely blushed, making herself look innocently cute. "I brought the trees," began Ze, "but it's in the car."

"That's cool, I got the money right—"

Nirobi was cut off in mid-sentence when the door suddenly opened and a light-skinned man wearing a diamond pendant that looked exactly like Talton's stepped inside.

Alize shot up out of her seat, "What the hell is this?"

"It's good," said Nirobi. "This is my cousin Yada. He's cool." He was surprised at the sudden change of plans. He wasn't sure what would happen next, but he hoped Yada had decided to hang out with the females before they did anything because he was dying for a chance to mess around with Alize.

Ze didn't like surprises, but her sister did. Brittany stood up, extending her hand towards the light-skinned intruder. "How you doing, Mr.Yada? I'm Brit-Brit, and this is my sister, Alize."

Yada took Brittany's hand and said, "Nice to meet you Brit-Brit." Then he turned to look at Alize; "My bad if I caught you off guard. I was just–"

"I knew you were out there. You were sitting in the scraper next to the trash bin."

Damn, she's sharp, thought Yada. "Yeah, I was rollin' a blunt. When I saw you show up, I came in to introduce myself. My cousin tells me you got pounds, but he didn't tell me you had a friend."

"She's my sister," said Ze.

"Shit... that's what's up," continued Yada. "Go ahead, get settled in. Let your hair down, have a few drinks, let's smoke some trees."

Alize did a quick inventory of the situation. Brittany was giving her a look of approval; it seemed like everything was on the up and up. She really didn't have anywhere else to be, and it had been a long time since she and her sister had partied together, so why not? *You only live once*, she told herself. "You know what... I can use a drink. And somebody needs to put on some music."

After that, it was on. Nirobi put on a J. Cole CD, and before long, everyone was tipsy. Alize found the thermometer and turned up the heat. In no time, the guys were in their boxers and the sisters were almost naked. Brittany was wearing a pink bra with matching boy shorts. Alize had on lace; Victoria's Secrets. Smoke was in the air, drinks were spilling, and the mood was festive.

It wasn't long before Brittany and Yada went to the bathroom to take a shower together. That's when Alize found herself alone with Nirobi. She hadn't had sex in months and couldn't think of a reason why a little casual sex shouldn't happen. Nirobi wasn't bad looking; in the back of her mind, she had always wondered what it would be like being with him. So, she went for it.

Somewhere in the background, she heard a phone vibrating. From the sounds of its location, she could tell that it was her phone. Nevertheless, she ignored it, choosing sex with Nirobi over business.

Nirobi was sitting on the couch watching Ze dance. Earlier they had moved the coffee table, so nothing was blocking her from seductively gyrating towards the young thug. He was memorized by the way she ran her fingers through her hair and manipulated her hips.

Alize worked her way towards Nirobi, eventually kneeling down in front of him. All the while, keeping constant eye contact with him as she took his boxers off. She then spread his legs and looked at his penis. That's when she found herself face-to-face with the smallest dick she had ever seen on a grown man. It was maybe two inches long, and as thick as her pinky. If she had had any goals of getting her cat beat up, they were crushed at the sight of his childlike manhood.

A part of her wanted to get up right then and there, but that would've been cruel. Instead, she took his penis between her thumb and index finger, holding it up while she put her lips on it. Alize had enough experience with different-sized men, but this was comical. His manhood wouldn't even reach to the back of her throat. Instead of deep-throating it, the only thing she could do was massage it with her tongue. She would've broke out laughing if it weren't so sad, so she did her best with what he had.

Luckily her mate was a premature ejaculator; she was saved by his lack of sexual control. The moment she tasted his cum in her mouth she quickly climbed his body and kissed him on the mouth, transferring his own fluids from her mouth into his. She would've never done that to a man she respected, but this was turning out to be a joke.

As they were kissing, Alize positioned herself beneath Nirobi. Then she pushed him down until his body was off the couch and his face was in between her legs. She then took off her panties and her bra and leaned back as far as she could, putting the bottom of her feet on the edge of the couch. After that she spread her thighs so that her wet pussy was in Nirobi's face.

Alize had thick pussy lips. So thick that they had to be physically parted in order for someone to see the entrance to her vagina. Before Nirobi spread open her lower lips, he saw her swollen clitoris sticking out like a tiny penis. And, once he did open them, he couldn't believe how small her pussy was.

Ze's sex cave was wet with eagerness. Nirobi was so close he could see the liquids slowly oozing out of it. He took two fingers and saturated them in her juices, then stuck them inside of her. The sudden penetration forced Alize to pull back, but not for long. Within seconds, she began rocking her hips to the rhythm of his foreplay. Then Nirobi put his mouth on her clit and started massaging it with his tongue like she had done to him only moments earlier

In the background Ze heard pounding coming from the bathroom. Her sister was yelling like Yada's dick was killing her. She would've been jealous if it weren't for the fact that Nirobi's tongue play was above average. He sucked her clit at the same time as he tickled her G-spot with the tips of his fingers.

With his fingers inside of her, Alize started rocking her body faster and faster. It felt surprisingly invigorating; so much so that she soon felt an orgasm mounting. All the while her sister was moaning loudly in the background. And, could that have been her phone vibrating again? She didn't care... she was about to cum!

All she wanted to do was reach that summit. "Keep going, Nirobi! Don't stop, God damn it!" She couldn't hold it any longer, she needed a penis no matter how small it was. Ze grabbed Nirobi roughly, pulling him on top of her, sliding his diminutive phallus into her tight subway. All in one motion she reached around his back and slid her middle and index fingers into his rectum. It all happened so fast, Nirobi didn't have a chance to react. Alize, then, used her tight grip to control his body, pushing and pulling him in and out of her as fast and as hard as she possibly could; the whole time, digging her fingers into his anus maliciously.

"Don't stop!" yelled Ze as she pulled him against her body. "Don't fucking stop!"

Nirobi couldn't have stopped if he wanted to. Alize had her eyes shut while she masturbated with his body. Then, suddenly she began shaking uncontrollably. She had finally reached the peak she had longed for. Wave after wave of ecstasy shot through her loins, shocking her senses. She didn't want the moment to end. She kept her fingers inside of him as if daring him to stop, not letting him go until she had sucked every ounce of erotic energy from his soul.

A few seconds went by... she heard her phone again. She also realized that the moaning in the bathroom had stopped. Her pussy felt good, but she had to snap back to reality. It wasn't the painful, dominating sex that she wanted from Talton, yet it was pleasing. Nirobi had been better than her fingers in the shower.

Alize disengaged herself from Nirobi, then gave him a little push, causing him to roll onto the spot next to her. Seeing the shocked expression on his face made her laugh out loud.

"What's wrong with you?" she asked. "It looks like you just got violated." Alize smiled as she stood up. Still naked, she walked towards the table where her phone was at. After picking it up she headed toward the bathroom. She didn't knock on the door; she was deliberately trying to catch a glimpse at the piece of flesh that made her sister scream so loud. But when she stepped in, all she found was Brittany kissing a towel clad Yada. "Girl, I gotta pee," said Ze as she walked around them.

Yada snickered when Alize sat on the toilet. Then he said, "I guess I'll give y'all some girl time." After giving Brittany one last kiss, he left the room.

As soon as the door shut behind him, the girls looked at one another and started giggling.

"Damn, bitch!" said Ze. "It sounded like he was killing you!"

"He's a beast, sis! Oh, my God... it was so big it was ugly. And he wouldn't stop. He just kept ramming that thing up in me! God, that dick was good. What about yours? You look like you just busted a good one."

"I'll tell you later."

"Tell me what?"

Alize had started checking her text messages. The first one read: Attached is a video from last night. If you recognize this guy, GET AT ME ASAP!!!

Ze activated the video link and gasped when she realized what she was watching.

"What's wrong?" asked Brittany.

"It's a video of my friend's brother getting killed."

"For real? Move, let me see!" Brittany leaned in and watched for several seconds before saying, "Oh fuck! Ze, that's Yada!"

Suddenly on alert, Alize said, "I know. Listen, go out there and get our clothes. Don't act suspicious, just get our stuff. Hurry up!"

"What're you gonna do?"

"Just get our stuff, we're leaving."

CHAPTER TWENTY

After picking up their things from Cita's sister's trailer, Talton and the girls were on their way to the beach. He had the spare key to his brother's place, so getting inside wouldn't be an issue. And Angelique had Anthony's car keys and cell phone, making the transition that much easier. Nevertheless, the loss overshadowed the gain; at least, in Talton's eyes... he would've given his life for his brother's.

They were almost there when Talton's cell phone vibrated. But, when he took it out of his pocket, Cita playfully snatched it out of his hand and answered it herself. "Hello... yeah... who's this? I asked who's this?... Alize? Why you callin' my man, bitch?!?"

Hearing the exchange, Talton took the phone from her. "What's wrong with you!? That's my fuckin' connect!" Talton put the phone to his ear but Cita wasn't having it.

"You got me fucked up, Talton!"

"Man, shut up!" he yelled at Cita before saying to Alize, "What's good? Did you get my text?"

"Yeah," replied Ze, "but, listen. Can you get to the Days Inn on U.S. 19?"

"Yeah, but what for?"

"The guy on that video is here right now! I'm in his bathroom."

"Are you absolutely sure it's him?" asked Talton, suddenly feeling as if he was just injected with a shot of pure adrenaline. Before Ze had the chance to reply, he was already in the process of making a reckless U-turn in the middle of oncoming traffic.

"I'm a thousand percent positive that it's him," she whispered. "He's even wearing a medallion like yours."

Talton's vision became blurred at the mention of his brother's necklace. He had to fight to hold the tears from falling. "What room are y'all in?"

"112; first floor, towards the back. But, you gotta hurry. I'm leaving right now."

$$\$\$\$\$\$$$

Alize had just ended the call when the bathroom door opened and in came Yada. She had no idea whether he had heard her conversation with Talton, and it must have shown on her face because Yada said, "What's wrong with you? My little cousin must've blown your mind out there. He's looking just like you. Like he just lost his virginity, or something." Yada squatted down to pick up his things from the bathroom floor.

Alize saw a pistol in his things as he scooped it up. Nevertheless, she slid a seductive smile on her face, and said, "Lost his virginity, huh? Well, maybe he did. You wanna smell my finger?" Ze stood up, still naked, and started washing her hands in the sink.

That's when Brittany came in with their clothes in hand. Yada stepped out the way so she could come in. She went to the toilet, put the seat down and sat down to put her clothes on.

Yada was still wrapped in his towel. As he stood there staring at Ze's plump backside, the sight of it was beginning to overwhelm him. It was obvious what was happening and the sisters watched as he slowly started to grow underneath the towel. From the long rising bulge, Alize could clearly see that he was working with over a foot of massive piping.

"Damn, sis!" exclaimed Ze. "I see why you sounded as if he was rippin' you apart!"

"I told you he was a beast."

"Oh, yeah, I'ma beast alright." Yada undid the knot in the towel, letting it fall to the floor. Without anything suppressing it, Yada's humongous member hopped around uncontrollably, twitching like it had a mind of its own, oozing with precum as if it were salivating at the prospect of more pussy. "If you want, we can make this a family affair."

Ze stared at the huge penis in front of her then turned and looked at her sister. After a few seconds, they both started giggling. Turning back to Yada, she reached out and grabbed the head of his hammer. Holding it like it was a doorknob, she gave it a light squeeze before saying, "I'll have to take a rain check on this one. But I'll definitely be calling real soon."

Yada's member fought against her grip, surprising Alize with its power. It was like an animal, with its own mind, spoiling for a fight.

Yada had never been turned on so much in his

life. He felt like he could cum, right there, on the middle of the floor. Yet, that would be a major embarrassment, showing that he had no sexual control. So he decided to leave the room before he had an accident. "Alright, then. I'ma give y'all some privacy." He quickly backed out of the bathroom, clothes in hand.

"You do that," said Ze. "We'll be out there in a minute." After shutting the door behind him she turned to her sister. "Hurry up, bitch! Get dressed! There's gonna be bullets flying all over the place!"

"What'd you do?"

"Don't worry about it. Just get dressed. We gotta get outta here."

They both raced to put their clothes on. Alize was in so much of a hurry, she forgot to put her panties on, stuffing them in her pocket, instead.

In the main room, Yada was getting dressed, too. Making sure to leave his newly acquired jewels visible. Nirobi still hadn't said a word, but that didn't bother the older cousin. He was on top of the world, feeling like he just hit the lottery, totally blind to the fact that by the end of the night, one of them would be dead, and the other would be handcuffed to a hospital bed...

CHAPTER TWENTY-ONE

Talton was speeding through busy traffic, already having narrowly missed several accidents. His body felt warm as the adrenaline raced through his veins. Reaching under his seat, Talton found his chrome Desert Eagle and placed it on his lap. He didn't have to make sure it was loaded because he kept it filled with hollow heads.

The mission was simple: Catch up with his brother's killer and murder him. Nothing he hadn't done before. Except, this time, he was with two women who had no experience in warfare. And, the fact that the one sitting next to him couldn't be trusted was a constant flashing red light in his head, yet his anger and bloodlust for the man who murdered his brother overrode any sense of self-preservation. His need for retribution was insular; the rest would have to be dealt with later.

From the moment he received that last call, Cita had watched his energy multiply a hundred-fold. Talton was like a dangerous snake, ready to strike at anything. But she didn't care, she felt out of control, and this ate at the deepest corners of her mind. "Where the hell you going? This ain't the way to the beach. I told you I'm tired, Talton."

"Angelique!" called out Talton. "Get up here and switch seats with Cita."

"You got me twisted," said Cita. "I'm not getting out this seat! Where the hell are we going?"

Talton was recklessly weaving in and out of traffic when he found himself at a red light. "Fuck!"

Angelique stuck her head between the front seats and said, "What's up, Talton?"

"My homegirl just found the guy in the video. He's at the Days Inn right now."

"How'd she do that?" asked Cita, cutting into the conversation.

Talton was debating whether he should run the light or not.

"I sent that video to everyone on my call list. She must've recognized dude, because she just called to tell me she was with him." The light turned green, giving Talton the right of way. He sped off without saying another word.

$$$$$

Alize and Brittany both came out of the restroom fully dressed. Nirobi was putting his pants on and Yada was sitting at the table, tying his shoe laces. The girls wanted to leave before the shooting started, but their suitors had different plans.

"Why y'all looking like you 'bout to run out on us?" asked Yada from the far end of the room.

"We gotta go," said Ze. "Nirobi, I just got another call, so I'ma go get your weed out the trunk."

"But we still got more drank. You ain't gotta go so soon, do you?" Nirobi asked, pleadingly.

Alize's phone sounded again. "See, that's them right now." She looked at her phone and read the text from Talton: STALL EM! Ze stared at the message for a moment, thinking of the possible ramifications of prolonging her involvement in what was about to happen. She knew she should leave; she had done enough, yet something more innate told her to stay. So, when she looked up from her phone, what she said next surprised everyone. "Forget that other sale. We can hang out a lil longer."

"That's what I'm talking 'bout!" called out Yada from across the room.

Brittany didn't seem to agree with her sister's sudden change of plans. "Ze, I think we better go. We can meet up with these guys later. At least, let's go get this money then come back."

"I got money right here," said Nirobi from his spot on the couch.

"A bird in the hand is better than two in the bush, right, Ze?"

"You damn right, baby. Go ahead and roll another blunt." With that, she walked over to the couch and sat down next to Nirobi.

Brittany stood in the middle of the room trying to make eye contact with her sister, but Ze wouldn't look at her. It was obvious that her sister was stalling for some reason, but she couldn't understand why. This had nothing to do with them; they needed to get out before things got too hot. It wasn't that she was afraid. On the contrary, Brittany was good under fire, but this wasn't making any sense. They hadn't been involved in anything like this since their teenage years, and now, Alize was forcing them to jump in head first.

"Brit-Brit, come sit wit' your boy," said Yada. "Why you over there looking lost?"

She tried to smile. "Hold on, I gotta use the bathroom. You put a hurtin' on this pussy, I don't know what's up with me." Brittany went back in the restroom with a sudden urge to urinate. On her way, she gave her sister one last glance, but Alize refused to look up.

$$\$\$\$\$\$$$

Cita screamed when Talton almost side-clipped another driver. "Slow down! You're gonna get us killed, Talton! You need to turn us around, now! I don't even know why you're going to this guy. Why don't you just call the police? This is crazy." Cita was getting nervous watching Talton squeeze his gun while he dangerously weaved through traffic.

Talton was on a mission. He was minutes away from the man who murdered his brother and nothing would derail him. "I need you to switch seats with Angelique."

"I'm not changing seats with no one. I'm calling the cops!" She then started rummaging through her purse.

When Talton heard Cita, something snapped. He'd given her too many benefits of doubt. And now, seeing her and hearing her openly ready to snitch brought the beast out of him.

Smack! Smack! Smack! Smack! He back-handed her with such speed and ferocity she didn't know what had happened. "You dumb-ass bitch! This what you want?" Almost losing control of the truck, he snatched Cita by the hair, and repeatedly slammed her face into the dashboard. Whack! Whack! Whack!

Cita's blood splattered all over the windshield. She couldn't see a thing; it was getting hard for her to breathe. When Talton finally let up, she couldn't focus on a thing, everything was spinning. He was yelling at her, but she was in too much pain, intermingled with shock to move or say anything.

Neither of the women had ever seen Talton in this state of madness. He was out of control, raving like a lunatic.

"Angelique! Get this bitch out my motherfucking face before I blast her brains all over the dash!"

Angelique helped Cita out of the front seat. Blood was flowing from her mouth and nose onto her chest. When she reached the back row, Angelique handed her a T-shirt from one of the bags of clothing they had taken from her sister's house. Then, Talton's voice boomed throughout the Suburban's cabin, scaring Angelique half to death.

"Angelique! I need you up here, *now*!"

Angelique climbed up front leaving Cita sprawled across the back row, crying. Talton gave her his phone and said, "Text the last number I called and put in, 'get out, now!'"

"Talton, let me go in with you. I wanna see you kill –"

"I can't do that, Ang. I need you behind the wheel." Talton turned into the Days Inn, quickly slowing down so as not to attract any unnecessary attention.

He knew exactly where to go. He'd been there on several occasions. The Days Inn was built like an apartment complex, with the driveway going all the way around its square layout. All the doors to the rooms faced the driveway. There was also a courtyard with a pool in the center, which was only visible from the rooms. Surrounding the motel was a wooden fence that separated it from a residential area.

Talton found Alize's car parked in front of room 112. After stopping the truck, he turned to Angelique, "If people start coming out of their rooms before I come out of the one I'm going in... drive away. We don't want anyone connecting the truck to this shit.

"If we get split up, I'll meet y'all back at the beach. But I should be in and out." With that, Talton cocked his cannon, prepared to leave the vehicle. But first, he looked at Cita. She was crying. Then to Angelique he said, "Watch her. Make sure she doesn't do anything stupid."

CHAPTER TWENTY-TWO

Alize had just taken a hit from the blunt when Brittany came out of the bathroom. When they looked at one another, Brittany shot her a glance that said, "Let's go!", and Ze replied with a look that said, "Give me a sec."

Then, their wordless conversation was cut short by Alize's phone. It was another text from Talton; this time it read: "Get out now!!!" It was all the prompting she needed. Alize hopped out of her seat, loudly announcing, "Well... it's time for us to go, guys. I'ma go get your weed, Nirobi–"

Before she could finish her statement, a deep banging sound came from the door to the room. It sounded like someone was trying to kick it open. Suddenly, the door snapped off its hinges and came crashing onto the floor. Everyone was caught off guard, giving Talton the edge he needed. It took a second for Yada, the sole person in the room with a gun, to assess the threat and reach for his weapon. Still, he was too slow.

As if his brother's OP medallion was a hone-in device, Talton zeroed in on it immediately. Ignoring everyone else in the room, he stepped in with his cannon in shooting position and quickly let off four deafening rounds. All of them aimed straight into his target's face. Upon impact, the bullets exploded, causing blood and brain matter to be grossly discarded in all directions, but mostly against the sliding glass door where Yada's lifeless body had fallen.

In Talton's mind everything was moving in slow motion. Alize ran towards another female, whom he didn't recognize, and they both sprinted towards the door. That's when he saw the dread sitting on the couch. This had to be the "Nirobi" character that the other one had called after killing Ant. Therefore, in Talton's eyes, he was an accomplice.

Talton slowly lifted his Desert Eagle wanting to savor the moment. When Nirobi realized what was happening, he dove off the couch, but it was too late. Boom! Boom! Boom! Fire shot out of the tip of the gun every time Talton squeezed his finger. Nirobi's torso flipped sideways as the bullets destroyed his upper chest cavity.

That's when Gangsta heard Alize trying to get his attention, but his mind didn't register what she was saying. He needed Ant's necklace; it was a piece of his brother and he had to have it. With only one thing on his mind, Talton dropped his gun and walked towards his first victim.

The headless body lay slumped against the glass door, still spitting blood from its main artery. The man's heart must have missed the memo. It was over; there was no way he was coming back from that. Talton walked up to the dead body, reached down and snatched Anthony's bloody necklace from the marauder's neck. He then put it on, letting it rest next to its twin.

That's when the world around Talton began to speed up. Now he could hear and understand what Alize was trying to tell him. From the doorway, she was yelling, "Hurry up! Come on, Talton!" Then, in the background, he heard a man's voice, "Call the police!" That woke Talton all the way up. Alize ran to her car. Talton followed, but he stopped just short of the door.

He saw his Suburban slowly creeping by with Angelique behind the wheel. He made eye contact with her and she got the message. She drove off, leaving him to fend for himself.

The Malibu was backing out of its parking space. Alize wasn't driving, though. She had her door open calling out to him but he ignored her. Instead, he took off running towards the back of the complex. After hopping the gate, and a few more fences after that, Talton found himself walking down a quiet street in the heart of someone's neighborhood. He then took off his black and red True Religion T-shirt and wrapped it around his head. He also took off both necklaces, putting them in his jean pocket.

Within minutes he emerged from the subdivision. Finding a Seven Eleven on the other side of a busy intersection, Talton headed straight for it. He knew from experience that it was better to hide in plain sight.

Brittany had driven away from the room in a rush. Alize was upset with Talton for not getting in the car, yet, deep down, she knew that he had made the right decision by running the other way. At the entrance of the Days Inn, the girls should've taken a left to head home. Instead, Alize told Brittany to go east and circle the area in search for Talton. After hitting a few corners they saw a man in a white tank top walking towards the Seven Eleven. It was him, so Brittany pulled into the convenient store's parking lot. When she stopped, Alize got at Talton and he got in. Seconds later they were safely driving away undetected by the law.

CHAPTER TWENTY-THREE

Nirobi was having a hard time breathing. He was going into shock and his chest was on fire. He needed medical attention but was afraid to move because of what he might see. Nevertheless, he had to get to a phone; he didn't want to die. Mustering all of his strength, he crawled towards the table where he last saw his cell phone. But, in the process, he found himself face-to-face with what used to be his cousin. However, all that was left of him was a grotesque torso with a bloody stump where the head should've been.

He needed to stand up, yet he couldn't. He was losing blood at a fast pace, thus making him light-headed. Then, something shiny caught his attention. It was the same gun that was used to shoot him and his cousin. It was on the floor next to his phone... within reach. Nirobi was able to grab his cell phone and call 911. When no one answered, he began to panic: "Oh my God! I don't wanna die! Please don't let me die, Lord." He tried dialing 911 again, but once again it was busy. Then he heard something. It was the sound of a man's voice. It had to be the same nigga who just shot him... he was probably coming back for his gun. Not wanting to be finished off, Nirobi reached for the gun and used the rest of his strength to pick it up.

$$$$$

Room 108 had been rented by a married lawyer who worked for the District Attorney's office. He had needed a discreet place to have an illicit tryst with his receptionist. After spending the majority of the afternoon having mind-blowing sex, he stepped out of the room for a quick smoke break. That's when he saw the blue and silver SUV pull in front of room 112. He wasn't giving it much attention until he saw a man with long hair get out of it carrying a silver missile launcher.

Suddenly the assistant D.A. was frozen where he stood. He watched the man with the gun run up to the door to the room and kick it down. Moments later there were gunshots. He wanted to dive into the safety of his own room but shock left him immobile. Then two girls came out of the same room, one of them calling for someone to come with her. At that point, he found his voice and yelled for his receptionist to call for help.

Moments later the same man who had kicked down the door came out the room, and the girls who had ran from that room were calling for him to go with them. The lawyer had seen it all. He even watched as the blue and silver Suburban drove away, leaving the shooter behind. He didn't get a chance to remember the license plate number of the truck, but he definitely got the one off of the burgundy Chevy.

By the time he turned back towards room 112, the man with the gun was gone. Assuming the coast was clear, he went to the room to see if he could help the wounded. Since the shooter was gone, he figured it would be safe.

When he entered the room, he immediately saw the headless body on the floor. He ran towards it, then suddenly a burst of flame shot out from the far corner of the room. It was accompanied by a loud roar, then followed by a feeling in his chest akin to being kicked, tackled, or maybe both. He lost his footing... On his way down, he heard the roar once more... Then he went blank.

$$$$$

When the responding officers arrived, they found a double homicide and their suspect was lying in a pool of his own blood, still clutching onto the murder weapon. Despite the horrendous gunshot wounds to the chest, he was still alive.

There were close to two dozen witnesses at the scene of the crime. However, upon questioning them, the police soon found out that no one had actually seen anything. The only witness to the crime was the perpetrator himself.

The news reporters were on the scene moments after the police arrived. They got there just in time to film Nirobi's body being carted away in the back of an ambulance. Yet, the only statement they were able to obtain from the officers at the scene was a confirmation that there had been a double homicide.

CHAPTER TWENTY-FOUR

On Clearwater beach, inside the beach-front cottage, Cita was in the living room, pacing back and forth. Shocked at what she had seen at the motel, she was a nervous wreck who was driving Angelique crazy.

"Oh, my God!" exclaimed Cita. "I can't believe he did that! And, who were those bitches that came out of the room?"

"It doesn't matter, they helped him find Ant's killer. That's what counts."

"How can you be so nonchalant about this? Talton just killed somebody! We need to do something."

"Do something?!"

"Yeah! We should call the cops or something."

Angelique didn't know what to do. He told her to make sure she didn't do anything stupid, and now she was talking about calling the cops. Anthony's big screen was on the news and by the sounds of it the cops didn't know what had happened. Nevertheless, the story was on every local station, which only fueled Cita's mounting hysteria.

"... Hold on, did you just say, 'call the cops'?"

"Hell yeah! We were in the truck with him when

he did that. Of course, we need to call the police! If someone saw the license plate on the truck, the police could be on their way right now! Then what? We go down as accessories? Hell, no... not me. I already caught a trafficking charge for that motherfucker. I'll be damned if I catch a murder case too! You saw what he did to me. Look at my face, Angelique! He beat the hell out of me!"

"Fuck all that! He hit you cuz you tried to call the cops. And look at you, now you're still talking 'bout callin' 'em. That man's brother was just murdered. He had to do what he did. Can't you see that? Not to mention that he's the father of your unborn child!" Angelique was in Cita's face. They were in the middle of the room, and her voice was steady getting louder. "You ain't even thinking about Anthony's kids. They just lost their father, and now you're talking about snitching on their uncle! The police don't even know what happened! Cita, that's your baby father, think about what you're saying."

"Father!" yelled Cita, only inches away from Angelique's face. "Are you serious? Talton isn't no fucking father! You need to get your act together! You're starting to make me think you were in on the whole thing! If I didn't know you were so dumb, I'd think you set this whole thing up!"

"What, bitch?!"

"You probably knew the guy that killed Ant! And you set this up so Talton would kill 'em. Oh... I see it now. You think you're gonna get all of this when Talton goes to prison, huh?"

That was it; Angelique couldn't take it anymore.

She swung, trying to take Cita's head off, but Cita anticipated the attack. Talton's pregnant girlfriend ducked and tackled Angelique. Both of them fell onto the glass coffee table, smashing it in the process.

This kicked off a flurry of punches from both women. They fought like a pair of rabid pit bulls, trying to kill one another with every swing. Neither of them scratched or pulled hair; this fight consisted of a series of close-fisted blows to one another's face and head. However, Cita couldn't match the rage spewing from Angelique. That and the fact that she was pregnant landed Cita at the bottom of the brawl.

Blow after blow, Angelique continued to pummel her adversary. "You fuckin' bitch! I loved him," she yelled. "I'll kill you, bitch!"

Angelique finally stopped after realizing that Cita was no longer fighting back. She was unconscious and barely breathing. Angelique's fists were bloody from punching Cita in the mouth. Then she remembered that Cita was pregnant. Suddenly she stood up, knowing she had made a horrible mistake. Her heart dropped when she saw the puddle of blood accumulating between Cita's thighs.

"Oh, fuck! What did I do?! Cita! Cita! Don't die on me, bitch!" Angelique ran into the kitchen, picked up the wall mounted phone and called the 911 operator. She gave him the address and told him there was pregnant woman lying bloodied on the floor. Then she dropped the phone and frantically searched the house for her keys. It was time to go. She had an aunt in Tennessee, it was her only option.

After finding her car keys, Angelique ran

outside, careful not to step on the broken glass. She tried ignoring the dying woman on the floor, yet the vision of Cita's lifeless body would stay with her forever. The scene she was leaving was like night and day when compared to all the other memories she had of the same room.

Angelique drove away without looking back. She headed north on I-75, at times with distorted vision caused by the salty tears that flooded her eyes. She wanted to call Talton, yet never did. She had probably just killed his unborn child, thus making her his enemy. And she had just seen what he did to his enemies, so she drove and drove...

Deep into the night, on her way out of state, Angelique pressed the button that controlled her window. The warm summer wind teased her face, forcing her tears to change directions. Then, she grabbed her phone; on its screen there was a picture of her and Anthony in a loving embrace. That life was over now, she had to let go. So, she tossed her phone out the window and closed it, vowing never to look back.

CHAPTER TWENTY-FIVE

Talton was staring at the Gulf of Mexico from his patio on the eighteenth floor of the luxurious Hilton hotel. The moon was shining bright over St. Petersburg beach, along with a sky full of stars. Under different circumstances the view would've been magical. Talton loved the ocean and its summer breeze. However, tonight wasn't the night to enjoy such things.

Inside, Alize and her sister were sitting at the edge of the room's king-sized bed. They were sweating the local news to see if the police had any details about what had taken place at the Days Inn. So far there was no mention of Talton or the girls. All it said was that local law enforcement officials had a suspect in custody who wasn't expected to make it through the night.

For the last hour Gangsta had been calling all of Cita's family and friends to see if anyone had seen her. Ever since the shooting, Angelique and Cita had fallen off the grid. That didn't sit well with him. For all he knew the police could've been bleeding the girls for information at that very moment.

Even though his face wasn't on TV Talton was

still worried. He knew of several situations where the media was fed bogus information so they couldn't tip off the real suspect. The more he thought about it the more he started to believe that this was exactly what was happening. Otherwise, why would the news tell the public that the suspect was in custody. None of it made any sense.

Talton also managed to call Mike and B.A. They told him they hadn't had any luck in finding Ant's killer, but that the weed was moving fast. Their consensus was that Talton needed to hurry up and drop off the product. Between the two of them they had seven pounds sold. They had been so busy juggling business calls that they had no idea of what had taken place at the Days Inn.

Talton set up a meeting for the very next day. He'd have to stop by Shannon's trailer because his Delta was still parked at her place. The duffle bag containing the marijuana was in its trunk. He also knew that he wouldn't be able to run around the city making money until he figured out what was going on with Cita and Angelique. Therefore, the fact that his boys were moving the product themselves was working out perfectly. Along with the weed, he also had all the cocaine he and Anthony had purchased the day before; all he had to do was go pick it up.

As he stared out at the ocean, he slowed down enough to take in the warm ocean breeze. The scene was picturesque, yet his life wasn't. On top of everything that was going on, the battery in his phone had died. Not having a phone cut him off from the rest of the world. That wasn't good; he made a mental note to himself to pick up a charger when he went by Ant's house in the morning.

Talton came in from the patio and sat between the girls, who were still perched at the edge of the bed. They had been surprisingly cool under pressure, giving Talton more than enough space to get his thoughts together while everything was going on. No one said anything until Alize turned away from the television to ask Talton what he was thinking.

Talton said, "I'm not sure. The news really ain't saying much. All that shit happened so fast, it might've been clean. But, then again, I can't get ahold of my baby mamma. My brother's girl ain't answering her phone, either. I just gotta wait till tomorrow–"

"I gotta go to work in the morning," said Ze.

"I know, and I can't risk driving around the city, either. What about you?" he asked Brittany. "You doin' anything tomorrow morning?"

"Huh? Me? No... I don't got nothing to do, but–"

Alize cut her off, "She ain't got no tint, though. You won't be safe in her car."

"No tint? What're y'all talking 'bout?" asked Brittany.

"He's gonna need a driver, Brit. Right, Talton?"

"Yeah. I got shit I need to do, but until I find out if things are really straight, I can't be driving around by myself. I might get pulled over. If you're driving, and we get stopped, I can give the cop an alias instead of my driver's license."

"I feel you, but I don't even know you like that. Not to mention the fact that I just watched you kill two people. I'm not too sure I should be riding around with you. I'm sorry, but I gotta keep it real with you."

"Brit-Brit, why are you trippin'?" asked Ze.

"Naw... she's right," said Talton. "I can't expect her to trust me after what she saw." Then, to Brittany, he said, "One thing, though. I can't be that bad if your sister's fucking with me. And, you can't be that uncomfortable, being as you're still here."

"I'm only here for my sister."

"That's cool, and I understand that," replied Talton. "I just need a ride to a few places. It's just a minor security precaution. As soon as I get ahold of my baby mamma, I'll be out of your hair. It'll only take an hour or two. Afterwards, you can drop me off and we'll part ways."

"Yeah, Brit," said Ze. "I'll even rent y'all a car with some tint. You saw the news, they don't have a clue, Brit. Why're you trippin'?"

Both Alize and Talton stared at Brittany. She was far from happy about being put on the spot. She wasn't as worried about driving a murderer around as she was for her sister's emotional instability. Several years earlier, this type of thing seemed to happen to them on a regular basis. Even after Ze came home, things were never normal, yet, at least Brittany knew what to expect. But, now that this Rambo-type thug entered the picture, her sister was suddenly morphing back into the Alize of old. From Brittany's view, she had no choice; she had to stay close just to make sure Alize would be OK.

"Alright," said Brittany. "But I'm only driving you around for a few hours. And, Ze, I'm keeping the rental till my off days are up."

"It's a deal! I'll rent you something for three days." Then, to Talton, Alize said, "Is that cool with you?"

"Yeah... sounds perfect. Now, I'ma take a shower and get some sleep. Gotta be on point tomorrow." Talton leaned in and gave Alize a kiss on the cheek. "Thanks. I really appreciate all the help you guys are giving me."

Talton got up and went to the bathroom. A few moments later, the girls heard the shower running. That's when Brittany took off her pants and started to get in bed.

"What're you doing?" asked Ze. "Talton's coming back out."

"So? I'm about to go to sleep." Brittany pulled the bed's comforter back then climbed into bed. "And when he gets out the shower, I'm totally gonna snuggle with him."

"Bitch, no you ain't!" spat Ze, while picking up a pillow and playfully throwing it at her sister. "Besides, you're not sleeping in the bed. Only me and Talton are."

"Not tonight, sis. I see how you been looking at him. You can't be serious about fucking 'em on the first night. Plus, you haven't even taken a shower yet... you nasty bitch. Did you forget you just had sex with one of the guys he killed? You ain't even told me what that was like."

"Girl, there's nothing to tell. His dick was the size of my pinky. I was hella mad till he put his tongue to work." Alize was giggling as she walked towards the bathroom. "You were right, Brit-Brit."

"About what?"

"I haven't taken a shower yet..."

$$$$$

As soon as Talton entered the restroom, he turned on the shower and took off his clothes. While he was undressing, his brother's chain fell out of his pocket onto the floor. When he picked it up, he saw that there was still blood on it. Since the murders he hadn't had the chance to look at it. Now that he was holding the bloody medallion in his hand, all the feelings of loss for his brother suddenly came flooding back into his mind.

Gangsta started sobbing. It was the second time since his brother had died that he lost control of his emotions. Talton killed several men in the past. He knew that taking the life of one individual wouldn't bring back another's. Yet, he always felt satisfied after killing a rival. Nevertheless, this time was different. He had lost a brother and the pain was horrific.

The reflection in the bathroom's fogged up mirror showed a picture of Gangsta holding his face in the palms of his hands. Anthony's chain dangling from the right one. When Alize came in, that's what she saw. With no hesitation, she stepped closer and put her arms around him. She felt his pain because hers was also near. But she knew that she had to be strong for the both of them. Talton needed her; maybe just as much as she needed him.

"Come on, baby. Let's take a shower..." Alize slowly undressed as Talton leaned against the wall, staring at his reflection in the mirror. She then pulled off his boxers and led him into the shower. The whole time, Talton held his brother's necklace in his closed fist. When they finally got under the water, she carefully took it from him and rinsed it off. Then, she slid it over his head, hanging his brother's charm next to his heart.

After that, Alize unwrapped a bar of soap and began lathering Talton's body; starting from his upper back to his calves, then she turned him around and went from his feet to his knees. From there, she worked her way up to his sex, from his sex she went to his chest. Talton eventually returned the favor. In a way what they were doing was a form of love making; even though, neither participant realized it at the time.

Afterwards they both went into the next room and climbed into bed. The day's stress had been too much for the trio. All three of them were asleep within minutes.

CHAPTER TWENTY-SIX

Talton was asleep when the phone next to the bed rang. By the third time, he reached over and picked up the receiver. Putting it to his ear without opening his eyes, Talton said, "What's up?"

The front desk informed him that a driver from Budget Rental had come and dropped off a key to a Hummer. It was parked, ready to be picked up whenever he was ready.

Talton put the phone back in its cradle, hoping to get some more sleep, yet knowing it would be next to impossible. That's when he realized there was another body lying across his. Talton looked down and saw that it wasn't Alize. It was Brittany who had an arm, a leg, and half of her torso strewn across his body. She was naked; then, Talton remembered that he was, too. That was enough to fully wake him.

After he tapped her on the shoulder, Brittany slowly started to stir. When she finally came to, she was also surprised to see their close proximity. Nevertheless, she made no attempt to disengage herself from him. She only looked up and asked, "Where's my sister?"

"She must've went to work," answered Gangsta.

"The front desk just called. We gotta get up."

Brittany felt her leg touching something smooth, yet firm. She figured it was Talton's penis, so she deliberately rubbed her leg against it before lifting herself off of him. She didn't remember him climbing into bed the night before. Therefore, she had went the whole night without knowing that she was sleeping next to a naked man.

When Talton got out of bed, Brittany's eyes feasted on his chiseled frame. Her gaze never once wavered as he walked to the bathroom in the nude, its main course being Talton's slightly aroused penis as it swung from side to side while he walked across the room.

After Talton stepped out of sight, Brittany laid in bed trying to make sense of what was going on. She was currently held up in a hotel room with a sexy killer. Her sister was obviously love struck. If all of this had taken place four, maybe five years beforehand, it wouldn't have surprised her as much. But, so much had happened since Alize had gotten out. She had finally been stabilized. Even though things weren't normal, in the true sense of the word, they had definitely become manageable.

It was time to get up, she had to start moving. However, as soon as she swung her legs off the side of the bed, she suddenly felt a soreness coming from her nether regions. She was feeling the aftermath from the sex she had had the day before. Yada really put a beating to her insides. For a second, it put a smile on her face. His dick was so big it was scary. But then other memories moved into her consciousness. Yada's face exploding, then splattering against the glass door. The fire from the muzzle of Talton's gun. The sound of impact... Yada's brain being disseminated. Brittany would never forget what she witnessed. The gruesome massacre would forever remain imbedded in her memory.

A little while later, Talton came out of the bathroom fully dressed. From his neck hung two identical chains, both with OP medallions. Brittany recognized them from the one Yada had been wearing the previous day. That's when it hit her; one of those pieces of jewelry was probably the reason for his death.

When Talton came in the room, Brittany was just getting out of bed. She was still completely naked and wasn't trying to cover herself in any way. At first, he made a valiant effort not to stare, yet, in the end, he couldn't help himself. Brittany had a perfect ass. Extremely large and round, just like he liked them. He wondered if the sisters had different fathers. They looked nothing alike; where Brit-Brit was short and stubby, Alize was tall and slim. Their only resemblance was their backsides. They both had perfectly shaped bottoms.

Brittany knew Talton was watching her. She could feel his eyes on her ass as she went for her clothes. So she decided to give him a little show by walking extra slow and pushing her butt out farther than necessary when she bent over the chair to pick up her clothes.

Gangsta watched as Brittany flaunted her God-given assets. He was enjoying the scene profusely, yet, knew he wouldn't act on it. Why would he? He had the older, more established sister. On top of that, he just didn't have the time or energy to play games. He needed to find Cita and make sure she hadn't done anything stupid, like contacting the police. He also had to pick up all his coke and weed, then head to B.A.'s apartment to drop it all off. He had a full day ahead of him.

$$$$$

Cita woke up in a hospital bed with only a vague memory of being rushed to the Emergency Room. Before she had the chance to fully grasp what had taken place, an older white lady came into her room pushing a food cart. "So, you finally woke up," said the nurse.

Cita tried to sit up, but was quickly thwarted by a sharp pain in her abdomen. "What am I doing here? What happened?" Her mouth felt sore, she put her hand to her lips and felt a cut scabbing over.

"We were all hoping you could help with the answers to those questions. All I know is, an hour after I came in last night, you showed up unconscious. You lost a lot of blood, and you almost lost your baby–"

"My baby! What happened to my baby?" Cita reached underneath the blankets to feel her stomach. It felt different; she pulled the covers away and pulled up her gown. There was a horizontal cut just below her bikini line. Her eyes began to mist up, a terrible sinking feeling came over her. "My baby... where's my baby?"

"Oh, honey, don't cry. Your son is fine. He came a lil' early, but the boy is tough. He acted like he was ready to come out anyway."

"Where is he?"

"He's in the maternity ward, on a breathing machine. He's fine. When you're feeling up to it, I'll take you to him."

"Does anyone know I'm here? Has my boyfriend showed up?"

"See, that's the thing. All we know is that someone called 911 and said you were having a miscarriage. The paramedics found you bleeding inside of a house, on the floor. You were half dead. They didn't bring an I.D. and no one else was with you. We haven't been able to call your family because we really don't know anything about you. The police were here, but you were out so they left a card with instructions to give it to you when you woke up. It's right there on the table next to your bed. I also have some forms for you to fill out. And, one other thing; your baby needs a name."

"Can I use the phone?"

"Yes, but I think you should eat something first. You lost a lot of blood. You need to build up some energy before you start dealing with things."

"I'm not hungry. I need to use the phone and the bathroom." She tried to get out of bed before she was hit with a bout of dizziness. She would've fallen if it weren't for the nurse coming to her aide.

"Hold on, baby. You need to understand that

you're not well. You lost a lot of blood before you came in, and the C-section put even more strain on your body. Just lay down, I'll get you a bedpan–"

"No! I don't want a bedpan. Just help me get to the toilet, I'll be fine."

There was a small bathroom a few feet away from her bed. It had a small shower as well as a toilet. As soon as she entered, the first thing that caught her attention was her reflection in the mirror. She didn't recognize herself. The person looking back at her had two black eyes, a swollen lip, and an ugly bruise that dragged down the left side of her face.

That's when it all came rushing back to her. The mirror became a video screen in which she was able to see everything that had taken place the day before. She watched as Talton back-handed her and repeatedly slammed her face into the dashboard. The next thing she saw was Angelique on top of her. Anthony's girlfriend was yelling something as she struck her over and over again. The mirror didn't have sound, it only showed action. Violent acts perpetrated against a pregnant woman who had never hurt anyone.

Cita sat on the toilet, feeling completely jaded. She also felt sad, but couldn't cry. Her soul had been commandeered by anger. Her body was sore from head to toe. She had internal wounds as well as external, physical as well as emotional. And the pain meds mixed with her loss of blood made it hard for her to formulate her thoughts. She was unable to hold onto any one specific idea. Yet, she was sure of two things: she hated her baby daddy, and she would be the best mother a child could ever have.

"Nurse... Nurse!"

"I'm right here, honey," said the older woman as she stepped in the doorway. "You ready to get back in bed?" She had seen hundreds of battered women throughout her career. Their first glimpse in the mirror were usually their breaking point. It would only go one of two ways; a deep depression, shattering the young woman's spirit. Or, a cold anger that made them hate the world. The look that she found on Cita's face was anger, pure unadulterated anger.

"... I need help getting back into bed. I also need to use the phone."

The nurse helped Cita get back to the bed. Then, after tucking her in safely she said, "Here goes the phone, baby. All you need to do is dial nine before you call out. When you're finished calling whoever you need to talk to, I'll take you to see your baby."

"I'd like that, but first, I'd like to talk to those police you were telling me about."

The nurse picked up a business card from the table next to the bed. Handing it to Cita she said, "Here it is. And, if you're feeling up to it, I also have some forms for you to fill out. I'll go get 'em. If you need anything, just press that button that's above your head. If you do, I'll come running."

The moment the nurse walked out of the room, Cita picked up the phone...

CHAPTER TWENTY-SEVEN

The black H-3 pulled up to the curb in front of the late Anthony's beach-front home. It was located on a quiet street of retirees with their manicured lawns. Brittany, who was behind the steering wheel, was surprised when she saw all of the shiny cars, motorcycles, and jet skis in the driveway. Gangsta studied the layout, searching for unmarked police cars. He didn't see anything out of the ordinary; the block looked safe. However, even though his Suburban was in the driveway, Angelique's Mazda was gone.

"Is this your shit?" asked Brittany.

"Well... the truck, one of the jet skis, and a bike. My big-wheel is at another spot. Technically, it's all mine now, but the rest was my brother's." Suddenly, Talton became sullen. Then, as if snapping out of it he said, "Let me go in alone. If my baby mamma's in there, she doesn't need to see me with another female. Regardless, I'll be back out in a few minutes."

"Alright, but if you ain't out in fifteen minutes, I'm leaving."

"Deal." Talton got out of the Hummer and walked up to the house. He was hoping the front door was unlocked. If Cita was still mad about the beating he gave her, she wouldn't be opening the door anytime soon. When he reached the entrance, the door was wide open. This irritated him to the core. He was constantly on Cita about keeping the house locked, but she never listened. Yes, he had hoped it would be open, yet it irked him that it was wide open like this.

Then, after stepping inside, all of his petty quibbles were snuffed out. There was glass all over the living room, the carpet was tracked with bloody shoe prints, and the big screen was on, yet someone had muted the sound. After seeing this, he rushed through the house, room by room, but found no one.

When he got to the master bedroom he sat down on his brother's bed. He needed time to think. In the process of gathering his thoughts, Talton noticed Anthony's cell phone charger on the dresser and remembered that his own phone was dead so he took the battery out the charger and exchanged it with his. In that exact moment he received a call. The screen read: John Hopkins Memorial. Talton answered it, "Hello."

"Yeah, motherfucker! It's over now! You're going to prison for life, bitch! I'm telling the cops everything! That'll teach you about putting your hands on me, you son-of-a-bitch!"

Then, just as sudden as the call began, it ended, leaving Talton in a state of vexation. Cita's words hadn't come as a shock to the seasoned criminal. He expected it, after what he had done to her. Yet hearing them still managed to throw him off his game. The mother of his future child had finally become his worst enemy. Something his brother had warned him about repeatedly.

Talton wasn't going to stick around and wait for the police to show up. He had to stay moving, which was the number one rule when it came to living life on the run. Underneath the bunk bed, in the kid's room, there was a hidden compartment where his brother kept all the work, weapons and money. Talton quickly ran to the room to get it all. It was all in backpacks and pillow cases, so he was able to carry it all out easily.

He then went outside and put the bags of illicit contraband in the back of the rented SUV. After that he went to the Suburban and pulled out two bags filled with his own clothing. He tossed them in the Hummer then ran back inside to look for any spare keys that might be lying around. He found a key chain hanging in the kitchen that contained copies of all of his brother's keys. Talton then hurriedly locked up the house and got back into the truck with Brittany.

He knew better than to panic. His whole life had been spent on one type of supervision or another; from juvenile probation to adult parole. Thus, he had spent most of his life on the run. He stayed calm by telling himself that this was no different than any other time he had eluded the law. The problem wasn't that he didn't know what to do, it was precisely the opposite. Talton knew exactly what he had to do: he had to kill Cita; it was now inevitable.

Talton had Brittany drive him to Shannon's

trailer park. It was a risk that he had to take since the ten pounds of weed that Ze had given him was still in the trunk of his Delta. When they arrived at the trailer park, Talton didn't let her drive him all the way in. He couldn't risk having anyone see the vehicle he was in. Instead, he got dropped off at the entrance and went in on foot. When he got to the trailer, he noticed that no one was home. It seemed peculiar based on what he knew of Cita's sister. She didn't have a job and she barely ever left the nest.

Nevertheless, he didn't have the time to ponder on that. He needed to get his things and leave. Talton kept an extra key to his Buick inside of a magnetic key holder in the wheel well. With that, he opened the trunk and took out the duffle bag of marijuana. He wanted to take his Delta too, but decided against it, knowing that it would be the easiest way for the cops to track him.

When he got back to the Hummer he gave Brittany the directions to B.A.'s apartment. For most of the ride there he stayed quiet, staring out the window in deep thought. Talton let the last few weeks of his life pass before his eyes as if it were a movie.

Then he thought about his past and how his life was a repeating cycle; every time he set up shop in a new place, something bad would happen. Someone he loved would die or someone he trusted would double-cross him. An unending cycle of strife.

Talton tried to formulate a plan as he watched the traffic from behind the tinted glass. Luckily, he still had Mike and B.A. He could still run his business through them. There was no way he could safely navigate throughout the city while on the run for a double homicide. The next issue he had to deal with was finding a secure place to lay his head at. Hotels were too dangerous; someone could easily recognize him and turn him in.

He couldn't believe he had been so stupid. Taking Cita with him to that motel was the stupidest thing he had ever done. However, it was still hard for him to believe that she would actually call the police like that. Anthony never trusted her, especially after the raid, but Talton didn't think she had talked on purpose. Cita had never been in trouble with the law, of course she was going to talk under the duress of a seasoned detective. But this was different, the cops didn't have a clue that he was involved in the shootings. Therefore, there wasn't anyone putting pressure on her to talk.

Something had to have happened after they split up that caused her mutiny. By the way the house looked when he got there, it was obvious there had been a fight. But with who? Had she fought with Angelique? He'd been calling Angelique the whole evening, yet she never picked up. He didn't want to think that she turned against him, but anything was possible.

Talton tried calling Angelique again, but the call went straight to voice mail. He needed to talk to her; however, he also knew that by her not answering his calls, she was telling him that she didn't want to talk to him. If that was the case, then every time he dialed her number, he took the risk of being tracked by the police. That's when he came to the conclusion that he had to get rid of his phone.

"Hey, Brit-Brit, can I use your phone?"

"Here," she said, handing it to him. With both phones on his lap, Talton started alternating between each one. He looked like he was texting people, but she couldn't tell. "What are you doing?"

"What you want for this phone?" asked Talton without looking up.

"It's not for sale. What're you doing with my phone?"

"I'm putting all my contacts in it. I gotta throw mine away. I can't risk getting tracked by my phone."

"Why're you worried about that? You weren't even on the news last night. They already have who they think did it."

"I know, but I can't be too careful. You never know what might happen. I remember when my homey Boss Hogg caught a FED case. The FEDS had tracked him, but he didn't know how they did it. Back then, niggas weren't up on shit like that. When he finally got his paperwork there were satellite photos of his car driving around the city. They used his phone as a beacon. I don't even take pictures on my phone when I'm on the run."

"It sounds like you're always on the run," Brittany commented sarcastically. "What does taking pictures have to do with anything?"

"Every time you take a flick with your phone, the image that you see is made up of a bunch of tiny pixels. Well, those pixels are actually tiny lil' numbers that give the exact coordinates of where the flick was taken."

"How do you know?"

"I saw it on Dateline. These guys from Jacksonville kidnapped a bitch, then sent a picture of her to her family. The FBI got their location by calling the phone carrier and requesting the information."

"Damn, that's crazy."

Talton smiled; they were pulling into B.A.'s apartment complex. "Shit... all the information is out there. Sometimes, all you gotta do is just slow down and listen, ya dig?"

Brittany drove towards the back of the complex to where Talton directed her to. "Why don't you wait till my sister gets off work before you start spending money on a new phone? She might just let you use hers." They finally got to their destination, Brittany pulled into an open space and parked. "And, since we're on the subject of my sister, there's something I need to tell you. I can tell that you like her, so there are some things that you should kno–"

"Before you get all into that, I want you to know something about me. Yes, I like your sister. I know she's not a saint, and I know she's got a past. None of which is any of my business. I also know that she's smart and beautiful and she's still riding with me, even though I just involved y'all in some bullshit. That alone warrants my loyalty. And that doesn't come cheap. Another thing... I noticed that neither one of you panicked when everything went down. What that tells me is, this silly shit isn't the first murder y'all seen. I need people like you in my life right now. But, check this out, if things get to the point where I'm putting you guys in a situation that might get y'all caught up, then I'll pull away. And, it won't be on bad terms, you can trust that." Talton locked eyes with Brittany, letting her see for herself how sincere he was.

She didn't say anything. He was spitting some real shit, but he had no idea what she was really trying to tell him. Nevertheless, it didn't sound like his intentions were ill, so she let it go. After all, it was family business and he might not be around much longer.

Talton reached into the backseat, grabbing the duffle bag and one backpack. Then, just as they were about to step out of the rental, Brittany's phone vibrated. On its screen there was a picture of Alize holding a newborn baby. "Here, I think it's your sister."

"Alright... Hey, I'll meet you in there. I gotta talk to her."

Talton opened the door and stepped out, carrying the bags. "I'll be quick anyway. I'll probably be out before you're done talking to her."

Brittany watched him go inside the apartment; making a mental note that he had entered the door on the right, on the bottom floor. "Sorry 'bout that, sis. We just pulled into an apartment complex and Talton went in to handle some business."

"So, everything's good, right? Did you guys find his baby mamma?"

"That's the thing, we went to his house on the beach and there was hella cars and shit. Sis, Talton's got money! But you probably already know that, huh? Anyways, he goes in, then a little while later he starts coming out with bags full of shit. At first it looked like he had guns and dope and stuff. But then he went into the back of the truck he was in yesterday and pulled out some garbage bags with clothes in 'em. Sis, what's up with this dude? I mean, don't get me wrong, he's fine as hell. He'd be a real catch if he wasn't running around killing people. But I think he's planning on moving in with us or something."

"Why; you think he's gonna ask to stay with us?"

"Asking! Oh, no, sis. This guy isn't 'asking' to stay, I think he's planning on moving in whether we say so or not. He already took my phone and put all his numbers in it. And, I can't be sure, but I think he threw his phone out the window while I was driving. The guy is smooth; smart, too. It doesn't look like he's trying to get over on us; he's obviously got his own money. I'm just worried that we're moving too fast."

"It sounds like you're the one moving too fast. He's probably got another place lined up. Anyway, I can't have a man staying at the house with the social workers coming by every few days. If they find out about Talton, I'll never get Shawn back."

"Sis, this is serious, are you listening to me?"

"I'm not trying to argue with your crazy-ass, Brit-Brit. I'll meet you back at the room around six."

CHAPTER TWENTY-EIGHT

Alize put the phone down just as a customer entered the main door of the bank's lobby. It hadn't been too busy that morning, which was good. She had too many things on her mind. Her thoughts were constantly revolving around Talton along with the whirlwind of sex, money, and murder he had brought into her life. However, she didn't dwell on the more pressing matters, such as the fact that she had literally seen him kill two people. Her daydreams consisted of the shower she took the night before and the softness of Talton's skin against hers as they slept in one another's arms. She couldn't remember a time when she shared such intimacy with another person.

When she woke up that morning and noticed her sister's arm draped over her naked friend, it didn't bother her one bit. She actually tried extra hard not to wake them. She knew they needed their rest, the day before had been stressful. Another woman would've been jealous, but not Ze. She trusted Brittany with her life, and she'd been around long enough to recognize a good man when she found one. Talton wasn't grimy. With what she knew about him, she couldn't see him trying anything with her sister. Not after what they had just went through. And, by the outcome of their shower together, she knew that sex was the last thing on his mind.

Alize was lost in thought when her coworker snuck up behind her. "Somebody looks happy today–"

Ze jumped, "God! Don't do that! You scared the hell outa me, Sarah!"

Sarah started laughing at her friend. "I'm sorry, Ze. I just saw you over here all quiet and I figured I would come mess with you. You alright?"

"Yeah... I just got a few things on my mind."

"Could it be that those few things are a handsome Puerto Rican guy, and what's hanging between his legs?"

"Oh, God, no. Sarah, you're crazy!"

"Yeah, whatever. I saw that guy that came in the other day. You were on cloud nine after he left. I know something happened. Come on, Ze... tell all. Did you slob on his knob?"

"You are so nosy!"

"Whatever. But, anyways, I came over here to tell you my sister's throwing a birthday party for her seven-year-old daughter. I told her I'd invite you and your little boy. All the kids will be about his age and it'll give me a chance to finally meet your little gremlin in person."

"Sounds good. Just text me the directions and time, I'll bring 'im."

"She's doing it at the Chuck E. Cheese in Pinellas Park, on Saturday, around one. That way we can all drink while the kids are running around. You can bring your new boyfriend, too."

"I'll come, but I doubt I'll be bringing anyone. I don't like the idea of having any men around Shawn."

"Yeah, right. You just don't want me meeting your new sex toy." Then a customer walked in and Sarah had to go back to her station, leaving Alize alone with her daydreams...

$$$$$

Talton was in the kitchen with Mike and B.A. The table was stacked high with thousands of dollars in cocaine, marijuana and drug money. Mike and B.A. had went ahead and picked up some cash from their customers before Talton arrived with the product. They had already amassed close to ten thousand dollars for the drugs that were currently taking up residence on the table.

Talton didn't tell them about the incident at the Days Inn, or the events connected with Cita. However, he did inform them that he would be fielding his personal sales through them, all under the guise that he was arguing with Cita, and had decided to lay low with Alize for a few days. They didn't question his excuse, partly because they were preoccupied with the prospect of generating more profits from Talton's personal clientele.

By the end of the meeting, Talton left ninety-eight-hundred dollars richer. And, with the drugs that he left behind, his boys owed him thirty-thousand more. Now that his money problems had been dealt with, he had one more issue to deal with. He needed to find a safe place to lay his head at while he figured out a way to get himself out of the hole he had dug for himself.

CHAPTER TWENTY-NINE

Cita never called the number on the business card. She did like the feeling it gave her when she threatened Talton, though. Therefore, the jury was still out on whether or not she would actually do it. Instead, after hanging up on Talton, Cita called her family. She wanted to share the good news of her baby being born. Cita had two sisters and a little brother. After calling them, she was told that her parents couldn't make it, but they would be on their way.

They arrived within the hour, and when they saw her they were shocked. Cita had obviously suffered a tremendous beating and no one had to tell them the details; they automatically assumed that Talton was the culprit. However, that didn't stop them from asking for the details.

Cita ad-libbed a tale immediately. She told them Talton came home drunk and started beating her for no reason. That this hadn't been the first time, but it was definitely the last. She showed them the card with the detective's phone number on it, assuring them that she planned on pressing charges.

In all outer appearances her siblings seemed to

believe her as they offered their sympathies. Yet, unbeknownst to her, they both had major doubts about the details of her story. They knew Talton, and the account Cita had given them didn't seem plausible. Nonetheless, they went along with the charade.

Cita's older sister, Teri, knew that Cita would never go through with filing charges against Talton. Cita wasn't about to give up her Sugar Daddy. Talton gave her everything she wanted, and Cita wasn't stupid. Yeah, she was dumb enough to get caught sleeping around, which was probably why he really beat her up. But she wasn't dumb enough to put him in jail.

That's why Teri took it upon herself to get the ball rolling. While the family coddled their precious Cita, Teri stealthily took the business card off the table and stepped into the hallway with it, where she made the ominous call herself.

Teri didn't really know why she was doing it. It certainly wasn't from an innate urge to protect her sister. Cita could take care of herself. It was more out of hatred towards Talton. At one point in time she thought she had shared something special with her sister's significant other. A lustful embrace where she held his pulsating manhood in her hand. A night in bed where they shared secrets and made love. But, in the end, he always went back to Cita. So, this was her form of payback.

The family eventually made their way to the maternity ward where they saw the newest addition to their family. Cita named the boy Marcus. He was small, but no one could deny his beauty. Little Marcus was born with big brown eyes and a crown of thick black curls. Even through the bubble he was housed in, one could easily see that he favored his mother's looks. His Mediterranean features promised to make him a handsome man in the years to come.

Right there from her seat in the wheelchair it was clear that something dramatic had happened to Cita throughout the night. It was far deeper than the cuts and bruises she brandished. For the last eight months she never once showed even an ounce of affection towards the tiny person in her stomach. She always felt that she was being completely honest with Talton whenever she told him that she planned on running the streets while he stayed at home with the baby. Yet, now that she was a mother, she didn't want anything more than to hold her baby in her arms.

Cita had suddenly awoken with an unexplainable instinct to watch over and protect her child. This feeling had never been explained to her and she didn't know such an emotion existed. Yet there it was, in her heart; a glowing sensation that threatened to explode with joy.

Finally all the excitement was beginning to wane on her energy. Cita was still weak from the recent blood loss, and all the commotion was wearing her down. She asked to be wheeled back to her room where she planned on taking a long nap. But the moment she entered her room, those plans were shattered.

A man wearing a grey suit was standing next to her bed, talking to the nurse who had been taking care of her all morning. No one had to tell Cita who he was. It was obvious he was a cop.

The nurse said, "Cita, this is Mr. Lopez. He's here to speak to you about what happened last night."

"Why'd you come?" Cita asked the man. "I didn't call you."

"Well, someone called and left a message on my phone a half hour ago. I was heading over here anyway. So, I decided to stop and talk to you first. Did I come at a bad time?"

Cita looked at her sisters, knowing that one of them had gone behind her back and called the detective. And Teri's smug stare told her all she needed to know. Now Cita would be forced to go through with the charges against Talton.

"No... no, it's OK. We might as well get this over with. My sisters were just leaving." She put extra emphasis on the last part, while giving her older sister an angry look.

That's when the doting nurse took her que. She quickly helped Cita into bed, then herded the family members out of the room. "OK, y'all, you heard the lady. Time for everyone to give her your hugs and kisses. Cita needs her rest..."

They all hugged Cita and promised to come back later. When it was time for Teri's hug, Cita pulled her close, whispering in her ear, "Thanks, sis. I couldn't have done it without you." Teri was surprised by the comment, not knowing whether she was being sarcastic or not. Teri's face clearly showed her confusion as she was led from the room by Cita's nurse.

The detective was a middle-aged Hispanic man with graying hair at the temples. Her first impression of him was that he would be easily manipulated. She'd give him the same story she gave her sisters and he'd be on his way. But then, she remembered what her face looked like; all of her self-confidence suddenly evaporated. Cita prided herself in having the ability to control any and every situation she found herself in. Yet, at that moment, she was at a loss for words. It was almost as if seeing the detective turned her into the victim she was trying to portray.

After the room was cleared Detective Lopez gave Cita a few minutes before approaching her bedside. As he stepped closer, studying her wounds, he suddenly became uncharacteristically overtaken with anger. At first he couldn't understand where the feelings were coming from. He had seen hundreds, maybe even thousands of domestic violence cases, and he couldn't remember ever being this upset. Maybe it was because he had a daughter her age who had also recently had a baby. In a different world, this poor girl could've been his daughter.

He started by saying, "I see you have a family that cares."

"Yeah, they got my back," she replied, dodging eye contact.

"Cita, I need to ask you a few questions about what happened to you. I came in last night and no one knew what had happened.

"There was no sign of sexual assault so I guess you were lucky there. But, you almost lost your baby, and I know that had to be scary. Is there anything you can tell me about who did this to you?"

"It was my baby's father who beat me up. He came home drunk and started hitting me for no reason." Cita covered her face and started crying.

The detective's eyes teared up as he watched the poor girl sob. "I know it hurts, but I need to know details. I need you to tell me exactly what happened. This way, I can put it on paper and file charges."

"It's just," started Cita, "there's been so much going on. It's like all the stress mounted up and he exploded."

"What kind of stress? What's been going on?"

"Talton sells drugs and our house got raided last week. Well... almost two weeks ago. Then his brother got killed. His brother had a house on the beach, so we were moving in since we lost the house that got raided. In the process, Talton got drunk and started beating me."

"Cita, by any chance, was your boyfriend's brother named Anthony Agosto?"

"Yeah. How'd you know?"

"A colleague of mine is the head of the narcotics unit. We have meetings once a week to discuss our bigger cases. We do that in case there's a connection between departments. Detective Krasinski and I were discussing the murder of Agosto, and the fact that he was connected to a case that Krasinski was working on came up. I was supposed to interview Agosto's girlfriend the other day, but she left the hospital before I could talk to her."

"I know her, too."

"Hold on... you said your house got raided. Did

you get arrested also?"

"Yeah. I'm out on bond."

"Krasinksi said the D.A. is already talking about dropping the charges against your boyfriend. Something about him refusing to talk the night the house was raided, and that they were going to prosecute you because you had admitted to knowing about the contraband being inside the home."

"Wait... what?! How is that? I told them it was all his stuff!"

"I don't know all of the details. But, I do know that the story regarding the arrest of your boyfriend doesn't match up between the officers at the scene. Something about Krasinski saying he was there when they kicked the door down, but a couple of the rookie officers said that your boyfriend was apprehended a few blocks away from the house."

Cita was livid. She couldn't believe Talton was about to walk on a case that she was about to take the fall for. All those nights that he left her alone while he tricked off his money on strippers, and now she was about to go to prison for his drugs! "Listen, sir. I need to talk with the other detective. I'll be his witness that Talton was there when they came in. I don't know what the other cops are talking about. He was there, and on top of that, I think he might have killed someone at the Days Inn, too."

"The double homicide that happened yesterday? How do you know that?"

"He was yelling it while he was hitting me."

"What exactly did he say?"

"He said, 'I just did a double homicide, and I'll

do it again.'"

"How did you know it's the Days Inn murders?"

"Umm... he said it was at the Days Inn," said Cita, hoping she sounded convincing.

"Ms. Wilford, are you willing to testify to all of this?"

"Yeah, but first, I need to talk to someone about my drug charges. I can't go to prison, I got a newborn baby. I need to talk to Detective Krasinski."

Detective Lopez took his phone out of his pocket and called Krasinski's number. No one answered, so he left a message, then put his phone on recording mode and told Cita, "I need you to tell me everything you know... from the beginning."

CHAPTER THIRTY

Alize used her key card to enter the room where Brittany and Talton were waiting. She had to struggle with the door because there was a wet towel wedged underneath it. The inside of the room was smothered in weed smoke and the towel had been put there to stop smoke from permeating into the hallway.

Brittany was lounging against the backboard on the bed with the TV remote in her hand. Talton was outside on the patio with what looked like a pistol tucked into the small of his back and a cell phone to his ear. Brittany's face lit up the moment Alize entered the room; this, Ze took as a good sign.

"What's up, sis?" asked Brittany. "What took you so long? We've been waiting for you to get back so we could go get something to eat."

Alize sat at the edge of the bed, then laid back, letting her feet dangle off the side. "Sarah's count was off again. We all had to stay longer to recount all of the deposits. What time is it anyway?"

"It's a lil' past seven–"

"Oh shit! I gotta call Shawn!" Alize quickly sat up and began rummaging through her purse.

When she found her phone she ran into the

bathroom, slamming the door behind her.

"Nobody's gonna answer!" called out Brittany.

Talton stepped in the room through the sliding door, just as the bathroom shut. He'd been on the phone handling business calling Ant's clientele, letting them know that he would be supplying them from now on. Already he was beginning to see a wave of Anthony's business, and it was way more than he was used to dealing with. Especially since it was only the middle of the week. He could only imagine what things would be like when the weekend came.

Talton had been forwarding his sales to Mike and B.A. all evening. He stayed in constant contact with them, even though they were moving their share of work just as fast. If it weren't for the looming danger from the police, Gangsta would have been on top of the world. But though he knew he was in big trouble; he masked his feelings with all of his might. Knowing how contagious negative energy could be, he didn't want to infect the girls with his cancer.

"What's up with Ze?"

"She had to use the bathroom; she'll be right out."

"Good," replied Talton. "I'm ready to get something to eat." He sat down at the table in the corner of the room and started lacing up his Jordans. "There's a lil' restaurant a few minutes away that got steak and lobster for less than thirty dollars a plate. You're gonna love it."

"Sounds good to me. And I know dinners on you, I saw that fat stack of money you made today."

Talton smiled. Earlier he had purposely let

Brittany see a roll of bills. He didn't do it with the intentions of showing off, it was more to show her that she wasn't dealing with a broke nigga. "It's funny, 'cause most of that money I picked up today goes to your sister. She should be the one paying for dinner. But, yeah, I be gettin' it though. Hey, Brit... thanks for everything. You and Ze are the only reason I'm not in jail right now. I appreciate that shit. Most females would've panicked if they would've seen what y'all saw. But, you didn't, and I appreciate that shit. So, hell yeah, dinner's on me."

"Don't trip, big bruh. My sister likes you, and I think you're cute... I mean, cool. I think you're cool, so we got you. But, man, yesterday was crazy. I hope the cops don't connect us to that shit. I'm really worried about my sister, because she's all I got."

"What about her lil' boy?"

Brittany didn't answer. She paused, looking into Talton's eyes as if she were searching for something. Then, Alize came out of the bathroom and sat down at the table, across from Talton.

"What's up, Gangsta? How'd things work out with the baby mamma?"

"Couldn't find the bitch. It's cool... she's probably at her sister's house waiting on me to show up with roses or something. I do got some good news, though." Talton pulled out two thick wads of currency. "Here's seven racks. I owe you eighteen now, right?"

"That's what I'm talking about!" exclaimed Ze, picking up the larger of the two stacks from the table. "Man, fuck your baby mamma! She can wait while we get this money!"

"That's what I'm sayin'," replied Talton. "I got eight more waiting for me at the homey's house that we can go get after dinner. I'ma need some more trees, too. My niggas is moving it hella fast."

"No problem. Before I got here, I got a call for three pounds. After I get rid of that, I'll have sixteen left. But, I wanna know what's up with the coke?"

"What'chu mean?" asked Talton, forgetting about their prior business arrangement.

That's when Brittany got off the bed and stood up in the middle of the room, yawning exaggeratedly loud. "Excuse me... this conversation is getting real boring, and I'm starving. I'm gonna use the bathroom, when I come out, you guys better be ready to go get some steak and lobster."

"Steak and lobster!" spat Ze. "Bitch, you might get a cheeseburger or something. I'm not gonna–"

Talton interrupted Alize, "I got it, ma. I already told her I was gonna take y'all out."

"Yeah! You stingy slut. My big bruh's gonna take us out to dinner," teased Brittany on her way into the bathroom.

Alize rolled her eyes at her sister before turning back to Talton. "So, what's up? What're we gonna do about the coke?"

"I was planning on buying another half a brick after my niggas sell what they got."

"How much will that cost?"

"Ten racks."

"Well... I got forty put up that we can use."

"Forty what?!"

181

"Forty thousand."

"You got what?!" asked Talton, a little too loud.

"Calm down, boy! What? You thought I was just hustling for my health? I save my money. So, yeah, I got forty G's plus the work in my attic. Not to mention the money you still owe me..."

CHAPTER THIRTY-ONE

Cita was in the bed, alone, in a dark hospital room. The only light came from a street lamp that shun through the window. She was exhausted from hours spent talking to detectives. When it was all said and done, she really didn't know how to feel. Ever since her baby had been born, she'd been experiencing emotions that she had never had before. Even now, as she thought of Talton, she was plagued with guilt. Along with the feelings of guilt came shame and confusion.

On the one hand, Talton was a direct connection to her baby. Putting him in jail was guaranteeing her child a life without his father. Yet, on the flip side, Talton going to jail put her on the fast-track to her ultimate goal. All the cars, jewels, and even the house on the beach would be hers. If she wanted, she'd probably be able to take over the drug business as well.

She was sure that he killed those men in that motel room. However, she hadn't actually seen him do anything. Nevertheless, it didn't stop her from fabricating a story for the police because they basically walked her through it by giving her all the details themselves.

Detective Lopez told her there were two people dead and one on life support. After that, all she did was give him back all the same information in different words, making sure to leave out the part about her being at the scene when it all happened.

Detective Krasinski showed up later and assured her that her drug charges would be dropped in exchange for her cooperation. In the end, Talton's face ended up being plastered all over the news. By all appearances, Cita was well on her way to the final checkmate.

So, why was she feeling like this? Sitting in the dark, feeling guilty for what she had done, she was confused. A large part of her wanted to see Talton; speak to Talton; even lay with Talton. Especially now that they had a baby together.

She knew she could find him if she really wanted to. Yet, she never told the detectives that. They kept having her call his phone, but she knew that wouldn't work. Talton was far from stupid. His phone was probably at the bottom of the ocean by now. In a way, she hoped he never got caught. He wasn't even from Florida, so he could leave whenever he got ready.

Cita thought of the previous day and how Talton had brutally attacked her. He had never hit her before, yet she always knew he was capable of it. She also understood why he killed those men. It was more out of love than anger. He loved his brother and they had taken him from Talton. There was no doubt in her mind that he would've done the same thing if it would've been her who was killed instead of

Anthony. Talton was real; when he pledged his allegiance to someone, he really meant it; unlike so many other people she had known over the years, including herself.

Cita cried. She cried because she now realized how much she really loved her baby's father.

$$$$$

Talton and the girls were back in their room at the Hilton. After the restaurant they rode around for a couple of hours, handling business. First they stopped at the girls' house to pick up a change of clothes and marijuana so they could deliver the work to their clientele. Then they went by B.A's apartment to pick up Talton's money and drop off more work. Somewhere along the way they picked up a bottle of liquor, then headed back to the room and spent the rest of the night smoking and drinking.

Talton had just finished his shower when he heard Brittany's phone vibrating. He thought he had turned it off earlier, but he obviously hadn't. In the back of his mind something told him not to answer it, but he did anyway. "What's up?"

"Bruh, where the fuck you at?!" asked B.A., sounding extremely agitated. "Why didn't you tell us you knocked them niggas down?"

"What the fuck you talking 'bout?"

"Turn on the news, fam! Your face is all over the place! They're looking for you for a gang of murders!"

Before Talton could reply, the bathroom door

opened and Alize stood there looking like she had seen a ghost. "You need to get out here." She was wide eyed, yet calm. Nevertheless, her body language told him the situation was ominous.

"Let me call you back," Talton told B.A. Then, wrapped in a towel, he went into the next room. Brittany was seated at the edge of the bed watching the news, her face was just as grim as her sister's. Talton walked up to the television and turned up the volume.

A female reporter was standing in front of room 112. It was dark outside but they had the place lit up like a concert. Forensic technicians were walking around in the background along with several nosy bystanders who were trying to get on TV. "I'm standing outside of the gruesome scene where a double homicide was committed over twenty-four hours ago. Earlier we reported that the Sheriff's Department had a suspect in custody, but now, our sources have revealed a different suspect and motive for this heinous crime. Our sources are telling us that these crimes are a direct result of an on-going drug war that is taking place throughout the Clearwater city streets as we speak. The Pinellas County Sheriff's Department refused to go on the record with any details. However, we have gotten word that there is an eye witness who places this man at the scene of the crime during the time of the murders."

Talton's mug shot was suddenly flashed across the screen. "The Sheriff's Department is asking that if anyone has any information on the whereabouts of Talton Robinson that they contact the secret witness hotline. The number is 727-678-1632. There is a twenty-five-thousand-dollar reward for any information leading to the arrest and conviction of Talton Robinson."

Gangsta turned the television off, walked over to the table and sat down. He tried to maintain his composure but he was having a hard time. He had been under investigation for murder on several occasions, but never had he been turned in by someone in his inner circle. As he looked around the room, he saw Brittany staring at him and she looked like she wanted to cry. He hadn't known her long, yet they had grown close over the last twenty-four hours. Then he looked at Alize, who stared back as if asking him what he was going to do. He had no answer.

Alize knew the situation was dire and that Talton was overwhelmed. Thus, she had to take control. "Talton, put some clothes on. We gotta get outta here now! By tomorrow morning, the whole city's gonna know your face." To Brittany, she said, "Get up, get all our shit, let's go! Come on–" Brittany's vibrating phone cut Ze off in mid-sentence. "And take the battery out of that phone. Talton... do you hear me? Come on, man! We gotta go!"

All their things were packed within minutes. After Talton got dressed, they all rushed out the room, down the elevator and into their cars. Brittany got in the Malibu, Alize and Talton took the H-3. They decided to go to the girls' house. On the ride, Talton called B.A. and set up a meeting for the next day. After that, he took the battery out of Brittany's phone.

In the Hummer's back row, Talton nervously clutched his nine-millimeter, Glock 17. Everything had went to hell in the last few weeks. He was trying to come to grips with what was happening. At that point the only stable aspect of his life was Alize. As he watched her driving the truck he thought of how calm she seemed under pressure. He knew he could trust her and Brittany above anyone else in his life. Nevertheless, in the end, he knew he would be alone.

As Ze navigated the small SUV she let her mind wonder, thinking of all the loved ones she had lost over the years. It seemed as if everyone she had ever loved had died or disappeared. All except for Brittany. She loved her sister, even though at times she was more like a daughter than a sibling.

Alize held herself together despite her inner fears. Her exterior was calm and collective, but on the inside she was going crazy. Not only was she angry at the people who threatened to take Talton from her, she also felt heartbroken, disappointed, and most of all... scared.

She looked at Talton through the rear-view mirror. He was silently staring out the window. At that moment she realized that she would do everything in her power to protect him, even if it meant trading her life for his. Then, as she was watching him, her worst fears materialized. She saw a police cruiser tailgating them. Seconds later, its siren sounded, and suddenly the inside of the Hummer was lit up by red and blue lights.

CHAPTER THIRTY-TWO

He heard the siren and saw the lights, yet didn't panic. Instead, he made eye contact with Alize, who was looking at him through the rear-view and said, "Pull over. But do it at an angle, so I can step out the passenger side without being seen."

"What are you gonna do?" asked Ze, as she did what she was told.

He didn't answer. He reached up, turning off the interior light switch so the light wouldn't come on when he opened the door.

The cop car was on their bumper with its siren going full blast. Talton knew he had to react quickly; either have Ze high-speed with the cop, or pull over and shoot it out with him. Regardless of what option was chosen, it had to be done fast; before the officer had the chance to call for back up.

The Hummer came to an abrupt stop, slanted from the curb just as Talton had requested. Without a second thought, Gangsta opened his door and surreptitiously slid from his seat onto the pavement. His Glock 17 was cocked and ready to shoot. With smooth and decisive movements, Talton made it to the rear of the SUV without detection. It was do or die, and he preferred the former.

Talton gripped the pistol tight. With his finger on the hairpin trigger, he stepped from behind the Hummer ready to shoot his way out of a life sentence. Then, just as he came out the cuts, he watched as the police car sped past him and the Hummer. When he realized what happened he let out a deep breath and leaned his back against the back of the truck, taking the moment to let the adrenaline slow its roll through his system.

It was a close call. But, from that moment on, he knew he couldn't afford to let his guard down. One mistake... any mistake could be deadly.

A short time later the trio arrived at their destination. No one said a word. Everyone understood the situation and were all preoccupied with their own demons. Ze went straight to her room and didn't come out for the rest of the night. Brittany did the same.

And Talton... he fell asleep on the couch that he wedged against the front door.

CHAPTER THIRTY-THREE

The next morning Cita was allowed to leave the hospital sans her baby. Little Marcus had to stay for a few more days so the doctors could keep an eye on him. Other than that, she was told that he would be fine.

The previous day, during the several hours Cita spent with the detectives, she told them she had been living at the beach house since her duplex was raided, but now that Anthony and Talton were gone, she had no way of paying the rent. Detective Krasinski started his career as a bounty hunter, and that experience taught him that the easiest way to catch a fugitive was to watch his girlfriend. Especially if the girl had a child. Realizing this, he talked with SVU Detective Lopez and secured Cita's rent money from the Special Victims Fund. Cita wouldn't have to worry about her monthly bills for at least the next three months.

Knowing that he'd have to stay close to Ms. Wilford, Detective Krasinski offered to give her a ride home from the hospital. Since Cita knew that Krasinski was the key to getting her drug charges dropped, she eagerly accepted. Thus, it was the beginning of a relationship based on exploitation.

When Cita was finally wheeled out the hospital, Krasinski was outside waiting for her. His unmarked 2015 Chevy Impala was parked near the exit. To Cita, Krasinski looked different. A bit cleaner, more attractive. In the sunlight he looked younger than she remembered, which was funny since she spent several hours with him the day before.

Today he had on a white, short sleeved polo shirt that accentuated his thick arms and wide chest. As he helped her out of her wheelchair and into his car, she also saw that he was a lot taller than she had previously thought. She was now officially beginning to feel a physical attraction towards him.

After they got settled in, Krasinski pulled the Impala into traffic. Cita seemed timid so he decided to initiate the conversation.

"How you feeling today, Ms. Wilford?"

"I'm alright. Just happy to be going home. It feels good to finally get some fresh air, too. I just can't stand the fact that I'm so pale right now."

"That's from the blood loss. A C-section will do it to ya every time. But then again, the doctors said you lost a lot of blood before you even got to the hospital. It's a surprise you're walking and talking."

"I still feel weak. Every once in a while, I'll get dizzy. I wish I could bring my baby home today, but it might be for the better. This way, I can take my time cleaning up the mess. Ya know?"

"Definitely... definitely," replied Krasinski as he glanced at Cita for a moment before turning back to the traffic. "Ms. Wilford –"

"Please, call me Cita."

"OK. Cita, I want you to know that you don't have to worry about a thing. I've got a team of undercover officers who'll be watching your house and I'm only a phone call away. There's a chance your boyfriend–"

"Ex-boyfriend. After what he did to me, I don't ever wanna see 'em again."

"Yeah, well there's a chance that he'll try and contact you. Especially after he finds out about the baby. When that happens, we'll be there."

"I really doubt he'll show up," said Cita, without looking at Krasinski. "Not after he sees his face all over the news. He's not stupid. I don't even think he's still in the city."

"Do you have any idea where he might've went?" Krasinski changed lanes, preparing to make a right turn.

"If I was him, I'd go to Puerto Rico or St. Croix. He's got family out there."

"What about Tennessee or California? He has a criminal record in both states. Has he ever spoken to you about any of those places?" Krasinski tried initiating eye contact with Cita, but each time, she looked away. It was obvious that she was self-conscious of her disfiguring cuts and bruises.

"This may sound cray-cray, but ever since you guys started asking me questions about Talton, I realized that I really don't know much about him. I mean... I know lil' things; like, how he likes his food cooked, or that he doesn't like waking up to cigarette smoke. I know about his kids in other states, too. But for the most part, I guess I didn't really know him that well. I couldn't tell you much about his childhood, or anything about his past. We just never talked about it much."

"It's probably for the better. Since I've been on this case, I've done my homework, and I can tell you... this guy's no good. His rap sheet shows a trail of blood and mayhem everywhere he goes. And, now that you tell me about the kids that he's left around the country, the picture's becoming more clearer. Being a career criminal is one thing, but leaving fatherless children across the country, destined to grow up in poverty is a whole different kind of shittiness. This guy's a freakin' class-A bastard. Look at what he did to you. You're the mother of his child, and he's trying to get you to take the fall for his drug dealing. Who does that? He almost killed you while you were eight months pregnant. If you ask me, you're better off without this guy. A lot of people will be better off when this guy's in prison."

"That's easy for you to say. You're probably happily married with your life in order. I'm stuck with a newborn baby, and now that my face looks like this, I'll never find a man."

"Ha! Are you serious? I know about ten guys on the force, including myself, that would kill to be with a women as pretty as yourself. Those bruises will be gone in no time, and having a baby just makes you that much more of a catch. Another thing, what makes you think I'm married? There's no ring on this finger. I've been divorced for years."

Cita didn't say anything, she just stared out the

window. Then, after a few moments of self-reflection she said, "I don't know... I guess you're right. All of this will be over soon, and then I can move on with the next chapter in my life. Who knows, I might go back to school or something."

Cita stole a glance at the detective while he was driving. After quickly looking away, she thought to herself, *Damn, why do I gotta have these black eyes!? This guy wants me, but I look like shit!* Cita pushed the button, rolling her window down. For the rest of the ride, she stared out the window with a sinister smile etched across her face...

CHAPTER THIRTY-FOUR

B.A. was behind the wheel of a 2015 Chevy Monte Carlo. Over the last week he had been enjoying himself as much as possible. Working with Gangsta had never been so profitable, yet B.A. still wanted more. Right now he was on his way to a bowling alley in a city called Pinnellas Park, just outside of Clearwater. He hadn't been able to sleep since finding out about the murders. Sometime throughout the night he came up with a plan, but he needed to talk to Mike about it before putting it into action.

Mike was outside standing next to his car when B.A. pulled into the bowling alley's parking lot. He was talking to a couple of good-looking females. This brought a smirk to B.A.'s face, knowing that if Mike managed to get either one of their phone numbers, chances were B.A. would be hooking up with the other one. That's how their crew worked. Whenever one of them met a new female, the rest of them would knock down their friends. Therefore, when B.A. saw Mike talking to some new tail, he automatically saw them as another possible conquest.

When Mike saw the candy-apple red Monte

Carlo and realized that B.A. was behind the wheel, his jaw dropped. Without excusing himself he stepped away from the girls and walked towards the spot where his friend was parking. "Damn, this bitch is clean!" said Mike as he approached the car. B.A. replied, "Get in, let's bend a few corners."

"I can't go anywhere; I'm waiting on a sale right now. Plus, I just met these females. Why don't you get out and meet 'em? They're Columbian and they're sisters."

"I'll do that, but first we gotta talk. Go get their numbers and come back. Tell 'em you'll get at 'em in about fifteen minutes. We might even bowl a few lanes wit' 'em."

Mike didn't want to miss the money he had lined up and the girls were enough to make him put off the average conversation with B.A., but the look on his friend's face told him he should listen. "Right, hold on." He walked away and said something to the females, took out his phone, entered what was obviously their contact information and went back to the Monte Carlo; this time getting into the passenger seat.

B.A.'s rented sports car was all red and had dark limo tint on the windows. The seats were black with red trimming making the car's interior look like the cockpit of a fighter jet.

"Bruh, this motherfucka is clean as fuck! Where'd you get it?" asked Mike as he ran his fingertips along the double-padded leather upholstery.

"I got a plug at the airport. My sister's baby daddy

works at the Budget Rental, so I get half price. They just got a few of these, too. If you want, we can get you one just like it."

"Come on, man. Same paint, same guts?"

"Hell yeah! We can go right now!"

"Let's go!"

"That's your word?"

"Let's go. I got the money and I'm ready to floss."

"What about that knock you got comin'?"

"I already made sixteen hundred today. He can wait. Let's go!"

This was exactly what B.A. wanted to hear. Without further ado, he put the car in reverse and pulled out of the parking spot. Now he'd have Mike all to himself with more than enough time to convince him to go along with his plan.

Awhile later, on the Courtney Cambell Causeway (the bridge joining St. Petersburg and Tampa), B.A. reached into his pocket, pulling out a sandwhich bag filled with weed. "Here, roll this," he said, handing the bag to Mike. "There's Swishers in the glove compartment."

"So, what's up with Talton ?" asked Mike. "I've been calling the number he gave us and it keeps going to voice mail." Mike split the cigar open, emptying the excess tobacco inside the paper bag the cigars originally came in.

"I know. I called 'em as soon as I saw that shit on the news and bruh hung up on me. I think he's spooked. That's what I wanted to talk to you about." B.A. paused to look at Mike, but he was concentrating on rolling the cigar. "Talton's cool, but bruh is wildn'. I'm not too sure he realizes where he's at. This ain't Cali... these crackers don't go for all that gunplay. And I think losing Ant was too much for him. I'm starting to think he's gonna fuck around and get us all locked up."

Mike sealed the blunt by licking its leaves and rolling it up. Now he had the lighter underneath it, using the flame to dry the leaves. "I feel where you're coming from, I'm just not sure where you're going. I thought about all that when he first came up with the whole murder thing. But, B.A., this is part of the game. He's the reason we're riding in cars like this. Yeah, if he gets caught–"

"When he gets caught," said B.A.

"When he gets caught, he'll be looking at some time. But, regardless, that's my boy. Before he got here I was selling nickel bags of brown weed. Now I'm supplying my old connect. I don't even leave the pad unless I got at least five-hundred waiting for me. Talton's the homey... point blank." Mike put the blunt to his lips and lit the tip of it.

"I'm not saying he's not the homey. I got stupid love for Gangsta, and Ant was my dog. But, damn, Mike... he's on every television station in the bay. The Sheriff's Department is tweeting pictures of him every hour, on the hour! On top of that, he's not even from out here. What would you do if you were him? Run. And, that's what I think he's gonna do. I think he's gonna collect this money we owe him and we'll never see him again. He has no reason to stay out here. He doesn't even have the connect that his brother had." B.A. took ahold of the blunt that Mike handed him. "We're basically hustling up all this cash just to hand it over to someone we'll never see again."

"So what? It's not like he's robbing us."

"That's not what I'm saying. I know he's not robbing us, but he will be leaving us with nothing. Look... Talton's gonna get got. And, when he does, he'll never see daylight again. We both know this. So, tell me, where's that gonna leave us? I know you're not trying to go back to telemarketing."

Mike didn't reply. He just stared out towards the body of water they were driving across.

"I didn't think so. So, this is what I came up with: I say we take these trees and coke he gave us and sell it. Then, instead of paying him back, we take the money and cop our own dope with it. That'll be fifteen G's apiece. That's not all, either. I'm thinking we might as well collect the reward money, too. In the end we'll have twenty-seven-five apiece. That's kilo money for each of us! We'll be able to front niggas just like he does to us. Since he don't really fuck with anybody else, we won't have to worry about anybody running up on us for it." B.A. then pulled the Monte Carlo over and stopped on the side of the bridge. With cars speeding past them, he looked at Mike and said, "So, what you think?"

While slightly shaking his head, Mike bit his bottom lip like he did whenever he had something serious on his mind. He weighed the pros and cons. B.A. had a point. In essence, it was grimy... scandalous even. But he had a point.

Then B.A.'s phone started vibrating. Looking at

its screen, B.A. said, "Speak of the devil; this is him right here..."

CHAPTER THIRTY-FIVE

With Alize at work, Talton and Brittany had the house to themselves. At the moment Talton was in the living room waiting for his brother's cocaine connection to call him back. It would be the first time that he dealt with Big Snoop directly. Big Snoop was also from the West Coast, just like Talton. He came up in Sacramento, and was the founder of the state-wide gang called Riders, aka Playboys. However, even though they travelled in some of the same circles, Talton and Snoop had never actually met one another. Therefore, Talton was anxiously waiting to find out if Snoop would return his call.

Alize's influx of cash had been a Godsend. With her thirty-thousand along with the money Mike and B.A. would have for him, Gangsta was able to put in an order for three kilos at twenty-thousand apiece. The money was a sure thing, but the transaction wasn't. Anthony had never ordered that much work at one time, so Talton had no way of knowing if Playboy Snoop would believe the deal was legit. If the brother of one of Talton's clients ever called him out of the blue to order three times more than his actual client ever even thought of ordering, Talton probably wouldn't serve him. Yet, now that he was on the other end of the spectrum, Talton hoped Snoop would trust him.

Then came the next issue; if Snoop did call him back to green light the deal, Talton had no idea how he'd pick up the drugs. His face was all over the news; there was no way he could drive to Jacksonville to pick up the work. At this point, he only had two options. Send B.A. and Mike with the money, or ask Alize and Brittany to do it. He was leaning towards B.A. and Mike. Up until that point they had never crossed him. He had no reason not to trust them.

While Gangsta was sitting on the couch, brainstorming, Brittany walked through the living room on her way to the kitchen. Talton, who had been lounging around the house in sweat pants, was caught off guard by what she was wearing. At a quick glance, from the corner of his eye, he thought Brittany was naked from the waist down. But after taking a better look, he saw that she had on a spaghetti string halter top with light tan panties. Her underwear was made from material that was so thin, it was transparent.

Not only were they see-through, making her ass-crack totally visible, they were also too small. Brittany was a thick girl; a normal pair of panties would've left little to the imagination. Thus, what she had on now gave the illusion that she was completely nude. For a split second Talton felt his manhood twitch. Her milky white flesh was enticing, yet he quickly remembered who he was looking at and adverted his eyes.

Moments later Brittany came into the living room holding a cup of orange juice in one hand and some fingernail polish in the other. Sitting down next to Talton she said, "What's up, big bro?"

"Ain't nothing, just plottin' on how to make a million bucks from the comforts of this couch."

"Well... while you 'plottin', you wanna help me with my toenails?" Brittany put her feet on the coffee table and began putting cotton balls between her toes.

"Toenails! You got me fucked up, Brit-Brit. What I look like painting your toenails?"

"Fine... I'll do 'em myself." She then took her feet off the table and placed her left leg on the couch; which opened up her body towards Talton. "I just figured since you ain't doing nothing... but that's cool."

Brittany's legs were wide open, with one foot on the couch and the other one on the floor. This caused one of her pussy lips to slide out the side of her small underwear; not that it really mattered since they were see-through anyway. Except her lips were now open, so her cat and clit were totally visible. And the fact that her panties were positioned the way they were forced the lining of her underwear to rub against her budding clitoris. Even the slightest movement teased it, causing enough friction to stimulate it.

"Hey, Brit, what are you doing this weekend?"

"I gotta go to work," she answered. Brittany noticed Talton's eyes open wide for a second when he looked between her legs so she looked down. That's when she realized how exposed she was.

Without as much as a thought she opened up wider. It felt good. She loved the control she had over men whenever she showed off her body. But this was more; she actually felt a tingle when she moved her legs. "I told you, I'm on four days and off three."

"Damn, you did say you had to go back to work." Talton didn't want her to catch him looking at her prize, yet he couldn't help himself. The girl had a fat pussy! He tried to act like he was watching TV, but continued stealing glances. Then he noticed a wet spot. However, his thoughts were redirected when her phone sounded. "Hold up, I gotta get this." It was the call he'd been waiting for.

When Talton stood up to take the call in the kitchen, Brittany looked at his crotch. That's when she saw the swollen imprint of his manhood and this aroused her loins even more. She began rocking her legs back and forth; each time, forcing the fabric of her panties to rub against her clit, stimulating her throbbing love button. It felt so good she started doing it faster, not realizing how wet she was becoming. After a few minutes her panties were saturated in secretion. So much so that it had started making a sloshing sound with every movement she made.

A few minutes later Talton came back into the living room with a smile on his face. Brittany slowed her rocking so that he wouldn't see what she had been doing, but it wasn't easy. She had already gone too far. And, now that he was so close to her, she couldn't concentrate. She tried to paint her toenails, but her heart was beating so fast her hands were shaking.

After sitting back down, Talton called B.A. He was feeling real good about his next move. Snoop had OK'd the deal; he had three kilos of fishscale cocaine as soon as he came up with the full sixty G's. All he had to do was quarterback the deal. When B.A. answered the call, Talton put the phone on speaker and sat it down on the coffee table.

"B.A."

"What's up, bruh? Me and Mike was just talking 'bout you. We're on our way to Tampa to pick up another rental. This nigga seen me pushin' this 2015 Monte and now he wants one."

"That's what's up," replied Talton. "Actually, I gotta situation where you guys can put them rentals to use." Just as he made the statement, Gangsta turned his body towards Brittany's. He then grabbed her left foot and put it on his lap. Next, he took the fingernail polish from her and started working on her toenails. He could see straight through her panties. She was so wet, he could've easily slid his rising member into her most deepest corners. From that point on, he made no attempt to hide the fact that he was looking at her salivating treasure.

"Hey, Talton," said B.A. "I'm gonna put you on speaker. It's only me and Mike in the car."

"It's good... What's up, Mike?"

"What's good, Gangsta?" called out Mike from the passenger seat.

Talton went on to say, "I just got the call I was waiting on. Which means I got a three-brick deal lined up for us. It's a go, so now all we're waiting on is for you guys to get rid of what you got. The catch is, I'ma need y'all to drive to Jacksonville to pick up the work."

Brittany's heart was beating a thousand times faster than usual. Just the simple touch from her sister's man was driving her crazy. She couldn't stop herself from rocking her thighs back and forth. And the fact that Talton was openly watching her was making her even wetter. The sound of her sloshing undergarments filled the room along with the aroma of her glistening vagina.

"Bruh, we only got thirty G's in work," stated B.A. over the phone. "How're we gonna get three bricks?"

"Don't trip, I got another thirty stacks right here. Just work on getting y'all end of the money and we're good. When you handle that, I'll tell you where to come and pick up the rest of the money. Then you can go get the work. When you bring it back, we'll turn those three bricks into five and we'll be on from there."

"A'ight," answered B.A. "We can do that, but it might take a few days. And... Talton?"

"What it do, bruh?"

"You good? I mean, bruh, you safe?"

"Yeah, I'm good. I think Cita went and lied to them folks. I fucked around and put my hands on her the last time I saw her. Then she disappeared. Next thing I know, my face is all over the news.

"What're you gonna do?" asked B.A.

"I'ma get it cleared up. But, right now shit is so hot, all I can do is lay low."

Brittany was about to cum. Talton wasn't trying

to hide the fact that he was loving every minute of it, either. In the midst of talking to the guys, he stopped messing around with the fingernail polish and just watched Brittany slowly lose control of her sexual inhibitions.

Brittany wanted that thick piece of meat that she saw hanging from in between Talton's legs at the hotel. She was so full of lust she felt like she would explode. The teasing her panties were giving her had worn thin on her nerves. Brittany reached between her thighs and moved them to the side, totally exposing her wet sex. She did this as she was reaching her climax; then she took both of her hands, placing her fingers on each side of her lower lips, spreading the skin apart. She wanted her pussy wide open so Talton could see inside of her sweet tunnel of love.

Gangsta stared into the pink hole as Brittany stretched herself open. It looked like it had a mind of its own. The more she pulled it apart, the more it seemed to come alive. The muscles just inside of the small entrance looked as if they were trying to seize and/or grasp for something that was just outside of their reach. He could only imagine how tight it would feel if he were inside of her.

Then, to the surprise of both of them, Brittany's pussy started spitting out cum. Her milky juices shot all over the couch and onto Talton's sweat pants. Her warm goo was everywhere, squirting spasmodically all over the couch they were on.

"... Talton... Talton, you there?"

"Yeah, yeah. Hey... I'll call y'all back in the

morning. Don't rush, stay low key, but remember that we're waiting on y'all."

Talton reached for the phone and ended the call. Then he got back to Brittany. Her cheeks were flushed; she looked as if she had just had the best sex of her life, and he hadn't even touched her yet. Talton pushed her foot out the way and climbed over her until he was laying on top of her. With his face only centimeters from hers, Talton looked into Brittany's eyes. If he didn't know better, he would've thought she looked afraid. He kissed her... He kissed her with a passion reserved for lovers. Then he slowly pulled away and said, "Brittany, you're sexy as hell. That pussy looks good enough to eat, and I'm feeling you real tough right now. But we can't do this..."

CHAPTER THIRTY-SIX

After the call ended, B.A. took a moment to process all the new information. Another thirty-thousand was incomprehensible; if Gangsta really came through with that type of money... they'd be rich!

Mike was in deep thought as well. He was on the fence when B.A. started stating his case. But now he was busy calculating the amount of money they were talking about.

B.A. was the first to speak. Turning towards Mike he said, "Now, you can't tell me the pieces of the puzzle aren't coming together like some butt cheeks! This dumb-ass nigga's 'bout to hand over another thirty-thousand! Not to mention, the connect of the century! Bruh... that's sixty-thousand, plus the twenty-five in reward money. We can buy them three bricks, turn 'em into six and still have twenty-five in cash!"

Mike put the blunt to his lips, inhaling deeply. He was quiet, but his mind was in motion. He felt like a guest in the "Big Brother" house, and that B.A. just cornered him with a plan to back-door Talton. It was a hard decision to make, especially with B.A. in his ear like he was.

"Mike," said B.A. "I know what you're thinking. Yeah, he's shown mad love, but he's a lost cause, bro. You heard 'em yourself; Cita told on 'em. Once they catch him and put his girl on the stand... its cookies!" Mike handed B.A. the blunt. B.A. took it, hoping the weed was clouding Mike's feelings of loyalty towards their homeboy. With the cigar now in his mouth, B.A. put the Monte Carlo in gear and pulled back into traffic. He drove a little while in silence before speaking again. "Talton's a sinking ship. There's nothing we can do for 'em. If we don't make this move now we will regret it for the rest of our lives. We'll either end up in Raiford, doing twenty-three and one, or we'll end up broke again. I'm trying to be out here, getting pussy... riding in clean shit-"

"Alright. You're right. I'm with it. But, for the record, I'm only doing this because life's a chess game. You gotta be three moves ahead, and this is the most logical move. Let's do it."

"You ain't gotta say anything else," replied B.A. before turning the music up and passing the blunt back to Mike. This was the beginning of a turning point in B.A.'s life. A crossroad in his journey to the top.

He thought he was ready for it...

CHAPTER THIRTY-SEVEN

Alize came home from work tired. The last thing that she wanted to hear was the loud music that was coming from the inside of her house. Yet, when she opened the door, she was greeted by the aromas of a clean home and roasted meat. Music was playing in the background and Brittany was on the couch playing video games in her sweat pants. Talton was in the kitchen, presumingly putting the last-minute touches on a full-course meal. It almost seemed as if they had lived together forever.

"Looks like somebody's been busy," remarked Ze after dropping her purse on the floor and finding a seat on the couch. "This place hasn't smelled this good since I moved in. I know this is all you're doing, Talton. Brit's way too lazy to do any housework."

"Tsst," sounded Brittany, still playing on the X Box.

"Actually, it was the both of us," replied Talton. "I had to do the cooking though. Brittany was talking 'bout putting pork and beans in the spaghetti so I had to take over in the kitchen–"

"Fuck you, Talton!" called out Brittany. "I was

telling you how to make chili, not spaghetti!"

"Yeah, a'ight. But, anyways, how was your day, Ze?" Talton opened the oven, pulling out a tray with baked pork chops smothered in mushroom gravy.

"It wasn't too bad, but I'll tell you one thing: I'm ready for the weekend."

After setting the tray on top of the oven Talton asked, "Are you picking up your son for the weekend?"

For a split second, in the midst of her video game playing, Brittany shot Ze a concerned glance. Then, just as quickly as it happened, she looked away.

"I don't think so," replied Alize. "Not with all of this craziness going on–"

"You're the only crazy one, Ze," said Brittany, without looking away from her game.

"Anyways, I don't wanna have him around while all this stuff is going on. I just spent half the day worried about you shooting it out with some cops or something."

Gangsta smiled before saying, "Ma, you trippin'. This house is probably the safest place on earth. No one knows I'm here, and no one even knows I know you. As long as I'm not out there paintin' da town, I'm good." Talton set out three plates on the counter and was now putting food on them. "I got the call from my partna... the deal is a go. All I'm waiting on now is a call from my boys telling me they got the money from all that work we dropped off." Talton brought the plates into the living room so they could all eat together. "When they get the money, I'm sending them to pick up the coke."

Alize took a bite from her plate, closed her eyes and said, "Ummm, damn, this is good!" She then took two more bites before speaking again. "So, basically, you're gonna give your friends all the money and have them go pick up all the coke?"

"That's the plan."

"Talton, you know we're talking about sixty-thousand-dollars, right?"

He took his time chewing his food before answering. "You guys want something to drink?"

"Yeah," replied the girls.

He then got up and went into the kitchen. From there he said, "You know... I really don't trust anybody. Not since I left California. It's just, right now, we don't have many options. Ever since I've been out here, I've been working with Mike and B.A. They never once came up short; the money's always been good." He came back into the living room with a two-liter of Sprite and three plastic cups. "I know it's a lot of money. And, I know it's not my money. But I think it'll be cool. Especially since we're all gonna eat off it."

"That makes sense," stated Alize. "I'm just not sure that you're taking everything into consideration. I don't know your boys as well as you do, I'll give you that. But, right now, anyone can pick up the phone and get twenty-five-thousand for turning you in."

"I know what you're saying. Here's the thing; in the dope game, anybody can cross anyone at any time. There's always a risk. If you run around paranoid, thinking the whole world is against you,

you'll never get anything done. In the end, you always end up trusting somebody with something anyway. Sixty racks is a lot of money. But this is my team we're talking about here. It's not like my niggas from back home, but they still my team. If I don't trust them, who can I trust? Your sister's gonna be at work and you can't take me cuz I'm wanted. It's our only option."

"Well, then," said Ze. "Since you say we have no other choice, when's the deal going down?"

"As soon as Mike and B.A. sell what they got. This way, we'll have the weekend clear for you and me to just hang out. I've been sending my clientele to their phones, and since they got coke and weed, they should sell out by the end of the weekend."

Alize took another bite from her plate and so did Talton. Brittany quietly ate her food without interrupting the two. If either one of them had asked her, she would've told Talton to cut his losses now and stop making investments until the murder cases were cleared up. Nevertheless, she kept quiet. Brittany learned a long time ago not to get involved in other people's business transactions.

"You know," began Ze, "I still gotta pay my connect for that weed."

"How much you owe?" asked Talton.

"Seventy-five-thousand. I should have most of it myself. It's just your boys have a lot of my work, and now I'm giving you the majority of my savings. If they did cross us, I'd be fucked."

"Ze, I give you my word; as soon as I flip this next batch of coke, we'll pay off your boy. It ain't nothing, don't trip. When it comes to gettin' money, I got this."

$$$$$

For the rest of the evening the trio sat around the house, smoking weed, drinking Johnnie Walker and playing video games, and ending the night with a romantic comedy from Netflix. No one watching them would've guessed that there was a fugitive amongst them.

After the movie, Ze and Talton took a warm bubble bath together, each taking their time to softly cleanse the other. The couple enjoyed every moment of their quiet time together. Around them the world was falling apart; Talton was on the run, Alize was missing her baby. Yet, during their time together, nothing else mattered.

Then, after drying off, they both went to bed. Talton fell asleep immediately. Having enjoyed the soothing warm water, he allowed himself to slip into nothingness the moment he got under the sheets.

An hour later Alize still hadn't fallen asleep. Lying next to Talton, she wondered how come he hadn't consummated their relationship. They had just spent the last forty minutes in the nude, in a bathtub together. His manhood had gotten hard on several occasions throughout the evening. Yet, now that they were in bed, he had went straight to sleep.

She wanted nothing more than to be made love to. She wanted him inside of her even though she knew it would hurt. But... there he was... dead to the world. As she layed there staring up at the ceiling she thought of masturbating. She couldn't do it, though. What if he woke up? What would he think then? Instead, she stepped out the room, still in the nude, and went into the living room where she found Brittany, still awake, playing video games.

"What're you still doing up?" she asked Brittany as she sat down next to her on the couch.

"Bitch, you just don't care about putting on any clothes, do you?"

"Why should I? It's my house."

"What's up with you?" asked Brittany, putting her game on pause. "Why're you sounding like you're mad?"

"Man, Brit, I don't know what's wrong with him. We didn't even mess around, and he's already asleep."

"Go wake 'em up!"

"And say what? Give me some dick or get out?!" Both of them started giggling.

"No, sis! That's not what I mean. Look, I know he likes you. He's just stressed out. You just gotta take it there with him. Shit... I'll go in there with you."

"Hold up, bitch! What do you mean you'll go in there with me? Ze stared at her sister, watching the light from the television illuminate her face. "Brit-Brit, you like him too?"

"It ain't like that... but, yeah. I wouldn't mind doing him. He likes you too much, though."

"Did you guys mess around already?"

"No... not really."

"Wha–"

"It's not what you think. I tried, but he wouldn't do it. He really likes you. I think this is the one. The only reason I said I'll go in there is because you need some help. Ze, you don't know what tomorrow will bring. This whole situation is crazy. He might go to jail at any time, and when they catch 'em he's not getting out. Do you understand that? If you really like him, you need to seize the moment. There's no time for games."

Alize looked at her sister long and hard, thinking about what she had just told her. Brittany was right; her time with Talton was not promised.

Brittany continued, "Whether he knows it or not, he actually needs it. You'll really be helping him if you give 'em some."

"OK, I'm doing it," said Ze, as she hopped of the couch. With a determined look on her face, she turned away and left the room.

Brittany smiled to herself. She was a tad-bit jealous, yet she was happy for her sister.

CHAPTER THIRTY-EIGHT

The next morning was the first time in a long time that Talton woke up in an empty house. Both Alize and her sister went to work without waking him; leaving him with only his thoughts to keep him company. Luckily, the sex that took place throughout the night had been so extraordinary that his thoughts mostly revolved around that episode. He replayed it in his mind so much that he found himself walking around the house with an erection that threatened to break through his sweats.

The rest of the weekend flew by like a honeymoon. Brittany had to work for ninety-six hours straight, leaving Ze and Talton to their own devices. Other than a few periodic calls to check on Mike and B.A., Gangsta and Ze spent most of their weekend in bed.

Then Monday morning came and he was at home, alone, again. That's when Talton's demons came home to roost. It all started with a call from B.A. He called to let Talton know that they had sold out and were ready for the road trip. This was definitely good news, yet Talton had woken up with other thoughts on his mind. While B.A. was on the line, in his ear, talking up a storm about how fast the money had come, that the sky was the limit, and how this was only the beginning, Talton's mind was elsewhere.

After assuring B.A. that he'd call him the second he got off the phone with Snoop, Gangsta ended the call and started scrolling through his contact list. But then, after finding Snoop's number, instead of calling it, Talton called a different number.

There he sat, in the same bed that he shared with Alize, staring at the screen on Brittany's phone. Before pressing the send button, he stopped himself. Cita was definitely the driving force behind his predicament. He was sure of that, yet here he was about to call her. There was an uncontrollable urge inside of him to speak to her. Not so much to hear from her as to find out what was going on with his unborn child. Or, at least, that's what he told himself, but he knew it was a lie.

Nevertheless, in the end, he didn't press send. Instead, he got out of bed and went to the bathroom to wash up. After doing his morning hygiene ritual, Talton went into the kitchen and fixed himself a bowl of Honey Nut Cheerios. From the breakfast bar, with a bowl of cereal in front of him, Talton called Snoop. Snoop was already up and moving. Most drug dealers were like that; early risers, especially the ones who had been to prison. To Talton's surprise he seemed upbeat, and everything went smoothly. Afterwards, he set the phone down and resumed eating.

He thought of Alize and their beautiful weekend

together, wishing he would've met Ze before Cita. Somehow, he knew that none of this would've happened if he had. Then his thoughts made their way towards more ominous subject matters. Someone had murdered his brother, he retaliated, and now Cita was the state's star witness against him. He was on the run, his face was on the news and he knew he was guilty. Things couldn't be worse.

Thoughts of denial intermingled with anger. He had to do something. He couldn't just sit back and watch as his problems metastasized. Talton picked up Brittany's phone, entered Cita's cellphone number and pressed the send button. Not knowing what he would say when she answered, he regretted the decision the moment he made it. When he heard the first ring he pulled the phone away from his ear, ending the call before it started.

He couldn't go through with it. Not at the moment, not with so many different thoughts shooting through his mind. Yet, nevertheless, he knew he'd have to. If Cita truly was the linchpin that held the case against him together, he'd have to reach out and touch her, some way, somehow. Just not right now.

So he called B.A. and gave him the directions to Alize's house. He let him know that Big Snoop had OK'd the deal, so he should come through with Mike and the thirty-thousand dollars they had. In turn, B.A. assured him that they'd be there within the hour and their call was ended.

Now all Talton needed to do was wait. His boys would show up, pick up the cash, then head to

Jacksonville. He'd post up, play some X-Box and spend the rest of the day getting high. All he had to do was chill, but that wasn't going to happen. Right then and there, at the breakfast bar, Talton picked up the phone and called Cita. This time he let it ring.

"Hello," answered Cita.

Silence.

"Hello?"

Silence.

"Talton... if this is you, I want you to know that I'm sorry. I love you, and I need to talk to you. Please... babe, talk to me."

He didn't answer. Instead, he pressed the end button.

CHAPTER THIRTY-NINE

The twin Monte Carlos turned onto Alize's street, one after the other. B.A. was in the lead vehicle with a beautiful Columbian girl sitting next to him. Mike was behind them with the sister.

After pulling up to the house, both men stepped out their rentals draped in brand-new clothes and expensive jewels. Everything about their appearance radiated wealth and they were enjoying every moment of it.

Talton opened the door looking just as clean as his comrades. The first thing that caught their attention was the second medallion hanging from Talton's neck. They knew it belonged to Anthony and that it was stolen the night it all happened. The only way Talton could've gotten it back was by taking it off the dead body of the man who had stolen it in the first place.

So, it was true... Talton had avenged his brother's murder.

"I can dig it. I can dig it. Kinda Martha Stewart, but it'll do," commented B.A. after coming inside and getting a good look around. "Where's the redhead?"

"She's at work, I got the house to myself all day," answered Talton. "My daily routine consists of cooking and cleaning, like I'm retired or something." Talton led his team into the kitchen where he had thirty-thousand dollars stacked on the counter extravagantly. "I already holla'd at blood. He's having someone meet y'all at the docks. All you'll have to do is exchange bags."

"So, we ain't meeting the actual connect?" asked Mike.

"Hell naw, he's acting paranoid, but what can you expect? We're lucky he's fuckin' with us in the first place." Talton noticed Mike and B.A. exchange what he took as a conspiratorial glance between one another. "He's kinda leery from the fact that I'm coming with so much money. Ant never spent this much, so I can see where he's coming from. I guess it doesn't really matter since the deal is going down anyway, right?"

Mike was fidgeting and B.A. wouldn't stop staring at the money. Talton was beginning to sense that something was wrong. For a second he thought of calling it all off, but that idea didn't last long. "So, what's up? You guys got the other half of the money, right?"

"Hell yeah! We got thirty racks, and we still got hella weed left," answered Mike, earnestly.

Then Talton saw it again. A glance between the two. However, this time it was a disapproving glare from the latter. Looking at B.A. Talton said, "What's all that about?"

"What?" replied B.A.

"That look you just shot at Mike. It looked like bruh said something you didn't like or something." Talton quickly eyed his Glock, which was menacingly perched on the counter next to the money. "Actually, you both acting kinda funny."

B.A. immediately sensed things going awry. He knew he had to do something fast or his whole plan would fall apart. "You're trippin', bruh. I just remembered we didn't bring any weed for the trip. We got two bad bitches outside and we ain't got no trees to smoke wit' 'em. If you think we're acting funny, you're probably right. We ain't ever picked up this much work before. What do you expect? We just hit the big time."

Talton stared at his boys, wondering if he really was overreacting. "How much of the weed do you guys got left?"

"About seven or eight pounds," replied Mike.

"That's cool. Maybe it's better y'all forgot it anyway. If you get pulled over, the smell is enough to get the car searched. So here goes the number you're supposed to call when you get to the docks. I'll call every hour to make sure everything's cool."

"You want us to come straight back here when we get back?" asked B.A.

"Yeah. Just make sure you get rid of the bitches. We'll probably be up all night rerocking the coke. You guys can post up with me. We'll have a lil' celebration while we remix the work."

Mike was looking calmer by then. "You really hit the jackpot with this redhead, huh? When we gonna meet the friends? Ever since you met this bitch, we've been getting twice the money we had before. And, now you got a big-ass house. I know she's got some friends."

Talton smiled, letting his guard down. "She really don't know nobody. She's kinda antisocial. And, it really ain't her that got us ballin' like this. It's our turn. This lil' shit we gettin' now is small change compared to the future. I'ma keep investing my money with her money and we'll be fucking with millions by the end of the year. Just watch. By the end of the summer, we'll be in whips with numbers on the back, and by winter we'll each have a condo on the beach. From now on, the weed is gonna be a regular thing. She's introducing me to her connect the next time she re-ups. We ain't gonna have no choice but to get rich." Talton started putting stacks of money into a backpack.

Mike watched his friend hand over the money, wishing he didn't have to double-cross him. Talton had always been a good homey, but B.A. was right. Talton was on his way to prison, and common sense told him that this move was the only logical option they had. As he left the house with Talton's money, Mike felt dirty. He knew he was looking at his friend for the last time.

After they left, Talton sat on the leather sectional with an optimistical mindset. At first, he started doubting his decision to trust them with the money, but then he changed his mind. Mike and B.A. would have to be idiots to cross him at such a pivotal moment in their careers.

That wasn't the only subject at hand, though.

Ever since he heard Cita's voice, thoughts of her and his seed plagued him. He kept wondering why she had sounded as if she wanted to speak to him just as much as he needed to talk to her. He was confused. He knew he needed to get in her ear to persuade her to recant whatever she told the police, but part of him was neglecting the inevitable. This whole time Talton had insanely told himself that Cita couldn't have really told on him, and that it was all a mistake. But facing her would force him to admit that the mother of his unborn child was the star witness against him in a murder case.

Talton sat on the couch with Brittany's phone clutched in his hand. Before he knew what he was doing, Cita's number had been put in and the send button had been pressed. The moment he heard the first ring, a rush of adrenaline shot through his veins. His chest constricted and his hands began to sweat. Then the call was answered.

"Hello."

Talton wanted to speak, but couldn't.

"Talton, is this you? If it is, just listen. I love you, and I'm sorry. The baby's OK. He was born the night we got separated. He's still at the hospital, but the doctors are gonna let me bring him home soon. Baby, he looks just like you!"

At the mention of his newborn, Gangsta's eyes teared up. All he could do was squeeze the phone tighter as he sat there in shock.

"All that stuff they're saying on the News is a lie. I was mad at you for leaving me with Angelique. She tried to kill me and the baby because I found out that she's the one who set up the whole thing. She's who got Ant killed. I woke up in the hospital the next day with my face all messed up so the nurse called the cops. I don't even remember talking to the police because they had me all drugged up. I'd never testify against you, Talton. You have to believe me. Please... Just say something."

CHAPTER FORTY

He sat on the couch with his head leaning against the cushion. Brittany's phone stationed on his lap like a portal into another world. A world filled with betrayal, confusion, and danger. When Cita started crying, Talton ended the call. He didn't want to fall weak, even though it was probably too late. Everything she said was exactly what he needed to hear, but was Cita telling the truth? His mind told him she wasn't. Cita had lied and cheated so much throughout the time they had been together that Talton knew better than to believe anything she said. Yet, his heart was heavy. It wasn't just about him and her, she had the baby. She had given him a son.

From an early age, Talton had a penchant for violence. He had murdered enough people to technically classify him as a serial killer. Nonetheless, he was still a man. A man with morals, and right now, he felt the need to see his newborn child as well as the woman who had given birth to him.

He picked up the phone and called back. This time he knew exactly what he would say.

The call was answered immediately.

"Talton! Please talk to me. I'm sorry, just please talk to me! Say anything!"

"Meet me at the art gallery on Ft. Harrison," said Talton. "I'm trusting you with my life right now, so don't cross me."

"I'll be there. I'll be there in a half hour. I promise. I love you, Talton."

He ended the call, taking a deep breath, wondering if he had made the right decision. It still wasn't too late, he didn't have to go. Though, he knew he would...

CHAPTER FORTY-ONE

At the Wachovia, Alize sat at a table inside one of the several offices. She was counting the cash that was deposited earlier that morning and things weren't going too well. Because her mind was wondering, she kept losing track of her count. Usually, all she'd have to do was take a few pills to calm her roving thoughts. However, she hadn't taken any of her antidepressants in weeks and wasn't planning on doing so anytime soon. Even if she were taking her medications, thoughts she was having now wouldn't have provoked her to take them anyway. These were the good kind, the ones that made her thighs moist.

Alize's thoughts were filled with erotic memories of what took place over the weekend she had just spent with Talton. Friday morning, before work, she found blood on her wash-cloth during her shower. Yet, the obvious internal damages hadn't thwarted her return to the bed she shared with her man. That night, she came back with a vengeance, set on showing Gangsta that she was his match.

Her coup-de-grace came the next night when she opened her back door for business. Any other woman would've ran from the idea, but Ze invited it. Taking him all in with the help of a lot of K-Y jelly, then refusing to stop as she squeezed the cum from his tree-trunk of a penis. In the end, she was sore, but the look on his face told her she had earned his respect.

She hadn't been this happy in years. Yet, the thought of losing her source of joy was menacingly crouched in the shadows of her mind. She tried not to think of the inevitable, the fact that her past was threatening to replay itself in a different form, yet the thoughts were there and they wouldn't leave.

For years her only access to her baby was through weekend visits and over the phone. And now, it looked as if the same arrangement would be set up with Talton. If he was arrested, the only contact she would have with him would be through weekend visits and collect phone calls. She tried to block it all out her mind, knowing that she couldn't handle another loss in her life. Maybe, before this past weekend, she would've gotten over it and been able to move on with her life. But not now. She loved Talton and wasn't about to lose him like she lost Shawn.

Which brought her to the next thought that fought with her blissful daydreams. Shawn. She had been neglecting her son to spend time with Talton. Never had she done such a thing. In all of their years apart, she never missed a phone call. Not that she actually got to speak to him, but at least she always tried. Because of her selfish lust for Talton, she not only forfeited her weekend with Shawn, but she had also forgotten to call. She justified her actions by telling herself that times were dangerous, and she couldn't have her baby around all the drama. And that Talton's business was much needed and would help get Shawn back.

Nevertheless, deep down, she knew the reason she was neglecting Shawn for Talton was because Talton was there. He was in her face, in her mind, and in her heart. Just having him around helped her deal with her depression. Where she was once lonely and isolated, she now felt whole. All because of Talton. The longer she spent with him, the further away she found herself from the pain that haunted her conscience.

As the minutes turned into hours, Ze found herself constantly checking her phone for missed calls. She was hoping to receive at least a text from her lover. Yet, the only messages she had were from Brittany and M.S., her weed supplier. She wasn't about to return any of her sister's calls. All she'd want to talk about was the sex Ze had had with Talton. However, the calls from M.S. were another matter. Ze needed to talk with him, yet she had been avoiding their inevitable conversation for several days now.

Ever since she moved to Clearwater, things had slowed down on her end. He never had a problem with that, but this was different. She had fronted most of her work through Talton to some people she didn't even know, not to mention that she had invested most of her savings through the same route. If something went wrong, she wouldn't know what to tell M.S. Still, she had to talk to him, so she decided to call him on her lunch break.

§§§§§

Both rentals were heading North towards Jacksonville. B.A. was in the lead, riding shotgun to his nineteen-year-old chauffer, one of the girls Mike had met at the bowling alley. In the trunk he had half of the sixty-thousand dollars, ready to be traded for the cocaine they would pick up once they reached the Jacksonville docks.

Mike and B.A. had been riding around with the Columbian girls all weekend. They were sisters, only three years apart. At first the guys had them around for leisure. This was until Mike came up with the idea of having them traffic their contraband. It was the perfect idea. They'd each drive North as a couple, then the girls would drive back with the work.

Throughout the weekend. Mike and B.A. found themselves at odds with their original, or better yet, B.A.'s original plan. B.A. changed his mind about going through with the deal several times. He wanted to pocket the sixty-grand and cash in on the reward money, never leaving Clearwater. But Mike was more strategic, arguing that it was in their best interest to go through with the transaction.

This was the one chance the duo had to make it to the big leagues. If they could somehow meet the connect, then they'd be set for life, even after Gangsta got locked up. And, if they didn't meet the connect, at least they'd have the coke. They could double the amount and each have three kilos to himself. In the end, Mike was able to convince B.A. to be patient by appealing to his greedy side.

What Mike didn't know was that in his own lust for riches, he was inevitably sealing his own fate.

B.A. was in his seat, mentally doing mathematical somersaults, thinking of how long it would take him to move three kilos if he were to break them down into ounces, then break the ounces down into grams. For some reason, in the midst of his calculations, he looked into the passenger side rear-view mirror to check on Mike. Mike was in his female's ear with non-stop chatter. That made him smile. Mike opening his heart and soul to that bitch. Crazy.

That's when he decided to make the call. One of his final moves to checkmate Talton. Pulling out his phone, he wondered how long it would take Talton to figure out what had happened. After scrolling through his contact list for the Secret Witness Hotline number, B.A. made the call. A few seconds later, someone on the other end answered and B.A. said, "Hello, yeah, I'm calling to talk about that guy that's been all over the news for the murders at the Days Inn... Yeah, his name is Talton Robinson."

Meanwhile, several car lengths behind the car B.A. was riding in, Mike was contriving a move of his own. From the beginning, he never liked B.A. He dealt with him because he seemed to come with the package that included Talton and his brother. Over the months they had hustled together, he saw how greedy and self-serving B.A. could be, yet he kept his thoughts to himself. Patiently, he waited for his chance to ultimately outmaneuver the leach of a man that B.A. truly was.

This was his chance. His one opportunity to rid himself of B.A. and come up drastically in the process. The fact that Talton was taking the brunt of the hit didn't sit well with Mike, but B.A. had been right on that note. Gangsta was through, his number was up. So Mike was going to make this his move to sever ties with everyone involved. He knew eventually he would have to jump ship, he just never imagined that it would be with so much money and product.

"... Do you understand what I'm saying?" Mike asked Carmen.

"Yes, but you have to promise me that my lil' sister will be OK."

"As long as you do exactly what I tell you, there won't be a problem. I just need to know that I can trust you."

"Hell yeah!" replied Carmen. "I'll do it exactly the way you're telling me. Don't worry about that."

"Alright then. Just sit back and relax. We'll be there in another two hours."

Mike proceeded to drive in silence, a firm smile making its home on his face. The plan was set; he'd be coming up, ending all the bullshit in a single stroke.

CHAPTER FORTY-TWO

Cita pulled up to the curb across the street from the art gallery. From the comforts of the Suburban's driver's seat, she looked for Talton. She knew he was there, somewhere. Watching her, looking for anything out of place. Talton was smart and there was too much riding for him to take her on face value. So she wasn't surprised when her phone vibrated with an incoming text. It was Talton, rerouting their meeting to the casino boat dock on the St. Petersburg side of Indian Rocks beach. Cita, having never turned off the truck, put the SUV in gear and pulled back into traffic.

From the back of a cab, Talton gave the driver another twenty to follow the blue and silver Suburban, cautioning him to stay at a safe distance. For the next fifteen minutes, Gangsta studied every vehicle in their immediate vicinity, including the air for helicopters and drones, but found nothing resembling the law. It seemed as if Cita had stuck to her word... the coast was clear.

Right before they reached the casino boat, Talton had the cabby pull up next to the truck at a stop light. After paying him, Talton slid out the side of the cab and crept up to the Suburban.

Before Cita knew what was happening, he was in the seat behind her.

"Oh, my God!" she yelled. "Don't do that! I hate when you do that! You scare me half to death!"

Ignoring the theatrics, Talton asked, "Who'd you tell about this meet?"

The light turned green, Cita went along with traffic. "Nobody. That punk-ass detective that raided the house was around all weekend, but I can come and go as I please. Talton," Cita said while staring at him through the rear-view, "I'm sorry. I can't believe I got you into this mess."

As Gangsta stared back at the reflection of Cita's face, he realized that something had changed. Cita wasn't the same woman he'd left the other day. Of course, he knew it was impossible for a person to change in a matter of days, yet something was different. She had black eyes, Angelique must've really gave her a beating, but what he was looking at was deeper than skin. "So what happened?"

"After we split up, Angelique tried to kill me! I swear, she tried to deliberately make me have a miscarriage."

"That's crazy, Cita."

"I'm serious!"

"Pull into the Hilton, it's a couple blocks down." He handed her a stack of twenties. "Get us a room as high as they got."

Awhile later, Talton and Cita sat on a bed in a room on the twentieth floor. There they caught up on everything that had taken place since they had been

238

separated. At least Cita's part, anyway; since Talton wasn't about to tell her he'd spent the weekend making love to a redheaded sex machine. The first thing he did do was take the batteries out of their phones. After that, he felt safe that they wouldn't be tracked. She felt safe that they wouldn't be interrupted.

$$$$$

Mondays at the bank weren't nearly as hectic as Thursdays or Fridays, yet Ze was spent by the time her day was over. She couldn't wait to get home and cuddle with Talton. By 5:01 she was in her car, on her way home. The prospect of being alone with Talton gave her a renewed burst of energy. Yet, in the back of her mind, she wondered if something was wrong.

She'd been calling his phone all day and never got an answer. Her calls kept going to voice mail, a fact that annoyed her, even though she understood the necessity of keeping the battery out of the phone. Security came first so she wasn't worried... just anxious.

She couldn't wait to get home to her man. The closer she got to her house, the more excited she became. Then, the moment she got ready to turn onto her usually quiet street, her whole world came crashing down around her. Her house was surrounded. Police were everywhere, some in all black, some in plain clothes, even a few in all blue. It was astonishing that no one noticed her passing by.

Alize took that blessing and ran with it. She didn't panic, just kept driving.

Seeing all the police surrounding her house took her to a different place in time. Another memory from when Shawn had first been taken out of her life. Alize remembered sitting in the back of a police car on a rainy night. The blue and red lights flashing everywhere while Sheriffs, EMTs and forensic investigators milled around her apartment.

She also saw Brittany, a lot younger than she was now, staring at her from the sidewalk, along with a group of her neighbors. Brittany didn't try to communicate with her, but they made eye contact. Ze couldn't understand why such a look of shock radiated from her little sister. She couldn't understand what she was doing, sitting there handcuffed in the back of a police cruiser, either.

Then came the cameras. The news people, reporters, all crowding around the car she was sitting in. Lights flashing and people yelling; asking questions, screaming obscenities at her...

Suddenly, Alize snapped back to reality. She couldn't remember how she got there, but she was safely some distance away from her neighborhood. Her only hope was that somehow Talton hadn't been there when the cops got there. But the odds weren't in their favor. Gangsta shouldn't have been anywhere other than her house. He was on the run, a wanted man, with his face all over the news. Still, she had hope. She drove to Show Girls, not having anywhere else to go. However, instead of going in, she found the darkest parking spot in its lot and parked there.

She called Brittany's phone, hoping Talton would answer. An hour went by, still no answers to her texts or voice messages. Then, after over seventy minutes of consistent calling, she finally got an answer.

"Talton!?"

"Yeah. What's good?"

"Where're you at? Are you OK?"

"I'm good. What's wrong? Why you sounding like this?"

"The house was surrounded. The police were everywhere. I thought they had you. Oh, my God, I thought it was over. Just tell me where you're at, I'll go get you."

Talton didn't answer. On a fluke, he went into the bathroom and checked his messages the moment he turned his phone on it started vibrating. The news that Alize was giving him was the worst information he could imagine. It opened the door to too many possibilities, questions he didn't want to ask, scenarios he didn't want to think of.

"Talton... are you there?"

"Look, I'm safe where I'm at. You need to go back to your house."

"For what?!"

"To find out what they know. Somebody had to tell them I was there." Just as the words left his mouth a sinking feeling hit him.

"I don't want to go back. I want to come get you. We can leave, I have family in Georgia. We can go there, I'll keep you safe." She couldn't stand the thought of losing another loved one. To her it wasn't about a new boyfriend getting locked up, it wasn't

241

even about the money she was losing. If the police caught Gangsta, her whole world would crumble.

"Don't worry," he assured her. "Just go back and play dumb. Remember one thing."

"What?"

"The cops aren't mind readers. They only know what you tell them. Ze, I gotta go. I'll turn the phone back on in a few hours."

"Hold on–"

Talton ended the call just as Cita started knocking on the bathroom's door. "Open the door, Talton. Why you locking yourself in there like that?"

His head was starting to hurt, signs of a massive migraine. He needed some time to process everything Alize had just told him, but he knew Cita would go ballistic if he didn't answer. So, he opened the door, masking his feelings with a smile.

When he opened the door, he found Cita completely naked. Enticing him with her perky breast and sexy hips. Her stomach had a new scar, barely healing, just below her bikini line, but that didn't bother him. It was proof that she had given him the gift of life. A few inches lower and he was staring at her cat. Talton love the way Cita's pussy lips hung nice and plump in between her thighs. At that moment, Cita was a Godsend, a gift to help him clear his mind from what he was going through. Like a drug addict who would drown his problems in the haze of a high, Talton welcomed Cita's body like a shot of morphine.

She reached out to him and he took her hand. Moments later they experienced the feelings that only lovers shared...

CHAPTER FORTY-THREE

Show Girls was located less than ten minutes away from Alize's house. Nonetheless, it seemed to have taken the Malibu a half an hour to get from the strip club to her street. As she approached her block, nothing seemed out of the ordinary. The spectacle of law enforcement that crowded her street earlier was all gone. Or, at least that's what they wanted her to believe.

The sheriff's cars and SWAT truck was gone, but the unmarked cars weren't. Both sides of the street was crowded with dark sedans. If Ze hadn't seen the show beforehand, she may have mistook the congestion for a house party. Instead, she saw it for what it was; an ambush.

Preparing herself for what she knew would happen the second she pulled into her driveway, she rolled her automatic windows down. She wanted anyone watching her to know that she was in the car alone. Then she turned up and started bobbing her head to the music. Later on, if anyone would've asked her what song was playing, it would've been impossible for her to recall it. She was more worried about the trigger-happy lawmen who were lying in wait for her to arrive.

She sat up straight as she slowly pulled into her driveway. Then just as she put the car in park, she quietly whispered to herself, "You ready for this?"

Suddenly, the whole block lit up. Law was everywhere, plain clothes men as well as the SWAT unit. Several vehicles pulled in behind her, blocking her exit. Officers jumped from behind her bushes toting semiautomatic assault rifles, and she even saw men coming out of her own house, pointing guns at her.

"Hands up!... Get out of the vehicle!... Get on the ground!"

Cops were everywhere, yelling orders at her. Within seconds she was handcuffed and someone was shouting in her ear, "Where's he at, bitch?!"

Her whole world was turned upside down. Someone pushed her to her feet, dragging her inside, and she didn't fight it. She stayed calm, knowing that she wouldn't say a word. If it were up to her, Talton would be safe forever.

CHAPTER FORTY-FOUR

Meanwhile, in Jacksonville, Mike and B.A. were parked at the north end of the docks. So far all of their communications with their supplier had been conducted through text messages. At any moment someone in a white Lexus was supposed to show up to make the transaction. B.A. was all smiles, knowing that his time to shine had finally come. But Mike was antsy. He couldn't keep still, smoking Newport after Newport.

After snuffing out his seventh cigarette, Mike asked B.A., "When you gonna make the call?"

"What're you talking about? They said they'll be here any minute. And crack the window, man. You gonna have me smelling like smoke."

"I'm talking about the call to turn in Talton."

"Man, you're hella late, Mike. I did that shit on the ride up here. Talton's either dead or in jail right now. That's a dun-dada!"

"I thought we were gonna do it together? So they'd get both of our names for the reward monies."

"It's good, ol' buddy, stop trippin'. I did it under my granny's name. That way it won't come back to us. The last thing we need is some paperwork with our names on it. Just relax, Mike. By the time we get back to Clearwater, Talton will be in jail and this dope will be ours."

Mike didn't say anything. This new twist irritated him beyond description. There was no doubt in his mind that B.A. couldn't be trusted, especially when he started changing plans around. He was so selfish it seeped from his pores. Mike knew that any reason for B.A. to change even the smallest aspect of their plan had to be self-serving in nature.

As he sat back and lit another cancer stick, Mike began subtracting his half of the reward money from what he planned on having when everything was said and done. If everything went smoothly, he'd be driving back into his city without B.A. The rest of their work and money that was still at the hotel room back in Clearwater, all that would be his.

He didn't like the fact that B.A. would end up with twenty-five G's, yet the more he thought about it, the fact that B.A. would have that money actually worked in his favor. He was already planning on starting a rumor in the streets saying that B.A. turned Talton in. If B.A. miraculously came up on all that cash, it would only back up Mike's accusations, ultimately stripping B.A. of any and all respect he had in the streets. Isolated and excommunicated, he would become a pariah within hours.

A few blocks away, in the second rental, two women were about to do some plotting of their own.

"...So, I'm driving down the highway and he grabs my hand and puts it on his dick. I felt it rocking up, so while I'm driving with my left hand, I'm unzipping his jeans with my right." Jesse paused for affect, something her sister Carmen hated.

"What?! Girl, say it!"

Jesse giggled, "His dick was stupid fat! I'm talking about, fat like a soda can. But it was short."

"What'chu mean?"

"Carmenita, his shit was probably four inches both ways!"

Carmen started laughing, "Stop exaggerating!"

"I'm serious, but an-e-ways, that's not all. While I'm strokin' his shit, he was on the phone, and I think he was snitching on somebody. He was asking 'bout reward money and all that shit."

"What a bitch-ass nigga!"

"I know, huh! He gave them folks an address and all. I can't remember the whole name, but I think it was somebody called Falcon or something like that."

Carmen stayed quiet for a moment, thinking of what Mike had told her on their ride up there.

"It all makes sense now."

"What?" asked the younger sister.

"I'm gonna tell you something, but I need you to stay calm and trust me."

"Just talk!"

"On the way up here, I was talking to Mike. He told me we were driving up here to buy some perico for their friend Gangster. But B.A. wanted to rob him and he didn't want to do it. He also told me that B.A. planned on putting the dope in our car and have us drive it back to Clearwater without us knowing it."

"What an asshole!"

"Yeah, but see, Mike's not like that. He told me

he'd pay us if we went along with his plan. On the way back, we're supposed to act like we don't know about the perico and just drive. Then, halfway there, I'm supposed to find a dark part of the highway and pull over like there's something wrong with the car. Mike's gonna get out their car with the keys, and he's gonna act like he's helping us, then we're gonna leave B.A. there once Mike gets in the car with us. He said he'll give us a thousand apiece if we–"

"That's easy!" said Jesse, sounding excited.

"Yeah, but that's not what I'm thinking. Jesse, Mike said they were spending sixty-thousand bucks. That's a lot of money. What if we leave both of them stranded and we take everything? We can do it just like Mike assumes we will, except we'll leave his ass too."

"You think we can get away with it?"

"Hell yeah!"

CHAPTER FORTY-FIVE

It was close to ten p.m. when the last police officer left Alize's house. After being dragged inside she was questioned for three hours. There had been several different detectives grilling her, but the most aggressive one was the one they called Krasinski. He kept accusing her of lying every time she told them that she never heard of a guy named Talton. He had a lot to say about her man, and it was obvious that he had a hard-on for Talton. Nonetheless, she stood tall under pressure, never saying a word about Gangsta.

After they finished questioning her and were convinced the tip was false, they all filed out of her home, leaving a disaster in their wake. Someone left a card on the counter with a number for her to call to make a claim so the city could pay for the broken windows they went through to get inside of her house. And, without the least of an apology, they left her alone in her broken home.

Ze was tired, yet she felt good about herself. The cops were gone and Talton was safe. All she had to do now was pick him up and flee the city. So she called Brittany's phone, and to her surprise, the call was answered immediately.

"What's going on? You good?" asked Gangsta.

"Yeah, baby. I didn't tell them shit... they're gone. Man, Talton, they questioned me for three hours straight! One of the detectives said he knew you. They tore the house up pretty bad, too. Luckily, they didn't go in the attic."

"Did you find out what brought them to the house?"

Cita walked into the bathroom where Gangsta was standing with the phone to his ear. "Who're you talking to?"

Talton quickly covered the mouthpiece and said, "Hold on, I'm handling some business right now."

Ze thought she heard a female's voice say something to Talton. She tried to listen but the line went quiet so she couldn't hear what they were saying. "Talton! Talton, you there?!"

Cita could see that Talton was hiding something, and that piqued her interest. "Well, I have to pee, so you can take your 'business' call in the other room."

He didn't argue. He stepped into the main room.

On the other end of the call, it was too late. Ze knew she heard a woman's voice and she snapped into a rage. "What the fuck are you doing with another bitch?!"

"What? what's wrong wit' you?!"

"I'm trying to tell you some serious shit and I hear some bitch in the background! Talton, they destroyed my house looking for you! I'm trying to get my son back! If the social workers find out about this shit, it'll ruin everything I've been working on for the last four years! On top of that, I'm over here worrying about you, and you're layed up with some bitch! Who the fuck are you with, Talton?"

"Calm down, Ze! I'm good, I'm with Cita."

"Cita!" Alize wanted to give Talton the benefit of the doubt, but hearing the other woman's name made her see red! "Are you fucking crazy? That's the bitch that got you in this mess! Tell me you just didn't say Cita... Myriam Cita Wilford!"

"Hold up, Ze. Let me–"

Cita entered the room and found Talton sitting at the edge of the bed in a state of vexation. Sensing the honeymoon was over, she walked to the side of the bed where her clothes were at and started getting dressed.

"Hold up, my ass, Talton! Let me tell you something, because you don't seem to be thinking with your head right now! There was a cop named Krasinski who said he knew you. He said he arrested you a few weeks ago. He also said that he has been in constant contact with your baby mamma, and that she had to have your baby early because you beat her half to death. She allegedly told him that you beat her because you were deliberately trying to kill the baby. When I asked him how he got the information telling him that you were here, he told me that one of your homeboys gave you up for the reward money. Talton, this guy basically told me that your whole inner circle snitched you out, and guess what? I still kept my mouth shut. I kept my fucking mouth shut, while you're layed up with the same bitch that got you into this shit! Talton, I owe seventy-five-fucking-thousand dollars for that weed! M.S. ain't gonna come looking for you, he's gonna come after me!"

Alize started sobbing, she couldn't hold it in any longer. "I can't believe you went back to that bitch!" She wanted him to say something, anything, but Talton didn't make any effort whatsoever to deny the accusations. Out of anger, Alize yelled into the phone, "Man, fuck you, Talton! Have her help you, then!" Then she ended the call.

Talton put the phone down, feeling defeated. If what Alize just told him was true, he was in a lot worse of a situation than he ever imagined.

Cita sat next to Talton, wearing only her T-shirt and panties. She had no idea what he had been told over the phone, but his sullen attitude told her that it was all bad.

Suddenly looking tired, Talton looked at her and said, "I'ma ask you some questions, and I need you to tell me the truth. Whatever you do, don't lie to me."

Sensing that the tides were turning against her, Cita asked, "Who was that on the phone?"

"Don't worry about that. I need to know if you told the police that I'm the one who gave you those black eyes? Cita, I just got some fucked-up information, and I need to know if the first part is true so I can find out if the second part really happened. Did you tell the police that I tried to make you have a miscarriage?"

Cita's eyes started overflowing with tears. For the first time in her life, she hated herself for something she had done. Anyone with a half a mind could look into his eyes and see that Talton was in love with her. He was the father of her child, and she had betrayed him. Betrayed him so badly that she might not be able to right her wrong. "Yes." She could barely stand to say it out loud. "Yes, I told them that." She then covered her face with her hands and started crying uncontrollably.

Talton looked away. The answer hit him like a bat to the face. It proved that everything else Alize told him had merit. He stared at the wall for a while before speaking again. "OK. What's done is done. Are you prepared to retract your statements?"

Cita looked up and said, "I already told you, I would never testify against you. I love you. What I told them before, I said out of anger. I don't care if I gotta do time; I'll never testify." Cita searched his eyes, trying to read his thoughts. Unable to read them, she asked him, "Would you tell me something?"

"What?"

"Who were those girls at the motel?"

Talton knew he could never tell Cita the truth about his relationship with Ze. "One of them was my dope connect. I haven't seen or heard from her since. But that's not an issue right now. I just got word that Mike and B.A. called Crime Stoppers and told them where I was at. I didn't want to believe it, but it makes sense because they have a lot of my money."

"You probably should believe it, Talton. I told you not to trust them, but you never listened to me. The only person in your crew that ever really had your back was your brother." Cita paused, briefly reliving her last tryst with Mike. "So, what're you gonna do now?"

"I don't know yet. But they probably think I'm in jail right now so I might be able to capitalize on that.

CHAPTER FORTY-SIX

Carmen had been driving for hours. The only things surrounding the stretch of highway they were on were trees and fields. If she was going to make her move, this would be the best area. There was an exit coming; secluded and abandoned, it looked as if it led nowhere.

Jesse noticed her sister studying their surroundings and asked, "You think this'll be a good place to stop?"

"It looks like it's as far away from civilization as we'll ever get. If we're gonna do this, it might as well be now." Carmen hit the button for the hazard lights, slowing the car down to a crawl while she was at it. "Now, remember; act cool with Mike until we get to the next stop. Then, we'll leave his ass, too."

In the second Monte Carlo, Mike saw the sign that his plan was in motion. Immediately he started feeling the rush of fear mixed with excitement that came whenever a soldier got ready for war. Except, in this case, Mike wasn't planning on going to war. In his mind, he was too smart for that.

As the lead car took the exit, B.A. immediately started showing signs of irritation. "What is these bitches doing?" he asked while following them.

Playing dumb, Mike said, "Something's probably wrong with the car."

"Then why didn't they pull over on the highway?"

When the girls' car stopped rolling, Mike felt proud of his new friend. She couldn't have chosen a better spot. There wasn't a light for miles. Even the moon was on break. It was so dark B.A. kept the headlights on to illuminate the scene.

After putting the Monte Carlo in park, B.A. turned off the ignition and took the key out. When Mike realized what he was doing he said, "Hey, leave the keys, bruh... it's hot in this bitch."

"Who cares, nigga. You gettin' out too. Ain't no tellin' what's wrong with the shit. If it's a flat, I'm not changing it myself." With that, B.A. stepped out the car.

In all of Mike's plotting, he had failed to factor in a scenario where B.A. took the keys with him. Mike got out of the car not sure of what he would do next. He only had two options: either abort the plan, or take the keys from B.A. He knew that whatever decision he made would most likely dictate the way he lived the rest of his life. If he aborted the plan, he'd spend the rest of his life playing second fiddle to people like B.A. If he took the keys, he'd be the master of his domain. With that thought in mind, Mike made his decision.

B.A. was already at the driver's-side door of the girls' car by the time Mike caught up to him. Mike, whose palms had started to sweat, approached B.A.

from behind. Before anyone knew what was happening, he put B.A. in a choke hold.

For several moments B.A. was helpless. Caught off guard, his brain was being cut off from its oxygen supply. All Mike had to do was hold on for a few more minutes and the dope would be his. But B.A. was a fighter, he wasn't. B.A. had grown up the youngest of three boys; getting choked out came with the terrain. Once he grasped what was happening, his counter-move came instinctively.

He dropped all his weight onto his knees causing Mike to renegotiate his grip. In that split second, B.A. reached over his shoulder and grabbed Mike by the back of his neck. Then he flipped him over his shoulder. Now, Mike was on the bottom, B.A. on top.

When the fighting started, Carmen pushed the window button, rolling up the glass, then watched in awe. This wasn't part of the plan, and it didn't look as if Mike was in control of the situation. Jesse, who was just as surprised at the sudden turn of events, leaned over her sister to get a better look. Both of them then watched in horror as B.A. destroyed Mike's face with a barrage of punches.

B.A. was like a rabid beast attacking his victim non-stop. Blood was everywhere; on the ground, against the car, and all over his clothes. Yet, he wouldn't stop. Not until he knew there was no more fight left in Mike.

To the women who watched in horror, B.A. looked like a madman with dirt all over his once brand-new outfit, and blood all over his face and hands. Then, out of nowhere, he stopped hitting

Mike. For a second it looked like the fight was over, but it wasn't.

B.A. stood up and jumped straight up into the air. When he came down, he landed on Mike's Adam's apple. Even through the closed window the sisters still heard Mike's neck bones snap, crackle, pop! Not only that, but the pressure of B.A.'s hundred-and-eighty-five-pound frame landing on his victim's throat caused Mike's left eyeball to pop out of its socket. The girls watched in shock as Mike's eyeball dangled from the side of his face.

Even that didn't stop B.A. from his enraged attack. Seeing Mike's eye dislodged from its socket only fueled his anger. "You thought you could play me! Fuck-ass cracker! Now what! Now who's the boss, bitch!?"

Inside the car Carmen and Jesse started to panic. "Go! Go! Go!" yelled Jesse.

Their car was in gear and in motion within seconds. Doing a U-turn in the middle of the two-lane road, dust kicked up, causing a cloud of dirt to momentarily blind B.A., yet at the same time awakening him from his murderous rage.

It didn't take long for him to realize that he was in a bad situation. Not only had he just murdered a man in front of those two fleeing bitches, they also had all his work in the trunk of their car.

He had to get them. If it was the last thing he did, he had to catch up with that car. B.A. ran to his car, got in and raced after them.

In the lead car, Jesse was already calling 911. Neither one of them had signed up for a murder, and it looked as if they were next.

"This is 911 emergency dispatch. What is your emergency?"

"Please, send somebody to help us! We just saw a guy kill his friend and now he's coming after us!"

"What is your location, ma'am?"

"I don't know! We're on the highway, going South, towards Tampa."

"What kind of vehicle are you in?"

"We're in a red car, there's a black guy chasing us in another red car just like ours!"

Then Carmen pointed at a highway sign and said, "Look, Jesse!"

Jesse looked at the sign and told the dispatcher, "We just passed a sign that said, Orlando forty-three miles. Please, send somebody! He's catching up to us!"

Before the dispatcher could give her any directions there was a violent crash against the door she was sitting next to. Carmen swerved to the left just as they were sideswiped by B.A., but the impact still managed to knock the phone out of her sister's hand.

"Carmen, do something!"

"I'm trying!" yelled Carmen while speeding down the dark highway.

No matter how fast she drove B.A. stayed right next to them. The interior light inside his car was on and they could both see his furious face yelling at them from only a few feet away. The speedometer on both Monte Carlos bounced uncontrollably at 140. Then, "SCRNNNCH!" Another sideswipe from

B.A.'s car. Spittle splashed against his window as he yelled at them to stop.

Carmen slammed her foot on the gas pedal even harder. They were now approaching a diesel truck that was pulling two large transport containers. As the girls sped around the left side of the eighteen-wheeler, B.A. slammed into them again. But this time, the sound of fiberglass being crushed was accompanied by a loud pop! One of the girls' car's tires had exploded, causing it to veer to the right.

B.A.'s car was suddenly sandwiched in between the diesel and the other Monte Carlo. That's when he lost control and slid into the undercarriage of one of the transport containers.

This caused the truck driver to lose control and his load fishtailed to the right, then left, then right again. Another vehicle then struck B.A.'s car from behind, spinning him into one of the tractor trailer's set of back tires. The front of his Monte Carlo was simultaneously crushed, causing the speeding muscle car to flip over itself into a deadly somersault. Metal smashed into metal. Glass shattered, imbedding its ripped flesh.

B.A.'s mangled Monte Carlo landed on its roof less than thirty yards from the massive pile up that he created. As he laid crumpled in the overturned rental, blood dripped from his mouth and nose. Nevertheless, he was alive; unconscious, but alive.

Carmen and Jesse's car managed to miss the five-car wreckage by sheer luck. When Carmen lost control, they spun out of harm's way, onto the dirt embankment. Surprisingly, neither one of them were seriously hurt. Yet they were banged up and stunned.

Within moments, Highway Patrol flooded the scene, along with paramedics and other emergency personnel. When the first rescuers reached the red Monte Carlo, they found two young women who were badly shaken up. And the first words they heard were, "The guy in the red car just killed someone... You have to stop him... He's trying to kill us too..."

CHAPTER FORTY-SEVEN

Around the same time as the crash on the highway, in a high-end hotel room, overlooking St. Petersburg beach, Talton finally drifted into a fitful sleep. Exhausted as he was, with the darkness of his life looming in the back of his mind, Gangsta drifted away into a dream world not unlike his current reality.

He was inside of a house that looked familiar, yet he couldn't place it. Next to him stood Anthony, except he was wearing an old devil mask. In Talton's hand, he held a Taser, and the brothers were slowly walking through the house. Finally, after quietly creeping down a long hallway, they approached a door. One of them kicked it open. Inside the room, a red-haired man was suddenly awakened out of his sleep. Talton ran towards him and put the Taser to the man's neck. From the corner of his eye he could see Anthony going through the man's closet. The next thing he knew he was inside of an old Impala, with Anthony, and they were both driving away.

Talton recognized the streets, or better yet, Avenues on which they were driving along. They were in his old neighborhood, Oak Park; streets he had grown up in. Then, all of a sudden, he and his brother were entering another house. Anthony was carrying a safe underneath his jacket and Talton was opening the door to the house with a key.

Once inside, they went straight into the kitchen, placing the safe on a table. He felt good, his brother was smiling, and the anticipation of opening the safe was kin to an early Christmas morning as a child. One where Talton knew that his wrapped gifts held exactly what he had asked his mother for.

However, the elation didn't last long. Talton felt the floor underneath him shake. All of sudden, all the cabinets started opening and slamming shut. Anthony, who had sat down at the table, suddenly fell onto the floor. Blood was coming out of his mouth while he fought for his life.

Then the people came. Police who had arrested him as a juvenile; friends he grew up with and put in work with. Alize was there and so was Brittany. Then B.A. and Mike. They all began to fight over the safe. The whole room became chaotic. Talton tried to find Anthony, but couldn't... he was gone.

That's when Talton woke up. To his surprise it was already morning. The light coming in through the open glass patio doors wasn't from the sun. They were facing the Gulf of Mexico, yet the room was bright. For a second, Talton tried to grasp onto his dream so he could go back and help Ant. But it was too late; he was back in the real world. A world just as volatile as any nightmare his mind could've possibly conjured up.

Cita was already up and moving. She would've

been fine with lying in bed for a few more days, but she knew Talton and he wouldn't be sitting still for much longer. Ever since he received that last phone call, he hadn't been the same. Of course, she was able to coax him into another bout of love making. But afterwards, Talton turned over, facing his back to her. She didn't get mad, though. Something was bothering him and who could blame him? It was amazing that he was as calm as he was.

Ergo, knowing the party was over, she got up early. She was putting on the finishing touches to her much-needed cover-up when she heard him calling her from the next room.

"Cita... did you take any of the keys off the Suburban's key chain?"

"No. Why? What's up?" she asked as she stepped out the restroom.

Talton was going through her purse. "Where they at?"

"They're in my purse, but I guess you already know that. What's up? You don't plan on driving anywhere, do you? Talton, the cops are really–"

"No. I'm not driving nowhere," he answered after finding the keys and looking through the lot. "I need you to take me to B.A.'s apartment."

"I thought you said B.A. and Mike snitched you out?"

"Yeah, but I thought about it and I came up with an idea. See, B.A. thinks he's smart, so he probably thinks his plan went down without a flaw. That I'm in jail, but I'm not. And guess what?"

"What?"

"Remember when he had to do them thirty days in the county over the summer? He gave me an extra set of keys to his apartment. I never gave them back. I hadn't thought about it until a few minutes ago."

"What are you planning on doing?"

Talton was now rushing to put his clothes on. "Him and Mike just came up on a major lick. Mike still stays at home, so they won't be there, and they need a place to conduct business from. They already told me they rented a room with some Columbian chicks. I'm almost positive that's where they're at now."

"So, you're telling me nobody's gonna be at B.A.'s place, so why do you wanna go?"

"Just get your stuff, I'll tell you in the truck."

A few minutes later, after safely tucking his pistol in his waistband, Talton led Cita out of the room; down the elevator, through the lobby, and out to his truck. Once inside the Suburban, from the passenger seat, Talton started talking. "I know they set me up because they haven't called. I sent them niggas outta town to go pick up some work, the first thing they should've done was text me. I didn't call either one of them after I got word the safe house got hit, for that precise reason. I was waiting for them to check in, and they didn't. That means they most likely think I'm in jail."

Cita was already navigating the Suburban through traffic, heading towards B.A.'s apartment, while Talton was talking. "The way I figure it is, I'll just post up in his shit for however long it takes for him to come home."

"Then what?" asked Cita. "You're gonna kill 'em like you did the guys at the motel?" Cita looked away from traffic long enough to glance at the bulge underneath Talton's shirt. "I'm not trying to get involved in another one of your psychotic outbursts, Talton. We need to specify what my part in all of this is gonna be, right now."

"I'm glad you asked that."

"I'm sure you are."

"After you drop me off, I need you to see a lawyer."

"For what?" asked Cita, suddenly reminded of her pending cases. Detective Krasinski already told her he was getting her charges dropped once they *caught* Talton. Caught Talton. That was the deal breaker, wasn't it? Maybe she did need to see a lawyer.

"…You said you ain't finna testify. You're gonna need a lawyer. That way, the investigators won't be able to trip you up. After you drop me off, get on your phone and google a lawyer. Get one from St. Pete, he'll have more connections in this county than one from Tampa. Set up an appointment; tell 'em you lied to the cops to get back at me for beating you up. He'll know what to do after that."

"That sounds good, except for one thing."

"What?"

"How am I supposed to see a lawyer without any money?" Stopping at a red light, Cita looked at Talton. "I don't got shit and you're telling me that Mike and B.A. just robbed you for everything."

"Money ain't a problem. I'll have way over a

hundred G's once I get my shit back. Until then, take this," Talton reached around the back of his neck, and unclasped one of the diamond necklaces that hung from it. "Pawn this."

He had never taken his chain off in the manner it was being taken off now. In his heart, he knew he was wrong, but this was an emergency. It had to be done. "It should get you more than enough for a retainer. Just make sure you keep the receipt, I gotta get that chain back."

Cita took it and put it around her own neck. The moment she grabbed it, Talton finally realized how dire of a situation he was really in. In a matter of two weeks, he went from living a hustler's life to running for his life. He'd lost his brother in a senseless murder, and the only other people he trusted had tried to set him up.

As he rode in silence, he looked at the streets, the stores, and the people in other cars. Everything in Florida was so different than the environment he came up in. Especially the people; in Cali, your boys never flipped on you. The mantra was "Family over Everything", and "Ride or Die". Aphorisms they lived by. In the South, he didn't see no loyalty. Everyone he had trusted had turned on him.

Except for Ze. Her and her sister risked their lives for him. And, how did he repay them... by losing everything Ze had trusted him with and then running off with the same bitch that put the cops on him in the first place.

Shit was fucked up. But Talton vowed not to give up. It wasn't over until he was dead or in jail. As long as he was free, and alive, he had a chance.

CHAPTER FORTY-EIGHT

Alize was at work and she still hadn't called her supplier. As she sat in her booth, she thought of ways to broach the subject. However, so far, she was coming up short. There was no easy way to tell M.S. that she didn't have the seventy-five-thousand that she owed him. In all the time she'd dealt with him, she had never once came up short. Her revenue slowed down since she left Orlando, but she had never taken a complete loss.

M.S. was a high roller. From the beginning he and Alize had hit it off. Ze was accustomed to dealing with violent drug dealers like himself, so she wasn't intimidated by his dark skin, long dreadlocks, and six-foot-five-inch frame.

M.S. came up in one of the roughest neighborhoods in Sacramento. Several years earlier, during a violent drug war, one of the main players was abducted by his rival. The drug dealer's wife immediately put out several million-dollar rewards. One for whoever found her man, and another for whomever murdered the person responsible for the kidnapping of her man. M.S., being the leader of a dangerous street gang called Underworld Zilla, used his connections throughout the city to track down the man behind the abduction, and within twenty-four hours, M.S. became a self-made millionaire.

After cashing in on the contract, he moved his operations to Las Vegas, where he eventually met Alize. When he found out that she wasn't from the West Coast, he really became interested in her. Instead of paying her for lap dances, they would sit at the back of the club and talk for hours. He asked her about Florida and she described the streets of Orlando. She told him about the neighborhood she lived in. OBT, short for Orange Blossom Trail, was a part of the city where hustlers made their money selling weed, crack, and women. M.S. saw an opportunity and seized it. After his first trip to Florida, he never left.

In the short time that he lived in Orlando, he turned his million-dollar hit money into a multimillion-dollar drug empire. He set up shop in the same neighborhood Alize told him about and turned the streets upside down. He went in with the full intention of shaking things up. He believed that in order for someone to conquer anything, he must first tear it down. So he brought some of his goons from his Underworld Zilla clique, and they kidnapped, murdered, and extorted the local hustlers.

It was easy for him because he had an unlimited supply of soldiers who would jump at the chance to make some fast cash in Florida. All he had to do was send for a crew, and within hours of their arrival, bodies would be laid out. This practice became so common, he bought a small passenger plane that he kept parked at a private airport just north of Orlando.

Alize knew she should have called him sooner, but she hadn't, and now, she had ran out of time. During her first break, she went to her car and finally made the call.

"So... let me get this straight. You're telling me that you got robbed for all the weed I fronted you. And, that you've got no money whatsoever to pay me back. This doesn't even sound like you, Ze."

"I know. I got done scandalous, and what makes it worse is that I know exactly who robbed me. I would've had at least forty thousand, but not only did they get the weed, they got me for three kilos, too."

"Three bricks! How come you didn't tell me you was pushing coke? Man, you're fucking up, Ze! You know I got work. You could've gotten the coke from me instead of messing with these broke niggas. You know better than that!"

"I wasn't actually pushing coke yet. I gave my money to this guy and he sent his boys to Jacksonville. They ran off with the money. Next thing I know, the police were kicking in my door. Come to find out, it was them who set it all up." Just talking about it made Alize upset.

"How do you know it wasn't a set-up from the beginning? Who's the nigga you handed the money to?"

"His name is Talton. I know it wasn't him who set it up because the cops were looking for him when they ran up in my house. We both got played and I don't know what I'm going to do."

When M.S. heard Talton's name, he was brought

back to a different time in his life. He grew up with a Talton, but they had lost contact years beforehand. The last he heard of his friend was that Talton left California and ended up catching some time, but he couldn't remember in what state. The Talton he knew was like a brother to him. It couldn't be the same guy. The Talton he knew was a hitter; he'd never let himself get played like that.

"...M.S., you still there?"

"I'm here. Look, I believe you, and I ain't trippin' off you, but them niggas that robbed you gotta be taken care of. On Zilla, when I get out there, somebody's gonna die. You know, Ze, I just don't get these Florida niggas. They all know what I do, but it seems like every other month one of these jokers force me to start another epidemic. When're they gonna learn they can't fuck with the Underworld?"

"See... that's kinda what I wanted to talk to you about, M.S. It's really hot out here right now, and it's not safe. I know who did this, but I need you to give me a lil' time to see what my friend is gonna do. If you give me a few days, and nothing comes up, then I'll call you."

"So, you still trust this nigga? Damn, Ze... this doesn't sound like you at all. Where is this nigga from?"

"I trust him 'cause he's real. It's just been a lot of drama out here. And I'm not really sure where he's originally from, but I know he travels a lot. He mentioned Tennessee, and I think, maybe California. I can't remember right now, but I know he's not from out here. He's different than these dudes out here."

Hearing her mention California struck a spark in his mind. M.S. didn't believe in coincidences. "Does blood got a brother?"

"No... well, yeah. He had one, but he just got killed. That's part of the reason we're all in this mess. Hey, M.S., can we finish this conversation later? I gotta get back to work."

"Alright, but call me the minute you get off work. I got a few more questions. Ze... make sure you call, or I'ma end up on your doorstep."

After ending the call Alize went back to work. As the day progressed, she started regretting giving M.S. so much information about Talton. Mark played with lives like they were chess pieces. If he thought Talton had anything to do with robbing her, there wouldn't be anything she could do to save him.

She had to find out where Talton's friends were. As soon as she did that, she'd give their location to M.S. and then they'd pay for double-crossing Talton.

CHAPTER FORTY-NINE

Most people have around three decisive moments in their lives. Times when a specific experience will mold their way of thinking, thus making them into the people they will be for the remainder of their lives. Cita's first "decisive moment" came at the tender age of nine.

By the age of nine, most little girls are already planning to one day marrying a man just like their daddy. Cita was no different. Her, her two sisters and her little brother were growing up in a happy home in Moline, Illinois. They had a mother and a father; it seemed as if they couldn't have been in a more nurturing environment.

However, if one were to take a closer look, they would find seeds of infidelity sprinkled all through the home. Cita's father had a best friend named Wayne. For as long as she could remember, Wayne was always around the house. So, while Cita's dad would be at work and Wayne was at the house with her mom, neither her nor any of her siblings ever thought anything of it. After all, why should they? They were too young to know what grownups did behind closed doors, with their best friend's wife, when their best friend was at work.

Then one afternoon, during the summer between Cita's third and fourth grade school years, there was a fight. Cita's mother managed to get the kids inside before things got out of hand. But they saw enough to know that Wayne and their father were mad at one another.

Outside, an argument turned into a fight, which meant the police had to be called. When they got there they found Wayne and Cita's mother on the porch; Cita's father bloodied and irate, in the yard. Cita's father was asked to leave, but he refused to leave without his things. So, the officers escorted him through the house and that's when the children saw their father, bruised and disheveled.

None of the kids begged or pleaded for their father to stay. Neither had he tried to take any of them with him. It wasn't that he was an abusive father, the kids loved him. They were just too young to truly understand what was happening.

After their father left, the kids were all sent outside to play. There was blood on the side of the house. Most likely their father's blood. Wayne stayed the night the next night and every night after. From that day on, he slept where their father had once slept, ate where their father once ate and paid the bills like their father once had. Life moved on like nothing happened.

Eventually they moved to Florida, thrived, and Moline became a memory. Nor Cita or any of her siblings ever heard from their father again. No one ever spoke of him, either. However, that day helped to mold Cita into the woman she was today. A woman with no set loyalties to anyone other than herself.

After dropping off Talton she had all her intentions set on calling a lawyer. But, after stopping at the closest pawn shop and trading Talton's necklace for thirty-eight-hundred dollars, her plans quickly changed.

First, she decided to get her hair done, which turned into a manicure and eventually led to an all-out shopping spree. The call to the lawyer was never made... and Cita was down to her last three-hundred dollars.

At one point, while strolling through the mall carrying several shopping bags filled with clothes, she thought of calling Talton. However, when she looked at her phone and saw what time it was, she forgot all about him. She was already late for her spray tan appointment, and it was on the other side of the mall...

CHAPTER FIFTY

Gangsta was sitting on B.A.'s couch waiting for him to show up. The TV was on, but it was on mute. His pistol was on his lap, ready to shoot. He'd been waiting for several hours and was well aware of the fact that he might be waiting for days. He didn't care, though. If he didn't catch B.A. or Mike, he was up shit creek. He had no other options.

Hoping Cita would call he periodically checked his phone for messages. But the only missed calls were from Alize. She'd been calling non-stop. He wanted to talk to her, yet refused to return her calls. He felt responsible for everything that was happening and didn't want to talk to her until he found all the money he owed her.

As he sat there all alone, he took an inventory of where he was at in the world. His main problem was Cita. She promised him she'd retract her statement, but he didn't trust her. Killing her crossed his mind. However, the fact that he was on the run and his son was still in the hospital stalled out all thoughts of murder. The baby would be lost if he killed Cita; there's no way he'd be able to get him out of the hospital with everything that was going on. That and the fact that somewhere, deep in his heart, he had feelings for Cita. He knew she loved him too. Otherwise, he'd be in jail already, instead of on B.A.'s couch, waiting for her to call him with news from a lawyer.

So, he waited. Things could only get better, he told himself. He had just finished checking his messages when a call came in.

The screen said it was an incoming call from "work", so he figured it was Brittany and answered it. "Brit."

"Talton! What the hell! My sister's going cray-cray! She told me the cops raided the house and your homies set you up. How come you haven't been answering the phone? She really needs to talk–"

"Slow your role, lil' sis. Yeah, them niggas pulled some shit but I'm on it. I'm at B.A.'s house right now and I got something for 'em the minute he steps through that door."

"Then what's this other stuff I'm hearing about you being laid up with your baby mamma? You didn't go back to her, did you?"

"It ain't like that, Brit. I had to find out what she knew about the murder charges. She told me that she told them folks a bunch of lies. I got her to retract her statements, too. She's talking to a lawyer right now. All I need is a lil' more time and I'll have everything straightened out."

"Then what? What're you gonna do when it's all over? You can't go back to that bitch. Talton, do you realize that we love–" Brittany caught herself before she said something stupid. "My sister loves you. You can't hurt her –"

"Brit, I'ma be wit' your sister."

"There's something that you need to know–"

"Man, I already know! She loves her son and all that! I don't care about all that. I got her back no matter what."

"That's not what I'm trying to tell you. This is important." Brittany was suddenly interrupted by the alarm system at her job. "I gotta go! I'll call you back later!"

"Damn, Brit-Brit. What's that sound?"

"It's one of the orderlies' personal alarms. Whenever someone gets out of hand, they'll sound their alarm. It's probably just this old Cuban guy named Bango. He likes to rub shit all over his body and run through the hallways butt naked. I gotta go! I get off work in a few hours, so keep the phone on, I'll have my sister call you."

"A'ight," replied Talton before ending the call. Then he leaned back and continued to wait.

$$$$$

Alize had had a horrible day. The suspense of not knowing what was going on with Talton was driving her crazy. As the hours passed with no word from him, her day became more and more unbearable. At one point she wondered if maybe he had gotten arrested so she called the jail, but he wasn't there. Then she got mad at herself for the way she spoke to him during their last phone conversation. With everything that was going on, she couldn't think straight.

When she got home from work she went straight to her bedroom. Inside her closet, all the way in the back, there was an old shoe box. The box held a pistol along with several bottles of psychotropic medications. She had vowed to never take another Thorazine, Seroquel, or Ritalin pill for as long as she lived. However, things had gotten so bad, she couldn't take it anymore. All she wanted to do was sleep.

She took four five-hundred milligram Thorazine pills out of its bottle then put everything back in the closet. After that, she went to her kitchen to find something to wash her medication down with. After taking the pills, she looked around as if for the first time seeing the mess the police had left behind. The disarray only reminded her that her life was in shambles.

The drug-induced fog started rolling in within fifteen minutes. First, she felt her tongue getting dry. Then her eyelids got heavy. That's around the time Brittany called. Brittany told her that she'd be home in a few hours and that she had spoken with Talton. But Alize was too far gone to understand what her sister was trying to tell her. All she wanted to do was sleep.

Maybe in her dreams Talton would be home and all their problems would be over...

CHAPTER FIFTY-ONE

Mark Sanders was at his house in Orlando with two of his closest comrades. All three of them were in the living room of the expensively-furnished home. Insane B and Killa Dirt were brothers. Street bred and state raised; they were both seasoned criminals who could be trusted. Therefore, M.S. kept them within arm's reach at all times. Since the day before, when Alize told M.S. what she was going through, he told his boys and they embarked on a mission to find their Talton. The Talton they had broken bread with on many occasions.

That evening led to the night and that night turned into the morning. They spent the whole time on their phones, calling people and sending out messages via Twitter and Facebook. They were anxious to find out if their Talton was the Talton involved in the drama coming out of Clearwater. Neither one of them were having any luck, though. No one in Oak Park had heard from or of Talton in years. The trail was completely frozen.

Then word came from an unlikely source. When M.S. realized that no one knew where his old running mate was, he reached into the California prison system to look for answers. He sent a text to Terauchi Golston... then waited. Terauchi was Talton's cousin; all of them grew up together. Even though he was serving a life sentence, Terauchi was still a major factor throughout the 'hood. While in prison he created a dangerous network of convicts and used them to control the streets. All from a cell phone inside of his prison cell.

M.S. was coming back into the living room from the kitchen when he got the call from Terauchi. It was the first lead of the day. According to the Folsom shot caller, Gangsta had stayed in touch with him up until the last six months. Terauchi had been getting money from Talton for years. However, it was always electronically transferred, so he never got an address. But he knew Talton was in Florida, though. He told him all about the strip clubs in Clearwater and Tampa. Terauchi also went on to tell M.S. that Talton and his brother Anthony had been out there getting money for a while now. After hearing this, M.S. thanked Terauchi for the information and promised to send him a few thousand for his commissary account before ending the call.

M.S. didn't believe in coincidences. The Gangsta in Clearwater was definitely the same Gangsta he'd known for most of his life. As he digested this information, he recalled one of their childhood memories, a time before all the money and the murders. He remembered how Gangsta had tried to pay some other kids in the neighborhood to rat pack him. He couldn't help but to smile at the recollection.

Killa Dirt was scanning an incoming text when

he noticed a change in M.S.'s demeanor. "What's up, blood? You got something?"

"I think so. I just holla'd at Rauchi, and blood told me Ant and Talton have been out here for years."

Insane B looked up from his phone and said, "Then it's him! Let's go get 'em!"

"It's gotta be him," replied M.S. "But Ze said blood's brother was dead... that he just got killed. That part doesn't make no sense. Ant was the calm one, never got into shit."

Then Killa Dirt said, "All you gotta do is google them niggas. Ze told you the police kicked in her door looking for Talton, right? If that's true, then there's gotta be something on the internet about it."

"You dead right!" said M.S.

Then all three men entered Talton's name into the Google search engine, and what they found brought a burst of energy into the atmosphere. They all stared into their phones while an array of news stories started popping up, story after story, describing the beginning of a drug war in Clearwater.

They all read about Anthony's murder and how it was connected to the now triple homicide at the Days Inn. Then Talton's mug shot came up on all three of their phones. Any doubts of this not being their friend were immediately disintegrated. After that, the remainder of the articles all emphasized the reward money being offered to help find Gangsta.

M.S. didn't need to see any more. Now that he had proof that one of his best friends was in serious trouble, he jumped into action. Mark owned several houses in his old neighborhood that he kept for his soldiers. Only top echelon Underworld Zilla were allowed the sanctuary of these properties. They all knew that when M.S. called, they would have to come. And usually, whenever he called, it was because he wanted someone killed.

K.P., short for Killa Pimpn', was at the house on 10th Avenue when the house phone rang. He was counting money from that day's take, along with two other Zilla goons, Staxx and Snubbz. When they heard the landline ring, all three of them looked up from the kitchen table. The only person who knew its number was M.S. Its familiar sound triggered a rush of adrenaline to shoot through all three gangsters. K.P. was the one who stood up from the table to answer the call. "What's hood, uz?"

"I got the plane coming to get y'all. Bring Staxx and Snubbz."

"We'll see you tomorrow then." K.P. hung up the phone, then turned towards his friends. "We're going back to Florida."

"What's going on?" asked the dark-skinned one called Snubbz.

"I don't know. But them niggas been callin' around asking people 'bout the big homey, Talton. It's probably got something to do wit' blood."

CHAPTER FITY-TWO

Over twenty-four hours had gone by since Cita dropped Talton off at B.A.'s apartment. All the money was gone and she hadn't made the least of an effort to contact a lawyer. To her surprise, Talton's calls had stopped coming earlier in the day. Not that she would've answered them anyway. Talton was now a thought in the wind. She already had everything she wanted, and was ready to move on.

It was eleven p.m. when Cita stepped out of the bathtub. As she studied herself in the mirror on the master bedroom's dresser, she felt reassured by her appearance. Her long, thick black hair hung loosely down her back; her skin was gaining its olive color back, and her wounds were healing nicely. She was feeling better than she had all week.

Then she heard the doorbell. Having no idea who it could be at such a late hour, she went to answer it, clad in only her bath towel. When she got to the front door, Cita called out from behind it and was surprised when Detective Krasinski answered.

Opening the door halfway she said, "How you doing, Detective?"

"I'm alright, sorry for knocking so late. I saw the

lights on so I figured you were still awake. I just wanted to let you know that I'm starting my shift. If you need anything, I'll be out here in my car."

Cita eyed the detective, standing on her doorstep, looking like he was dressed up for a date. This was the first time he'd ever knocked on the door to let her know he was "starting his shift". No one had, especially not this late. She knew what he was there for... she wasn't stupid.

She opened the door a little wider and said, "Why don't you come in for a while. I was about to watch a movie, you can keep me company."

"Oh, I couldn't do that. I was just letting you know–"

"Man, fuck that," said Cita, with a seductive smile. "Come inside." Then she stepped away from the door. "What do you want to drink? I got some soda, or do you want something stronger?"

Krasinski stepped inside, shutting the door behind him. Without being told, he took a seat on the couch. The big screen was on, but no one was watching it. "I'll take a soda," he said, glancing towards the kitchen. She had the refrigerator open and was bending over, reaching for something. Her towel left little to the imagination, triggering a lustful stirring below his waist.

Krasinski had been sitting outside for the last fifteen minutes, debating whether or not he should knock on the door. And, now that he had, he was glad. She hadn't even made an effort to get dressed, which he took as a good sign. He knew from past surveillance how promiscuous she was, so he tried his luck.

Cita came back to the living room with two glasses of Mt. Dew. After handing one to Krasinski she sat down next to him. Then she said, "You're gonna have to meet me halfway on the drink, Detective. It's soda plus a lil' gin. I hope you don't mind."

Krasinski took a sip from his drink, barely tasting the soda and said, "That's OK, it's good. You know, you look nice, Cita. There's something different about you."

"I got my hair done yesterday. Along with a few other things." Showing him her nails, she said, "Got my nails done and a massage and a bikini wax. I had to treat myself. After all I've been through, I deserve it."

Krasinski stopped listening to her around the time she mentioned the bikini wax. He let his eyes wonder down her body and was suddenly aware of her nakedness. Other than her towel there was nothing in between him and her soft skin. His eyes betrayed his lust.

Seeing this, Cita made her move, "You like what you see, Detective?"

"Uh... uh, yeah," replied Krasinski, before getting ahold of himself. "Actually, I've liked what I saw from the first time I met you."

Cita leaned back and pulled the bottom of her towel up high enough for him to see her freshly manicured cat. "Then come and prove it to me, Detective..."

Krasinski wasted no more time. He dove face

first into her lust-filled pool of honey, greedily eating more than his share. For the rest of the night, the Detective who hunted Talton made love to the woman he was being paid to protect.

CHAPTER FIFTY-THREE

Brittany had been home for close to thirty-six hours and hadn't spoken to her sister the whole time. The only times she saw her were a few short glimpses whenever Ze went to the bathroom.

The rest of the time Ze stayed locked away in her room. Brittany tried calling Talton but all her calls went straight to voice mail. She wished she could say this wasn't normal for Alize. However, the truth of the matter was that the talkative, outgoing Alize was the real stranger. For years, the dark, depressed and distraught Ze was the only sister she knew.

Their life hadn't been easy by far. Even when they lived at home Brittany's memories were of being molested by their stepfather. Time after time they would corner their mother and tell her of the abuse. Yet, she never listened and the abuse continued.

Then their brother killed himself. A shotgun blast to the face ended his life. Brittany was out shopping with their mother when it happened, but Ze was there. No one ever told Brittany all of the details, she was too young to be told. However, she was old enough to hear and understand the grownups talking. The suicide had been a plan between her sister and her brother. Ze was supposed to have killed herself also, but the gun jammed.

As the years went by, not much changed. Other than Ze getting older and more rebellious. No longer willing to take the abuse that came in the form of their stepfather's penis, Ze started running away. Brittany was now older, yet not old enough. So, when Alize came back from one of her "trips", no one told her what had taken place, but Brittany was able to piece it together.

Alize had ran away with one of her friends. Her friend told her that she had an uncle that would help them... give them a safe place to eat and sleep. But it was all a setup. That "uncle" ended up being a pedophile. A trucker with a penchant for young runaways. After being raped several times, and left at an old, rundown hotel, Alize managed to get away. Yet, the scars came with her. When she finally got home, something had changed. She was stronger, more mature. The streets had made their mark.

As soon as Brittany hit fourteen, she followed in her sister's footsteps. Except, this round, she wouldn't have to depend on two-face wolves in sheep's clothing. She had Ze. Of course, things were hard. Family Services caught her a few times. Nevertheless, in the end, there was always Ze.

Until that one night.

Brittany was out all day. She had a friend from the neighborhood, with cool parents, who gave her the run of the house. She loved being there; it gave her the sense of what a real home was supposed to be like. Plus, Ze had been acting erratic for some time.

It almost seemed as if her older sister had split personalities. One was a warm, loving sister; the other a cold, unpredictable bitch.

Brittany never forgot coming home that night to an army of news reporters, police officers, and paramedics. The whole block was crowded with onlookers and Alize had somehow become the main attraction. Brittany knew better than to let anyone know she was there. She would've been taken too. So, she faded in with the crowd. This time there were no hushed tones, and she was old enough for people to tell her exactly what happened.

Now, years later, after moving and becoming successfully established, Alize had become stable. Brittany watched and helped as Ze got her job, moved a lil' weed and pretty much enjoyed life. But now, after meeting Talton and witnessing those murders, Ze had taken a major setback. And she wasn't handling it well at all.

So, Brittany gave her sister all the space in the world. She spent the whole day before, cleaning the mess the police had made. Even finding a local handyman on Craig's List to replace the kitchen window and back door. But now, on her second day, she was hoping that Ze would snap out of it. The longer she isolated herself, the harder Brittany knew it would be to get her back to functioning mode.

When Brittany got up, she quickly brought the house alive. She pulled open the curtains, turned on some music and started breakfast. She knew that Ze hadn't eaten in days, so she started on a good ol' country breakfast with eggs, potatoes, biscuits, gravy, hash browns, ham, bacon, and more. Brittany dared her sister to ignore the sounds and aroma of a loving home in progress.

Before long, her plan began to work. She heard the bathroom door shut and water running from the inside. Alize had awakened, but would she go back to her depressing lair? Minutes later, she came out of the bathroom and into the kitchen. Completely naked, she went straight to the refrigerator and pulled out the gallon of milk. Brittany didn't say anything, afraid to scare her off. Instead, she fixed a plate and placed it on the breakfast bar. Then Ze sat down and quietly stared at the food.

She was a mess. Her hair was tangled and her face was oily. Brittany could smell her B.O. from across the room. Nonetheless, she kept quiet, allowing Ze the luxury of controlling the scene. Instead of rushing into a conversation, Brittany fixed herself a plate of food, leaned against the kitchen counter and ate her food while standing up; as if there was nothing wrong... just two sisters enjoying a hearty breakfast.

Alize didn't touch her food. She just sat there, obviously out of it. Then, out of nowhere she said, "I don't know what I did wrong."

"What are you talking about?" asked Brittany, before taking a bite from a slice of bacon.

"I'm talking about Talton. I treated him like a king. Brought him into my home. Hid 'em from the cops and gave him my money. Then he runs back to that bitch. I just wish he'd call and he won't even do that! That bitch he's with doesn't even love him like

I do. And what do I get? I'm the one alone, and she's laid up with him."

Brittany took her time before answering. When it looked like Alize wasn't going to say anything else, Brittany said, "Sis, it ain't like that. I can almost guarantee that it's not what you think. Talton has feelings for you. I know he loves you more than his baby mamma. You gotta look at the whole situation, though. The cops just came around here looking for him and he knows this. Of course, he's not gonna come here. About him not calling you, I bet it's because he lost that money and he feels bad about it. That's all. I bet he'll call the second he tracks down his fake-ass friends and gets it all back. If anything, Talton needs you more than ever. But you can't help him if you're moping around the house like you've been doing. Ze, we all need you right now. If you don't get yourself together, you'll be letting us all down."

"Do you really think he needs me?"

"Come on, sis! Look at the situation he's in. His brother just got killed, his baby mamma snitched on him and his closest friends robbed 'em. We're all he's got right now. Instead of lying in bed with the lights out, and the windows all blacked out, you should be trying to figure out a way for us to help him."

Brittany stared deeply into her sister's eyes. Alize was always slim, but not eating for the last few days had given her a sullen and gaunt look. Her tiny breast were as perky as ever, but her shoulder bones and rib cage were visible. Brittany was sad to see her in such a state. "Ze, you need to eat something! At least take a couple bites so you can think like a normal person."

Suddenly Alize looked up with wide eyes and said, "You're dead right!" Then she scooped a large chunk of eggs into her mouth, topping it off with a slice of bacon. "We need to help 'em get out this mess. His main issue is this murder case. It seems like the only thing they got on him is his baby mamma's statement. So, we need to deal with that first." Ze scooped more eggs into her mouth then rushed out the kitchen and into her bedroom.

Yelling from her room she said, "Hey Brit, do you remember how to get to that house where he picked up his clothes?" Ze rushed to put on a pair of sweat pants, totally disregarding the fact that she hadn't put on her panties.

Brittany stepped inside her sister's room. "Hell yeah, I remember how to get there! You can't miss it, with all the cars out front. But, why you wanna know if I remember how to get there?"

"That's the epicenter of all his problems. I need to see for myself if he's there or not. If he's there, then he probably does have the situation under control, but if he's not, then I'll handle it myself."

"You know what, sis... under normal circumstances, I would say that this is definitely a bad idea. But I'm kinda curious to see if he's laid up with that bitch too. We're over here stressed out the game, and he could be over there with that punk rock bitch right now!"

"Alright then. Let's do this!"

Brittany rushed out the room to go get dressed also. She found an old pair of loose-fitting jeans just in case they ran into Talton's girl. Ze and Brittany had beat up their share of females over the years, and this was the makings of one of those exact situations. But they were far from prepared to deal with what they were met with the moment they stepped out their front door.

All that energy that had suddenly been aroused was now deflated. Brittany finally managed to breathe some life back into her sister, yet the devil in their driveway was about to take it all away.

M.S. was standing in front of his cream-colored Lincoln Navigator, along with five other Underworld Zillas, all strapped and harboring malicious intent. Things had just changed for the worse... Definitely for the worse.

CHAPTER FIFTY-FOUR

Talton was tired of waiting for the traitors to show up. He'd been sitting around doing nothing but waiting for three days. Then, finally, he decided to call the one person who always knew where B.A. was at. His grandmother. And, what he found out gave him the feeling of overwhelming defeat. B.A.'s nana told Talton that her grandbaby was languishing in a Sarasota County jail on a trumped-up murder charge for the death of his white friend Micheal.

B.A.'s nana also told Gangsta that she was planning on bailing her grandson out of jail soon. When Talton asked her how she could afford to bond him out, she told him she was putting her house up along with twenty-five-thousand dollars that B.A. had coming. That told Talton all he needed to know. He wasn't sure of what happened between Mike and B.A., but it was obvious that they had gotten into it during their trip.

After Talton finished talking to B.A.'s nana, he sat on the couch clutching his pistol. He tried calling Cita again, but he knew she wouldn't answer. She had crossed him too. She took his chain and went back on her word. Now, as he sat alone thinking of his mistakes, he wished he would've killed her when he had the chance.

Talton went into the kitchen to pour himself a glass of Brandy. As he stood at the counter with a bottle of dark liquor in front of him, he continued to ruminate on his situation. All of his closest friends had betrayed him, set him up, and left him for dead. Niggas he ate with had turned him in for reward money. A woman he had taken care of, slept with, and made a child with was the state's star witness against him. Talton was in a dark place; a real lonely and damp place.

Then he started thinking of Alize. She was the one person in the world who had his back with no strings attached. And she had just lost most of her savings because of him. How could he have done this to her?

He couldn't help but think that, if he would've been in California, none of this would've happened. Talton looked down at the platinum chain that hung from his neck. The OP medallion immediately triggered emotions that threatened to incapacitate him. Part of him just wanted to go to sleep, leave this mess behind, but he couldn't give up like that. He had to stay strong and keep pushing.

Talton took the contents of his glass down in one gulp. He needed to keep moving; he had to come up with a plan. He wasn't going to sit around and allow the haters to dictate his future. Then, just as he became motivated to move, Brittany's phone vibrated...

CHAPTER FIFTY-FIVE

M.S. and his clique made themselves comfortable in Alize's living room while she explained everything that took place over the past several weeks. She already knew Killa Dirt and his brother, Insane B. They lived in one of the houses M.S. owned in OBT. But she had never met the other three guys he had with him.

They all looked dangerous, though. They all had long dreadlocks in different colors, ranging from red to bleached blond. Their whole crew was tattooed and muscular like they spent most of their lives in prison. Ze knew that M.S. was a powerful person; that he had an army of killers who would do anything he ordered, yet she had never been in the midst of them like this.

While she explained everything to M.S., Brittany made herself useful by offering them something to eat. She tried to look busy but she kept eyeing the two younger looking gang members. They were introduced as Staxx and Snubbz and they seemed closer to one another than the others. Snubbz was the darker one. He had a stocky build, with tattoos all over his face. He was the only one with red dreadlocks. Staxx had dreads too, but he didn't look as mean as Snubbz. He had an aura that said he was more thoughtful than his friend. Nevertheless, they both looked scary and that caught Brittany's interest.

Neither one of the girls were put off by the fact that M.S.'s whole ensemble carried guns. They all had pistols with long clips that caused bulges in their clothes or menacingly stuck out from their waistbands. Anytime M.S. was around, there were guns. He had had so many people killed throughout Orlando there was no way of knowing when there would be an attempt on his own life. The guns were a natural extension of the man himself. Nonetheless, this many Underworld Zillas in one place at one time was bad.

"Blood, that Days Inn shit sounds just like Talton," said Insane B. "He loves using females to set niggas up. But what I don't understand is how we're gonna find 'em if he doesn't wanna be found?"

M.S. was thinking the same thing. "I'll call 'em. Just cuz he ain't answering his phone doesn't mean he ain't listening to his messages. The nigga thinks he's out here alone. If I call 'em and let 'em know we're out here, blood'll call back. And... I keep hearing about his baby mamma, and that house on the beach. Somebody's gotta go check that out. As a matter of fact," M.S. turned to K.P. "Take the truck and ride with Brittany to the beach house." Then, to Staxx and Snubbz, "Y'all go wit' 'em. When you get there, go up to the door, if they don't answer, look in the windows. Find out if that nigga's there, or not. If he's there, bring him back here. No matter what... do *not* bring his bitch! You might have to off the bitch. It sounds like she's gonna have to die anyway."

"Excuse me, M.S.," said Brittany. "I never said I'd go anywhere with your boys. I don't even know them like that."

Without saying a word, M.S. just stared at her for about three seconds before diverting his attention towards Alize.

K.P. saw the short exchange and laughed out loud. M.S. was the person that taught him the art of pimpin' and the move he just pulled on Brittany was a classic "Your say means nothing" move. K.P. loved it; he was the pretty boy out of the crew with the longest dreads and the smoothest mouthpiece. Any real pimp respected pimpin' when he saw it and the protégé had just seen the teacher in action.

Ignoring his tickled student, M.S. told Ze, "Give me Talton's number. I'ma call 'em right now." He gave his phone to Alize, she put in Brittany's number; pressing the send button before handing it back to him.

After several rings, the call went to voice mail. "Gangsta, this is M.S. Yeah, nigga, Oak Park's finest. I'm out here. When you get this message, call me back!" He put his phone back inside of his pocket, knowing his number was now in Talton's phone. "Now, y'all need to hurry up and get to that house." To K.P., he said, "Keep me posted. I'll let you know if we get any news on this end."

Brittany stayed quiet. She felt stupid for the way she had acted, and the truth of the matter was that she really did want to go find Talton. Within minutes she was outside of the house and inside the Navigator, on her way to the beach.

After they left, Alize settled in with Mark and the others. She was curious about Mark and Talton's relationship though. Now that she was paying attention, she noticed that they shared a few similar mannerisms, so she believed they knew each other. But, then again, this could all be a ploy on M.S.'s part to fish out the man he thought was responsible for the loss she had taken.

"You know," began Ze, "I know the world isn't as big as most people think, but this is cray-cray. I can't believe you guys really know Talton."

M.S. looked up from his food, washing down a mouthful with a drink of orange juice before saying, "Really, it ain't that crazy, Ze. I just didn't know the nigga was in Florida. If he was really getting money like you say he was, which doesn't surprise me at all, then we were liable to run into each other eventually. I thought blood was locked up and he probably thought the same about me. When he gets my message, I guarantee he'll call back."

Then he asked, "So, you have no idea where his punk-ass partnas are at? I'd hate to leave the city without my money. That jet fuel's a motherfucka. This whole trip's costing me a lot of money."

"I really didn't know them. I figured since they just came up on all that work, they'd have to come up for air sometime. They have to if they plan on selling any of it. I'll tell you one thing, though: if anyone can find them, it'd be Talton. He knows them best."

That's when Killa Dirt cut in, "That's on U.Z.,

when we find them fuck-boys, I'm knockin' 'em down! They not getting away with trying the homey like that, blood!"

"I know," said M.S. "But we gotta find Gangsta first. Especially since the police lookin' for 'em... then we'll have some fun."

"You know what," said Insane B, from the other side of the room. "Why don't we run a check on his phone's GPS?"

Everyone looked at Alize.

"I didn't think about that. But, I don't see it working because he usually takes his battery out of his phone. He does it for that exact reason, so people can't track him."

"Does he take the sim card out?" asked M.S.

Alize was quiet for a moment, and then as the thought hit her she jumped out of her seat on the couch. "No! He never takes it out!"

Then she ran towards her room where her laptop was. M.S., Killa Dirt and Insane B all followed.

CHAPTER FIFTY-SIX

Talton was sitting on the couch when the phone started dancing across B.A.'s coffee table. Before reaching for it, he eyed it, hoping it was Alize. He wasn't sure if he would answer it, if it were her, yet he hoped it was her. For some reason it would've eased his worries a little if she gave him a sign that she was still in his corner.

So, he reached for it, picked it up and looked into its screen. Not recognizing the number nor the area code, he sent the call to voice mail. With everything that was happening, he wasn't about to answer a call from an unknown number.

By now Talton was beginning to feel the effects of the liquor he was drinking. The slightest movement felt as if he were dragging himself through the Matrix. He would've preferred a weed high, but he didn't have any, and B.A. hadn't left none laying around.

Then the phone beeped. When he looked at its screen, he saw what it was trying to tell him. The battery was low. Extremely low. With one missed call. If he planned on checking it, he had to do it now.

Gangsta put the phone on speaker and played its

message: "Gangsta, this is M.S. Yeah, nigga, Oak Park's finest. I'm out here. When you get this message, call me back!"

He was sure he heard the message wrong. The phone was about to die and B.A. didn't have a landline. Still, he had to check it again. "... this is M.S... I'm out here... call me back!"

This was too good to be true. He had to call him back. Gangsta quickly scrolled back to the call log to retrieve M.S.'s number when suddenly the screen went blank. With the death of its battery went any chances of getting M.S. back on the phone. Now, even if he had access to a landline, he had no way of getting the contact number out of his phone.

"Damn!" yelled Talton as he stood up from his spot on the couch. For the first time in days, things were finally going his way and the phone dies. He had to get ahold of M.S., but how? Then it came to him. The only way Mark would've known to call that number for him was if Alize or Brittany had given it to him.

That's when he remembered Alize calling her connect M.S. Even Brittany had said the name. How could he have missed the connection? Alize's M.S. was Oak Park Mark, his mans from back home!

Gangsta now had one mission and one mission only. He had to get to Alize's house immediately!

CHAPTER FIFTY-SEVEN

While Killa Pimpin' was behind the wheel of the Lincoln, navigating through traffic, he was also searching through the truck's playlist. "Man, this nigga M.S. is on some other shit. All he got is some R&B, and the little rap he do got is Ricky Ross. Where the fuck is the West Coast shit?"

Brittany was supposed to be guiding K.P. to the beach house. Instead, she was in the passenger seat, wondering how long it would be until they crashed into someone else's car. She was also praying they didn't get pulled over. There was enough firepower in that truck to supply a small militia. It'd be impossible to hide their guns if they were stopped by the cops. The extended clips that stuck out from their guns were at least twelve inches apiece. Brittany figured, either they didn't know about Florida's ten, twenty, life laws, or they just didn't care. This wasn't the first time she rode around in a car with guns. Yet, the way this team moved just made her plain nervous.

"Hey, Snow," called out Staxx from the middle row. "How long till we get there?"

Brittany turned her body to face him staring at

him longer than necessary. She said, "We're almost there, and my name ain't Snow, it's Brit-Brit."

Staxx' ace, Snubbz, who was seated behind him, smiled to himself. He'd been around the block enough times to recognize the charade. He started wondering if they'd be in Florida long enough for him to hit that.

Ten minutes later they were turning onto the late Anthony's street.

From behind the tint, Brittany pointed and said, "That's the house... the one with all the cars out front."

K.P. slowed the Navigator to a crawl and asked, "Who's that?"

They all looked and saw a white man with a bag of what looked to be Chinese take-out in his hand. He knocked on the door and a woman answered it, greeting him with a hug and a kiss. Instantly K.P. lifted his phone, snapping a photo of the two. A second later the couple stepped inside.

"Was that the homey's bitch?" asked Staxx.

"I think so," answered Brittany. "She was one of the girls in Talton's truck the day we were at the Days Inn. But I don't know who the man was."

Now it was Snubbz turn to cut in, "I'd call that a positive identification. Me and Staxx can go in through the back and catch her wit' her panties down... her and dude."

"Hold-up," said K.P. "I'ma call M.S. and see what he wants us to do. Till then, we'll wait up the street." He started driving up the block just as his phone started vibrating. When he looked at its screen he saw a picture of the Japanese sea monster, Godzilla. "This is him, right here," he announced before answering the call. "Bruh, we got an ID on Talton's bitch. She's not with blood, though. I just took a flick of her kissin' on a cracker. We can sleep her and the cracker, just make the call."

"It's a no-go," replied M.S. We just got a beam on Gangsta, but send the flick anyway. We found his phone from its GPS. Ze says her sister knows where he's at. He's at the spot where them niggas that set 'em up stay at."

K.P. turned to Brittany and said, "They say Gangsta's at the spot where his homies be at, and that you know how to get there."

At first, she didn't know what he was talking about. Then she remembered taking Talton to B.A.'s apartment. At the same time she recalled their last conversation, when Talton said he was waiting on someone to walk through the door. "Oh shit! I do know where he's at! He's at this big-ass apartment complex on U.S. 19!"

Back to the call, K.P. said, "She said–"

"I heard her, that's the spot. Go get 'em and bring him straight here!"

"A'ight, uz! We on it!" K.P. ended the call, then said, "Tell me where to go, Brit."

$$\$\$\$\$\$$$

Meanwhile, inside of the house, Cita was passionately kissing the detective. Not giving him any space to put down the Chinese food, she took the bag and let it fall to the floor. Then she led him to the couch.

"Cita, let's eat first–"

She put her index finger to his lips, then "Shhh'd" him. With her guidance, Krasinski fell onto the couch. That's when she went for his pants, unbuttoning his khakis. When she had them loose, she pulled them down, along with his boxers, exposing his flaccid penis to the living room's cool air. She then took it in her mouth.

"Cita... we need to talk."

"Umm-hmm," sounded Cita, with his member in her mouth.

"We need to figure out a way to flush your boyfriend out of hiding." Krasinski squirmed as he made his statement. His man had been awoken, threatening to throw off his concentration.

When Krasinski's rod grew to the size and stature Cita was working for, she took it out of her mouth and started stroking it. Then she said, "Why do we have to 'flush him out' if I know exactly where he's at?"

Suddenly, Krasinski sat up and said, "What'd you just say?"

Cita smiled at him from in between his legs. "You heard me. But, you don't get nothing till I get what I want."

"Cita, I'm not in a position to play with you. If you know where he's at, you need to tell me right now!"

Ignoring him, Cita put his throbbing penis back into her mouth. When she came up for air, she took the palm of her hand and rubbed her saliva all over it. Then she said, "I'll tell you where he's at after you put this fat dick in my ass and fuck me all crazy."

Before he could reply, Cita turned around and got on all fours. Then, with the hand she used to stroke his spit soaked penis, she started lubricating her rectum, hoping to have it rammed inward by his thick hammer of love.

Krasinski couldn't handle anymore. All the stress from this case suddenly blew a gasket. He snatched Cita by her hair, turning her around so she was facing him. Then he slammed her head onto his cock, causing his member to ram mercilessly into her throat, violently choking her in the process. She tried to stop him, but he overpowered her by knotting both of his hands in her long, black hair.

Over and over, Detective Krasinski rammed his rod into Cita's throat. She couldn't breathe; she was gagging, and thought she would die. The more she fought, the harder he forced himself into her. Then, suddenly the detective began to shudder. There was a moment when he pushed himself into her face as hard as he could, but then he let go. Yet, she still couldn't breathe, because now she was choking on a mouth full of salty goo.

That's when the law dog pushed her. Still dizzy from the assault, she hit her head on the corner of the coffee table before falling to the floor. Like a drowning victim fighting for a gasp of air, Cita fought through the cum in her mouth to get a breath of life.

"Now, tell me where that motherfucking nigger

is at or I'm taking you to jail for accessory to murder!"

"I'm not telling you shit, bitch!" yelled Cita, defiantly.

Krasinski pulled his pants up, then stood up and kicked her in the chest, knocking all the air out of her lungs. Next, he flipped her over, onto her stomach, and slapped the cuffs on her. "You have the right to remain silent... Anything you say, can and will be held against you in a court of law..."

CHAPTER FIFTY-EIGHT

He felt as if he had just been given a new lease on life. If that really was M.S. who had left that message, then there had to be more "Park Gang" in Florida. If there was one thing he knew about Mark, it was that he never travelled alone.

He couldn't believe he hadn't put it together before. While he was in jail, in Tennessee, he heard about M.S. hitting on a million-dollar lick. Then he heard his homeboy moved to Vegas, but he never guessed that Mark was the connect Alize had told him about.

Now all he needed to do was get to M.S. Once he did that, he was sure he'd be OK. The least he'd get was a trip back to California, and that was better than running around Florida; broke, with no assets.

Since B.A. didn't have a house phone and Brittany's cell phone battery died, he needed to find another way to contact his comrade. The idea of going from door to door asking for a phone crossed his mind, but he quickly jettisoned the thought. His face had gotten way too much airplay on the news. His only hope was the gas station across the street from the apartment complex. There was a pay phone there. It was risky, but he had to go for it.

With a renewed gusto, Gangsta rushed into B.A.'s bedroom, searching for an outfit. He found a black hoody with a matching fitted cap. After putting it all on, Talton looked at his reflection in the mirror. The person he saw staring back at him had his back against a wall. With nothing to lose, he was dangerous and he looked it.

$$$$$

It was hot and sunny outside as the cream-colored Navigator pushed through traffic. K.P. didn't need the GPS to find the address to the apartments they were heading to because Brittany knew exactly how to get there.

The crew of gun-toting lunatics became anxious the moment they got word of Talton's location. To Brittany, the vibe was confusing. She expected them to be as delighted as she was, but that wasn't the case.

What she didn't understand was that they were glad to find Talton, but they knew that there was no reason to become festive until they had him safe from harm's way. At any moment things could go bad, and they all knew this.

When K.P. turned the SUV onto the long driveway that led into the apartment complex, he noticed a lone man walking towards them in the distance. If he wasn't wearing a black hoody on such a hot day, K.P. would've passed him by without a second thought. But this guy looked grimy. He looked as shady as they came.

Upon closer scrutiny, Killa Pimpn' recognized a familiar sway in the thug's stroll. Everything about him screamed Oak Park. K.P. began wondering if the shady-looking hooded fella was Gangsta. He slowed the truck down as he got closer, and when they were close enough to make eye contact with one another, the man in the hoody reached under his sweater for what K.P. assumed was a pistol. That's when he knew it was Talton.

"That's the homey, y'all!" yelled K.P. while slamming his foot on the breaks. After putting the truck in park, he hopped out and told Talton, "Blood, it's me! Lil' K.P. from 4th Ave!... Big K.P.'s son!"

When Talton realized who K.P. was, he let out a deep breath and ran towards him, greeting him with a hearty embrace. During all the excitement, the other two got out of the truck and Talton recognized them as well. The last time he saw them, they were terrorizing the neighborhood on their BMXs.

"What the fuck is y'all doin' out here?" asked Talton, while handing out bear hugs. "Q.Q. and May-May, you niggas done got big as hell!"

"People don't call us that no more, bruh. They call me Snubbz, and May-May's Staxx. We're running shit now, big bruh. We got the "P" on lock."

Brittany watched most of the exchange from the inside of the SUV. She had purposely waited to get out last so she could see what kind of reception the men gave one another. She was now fully confident that they really knew Talton from a previous life. So, she stepped out and said, "Yeah... this looks like a really nice gangster reunion, but I think you all forgot that Talton's America's most wanted right now. We need to get him off the street, quick."

Talton's eyes lit up the moment he saw her. He ran up to her and gave her the tightest hug of all.

Heading back to the truck, K.P. said, "She's right, blood. We need to get back to M.S. Then he ushered everyone into the Lincoln and tried to make a U-turn, but the driveway was too narrow. He was forced to make a three-point turn. Then, after turning the truck around, the whole crew was taken by surprise. The driveway had been suddenly blocked off by an armada of law enforcement. The police had caught them all off guard.

All of a sudden, the inside of the Navigator was filled with the sound of semiautomatic weapons being cocked. This was precisely the reason why they hadn't gotten excited when they first heard of Talton's whereabouts. They all knew the risk they were taking, and now that they found themselves in the worst situation possible, going out in a hail of gunfire seemed like their only option.

Immediately Brittany realized what was happening. She knew that she had to do something before she was caught in the front seat of a shoot-out between the Zillas and the cops. Brittany softly placed her hand on K.P.'s right forearm and said, "K.P., slow down and think about this; if they were coming for us, they'd be out of their cars already. All you gotta do is pull onto the grass and let them pass. I promise you... they're not here for this truck."

He looked at Brittany then turned towards Talton, who was seated in the second row. Talton slightly nodded, signaling for him to listen to her. So, K.P. drove onto the grass. As soon as they moved out of the way, the parade of law enforcement vehicles drove past them ascending towards the interior of the apartment complex.

Brittany turned and faced Talton after K.P. started driving again. "Does your baby mamma know you're here?"

"She dropped me off, but that was three days ago. She was the only person that knew where I was at, though. Then again, how'd you guys find me?"

"M.S. found you by your phone's GPS," replied K.P. "He's at Alize's house with Killa Dirt and Insane B right now."

Talton didn't say anything else. He was thinking about his young homies and how much they had grown since he had last seen them. They were men now, drafted by Oak Park's war machine. And obviously ready to ride, or else M.S. wouldn't have had them in Florida. Finally, in the midst of killers, Talton felt safe.

"Hey, Talton," said K.P.

"What's crackin' ?"

"Take a look at this flick." Handing him his phone; "You know these two?"

"That's my baby mamma. I don't know the cracker she's kissing. That looks like my brother's house, though. When was this taken?"

Before K.P. could answer Brittany said, "About thirty minutes ago... Talton, that bitch is dirty."

CHAPTER FIFTY-NINE

Cita told it all before the detective even had the chance to finish reading her her Miranda rights. It didn't take long for him to rally the troops, either. He could've gotten the information he needed without the fake arrest, but he was tired of the games. Other than wanting to have sex with her, Krasinski disliked Cita from the moment he met her. He had lost all respect for her the moment she started giving up information on the man who fathered her child.

The fact that he had had sex with her would definitely compromise the case if it ever came out. Nevertheless, he was confident that he had everything under control. No one was going to believe a money hungry snitch that changed her story every few days. With his impeccable service record, he had nothing to worry about.

Within minutes of receiving the address, Krasinski called his superiors and got the green light to raid it. Still, that wasn't enough for the detective. On his way to the apartment complex, he called all of the local news stations, leaving an anonymous tip that something big was about to happen. By the time he arrived at the location, he was at the tail end of an army of anxious officers, and they were being followed by several news vans and helicopters. Exactly what Krasinski had been shooting for; he wanted the biggest bust of his career to be televised.

Krasinski was strapping on a bulletproof vest as the SWAT team quietly surrounded the unit their suspect was allegedly hiding out in. Talton was deemed armed and dangerous, so the powers that be had authorized lethal use of force. In other words, Mr. Talton D. Robinson was not supposed to leave the premises alive.

Two burly officers clad in black SWAT gear held a battering ram, ready to knock the door off of its hinges. There were also a number of ski-masked lawmen surrounding all the windows to B.A.'s apartment, including the back, sliding glass door.

In a situation like this, the lead officer had the option to use concussion grenades. However, they weren't recommended for use in small confined areas such as the one they were going into. Krasinski was well versed in these procedures, nevertheless he called for them. Since there were so many reporters covering this spectacular event, he decided to shine. Figuring that the loud explosions would add dramatics to the simple raid.

When the time for business came, Krasinski stood behind two battering-ram-toting officers with his gun drawn. With his earpiece activated, he counted down, "On my go, all units are to enter the residence. Use of deadly force is authorized. I repeat, use of deadly force is authorized. One... two... three... go! All units go!"

The moment he called for action, grenades were propelled into the small, one bedroom apartment through the bedroom, bathroom, and kitchen windows. What followed were a series of loud explosions that were heard throughout the six-acre complex. The explosions worked wonders for the dramatic effects. Yet, what Detective Krasinski failed to consider was what the grenades would do to his own men.

As soon as the flash bombs were shot into the apartment, the team with the battering ram smashed their way into the unit. That's when the chaos ensued. Suddenly they were all blinded by the bright explosion that came from having three different concussion grenades activated in such small vicinity. Every single officer that entered the apartment was affected in the worse way.

Then somebody accidently pulled their trigger just as both teams rushed the apartment from opposite ends, triggering a barrage of blind gunfire. All of a sudden, the scene became cryptically unruly. In a matter of seconds, there was an all-out slaughter between twenty different law enforcement officers; all within the confines of a one-bedroom apartment.

Based on the fact that there had been so many media representatives in the area, the whole country was soon watching the violent fiasco play out from the luxury of their living rooms, computer screens, and smartphones. In the end, there were sixteen wounded officers and three of them were dead from the botched raid. All of this conveniently recorded by the media.

Instead of sending a message to Florida's underworld, the Pinellas County Sheriff's Department made fools of themselves. Of course, no one with a badge would take responsibility for the blunder. Instead, they looked for a scapegoat and a cause; which easily came in the form of a drug-dealing murderer named Talton.

CHAPTER SIXTY

Cita was on the toilet, dabbing antibiotic cream on her C-section wound. She was hurt, yet she felt lucky that Krasinski hadn't struck her in the stomach. The cut wasn't fully healed, it was still oozing clear, gooey liquid; one kick and she would've opened back up. She was OK. She didn't get arrested, and once she told him what he wanted to hear, he took the cuffs off of her and left.

However, now that she was alone and had had some time to think about it, she became livid. Yet, instead of directing her fury towards the man who had just attacked her, she got angry at Talton. The longer she thought about it, the more she became enraged. Blaming everyone except herself.

On the surface it seemed as if she had everything she had wanted. The problem was that she was broke. The cars, the house, and all of the other things didn't matter if she had no way of sustaining it. Immediately thoughts of her sister's lifestyle crowded her mind. She had to do something; ending up in a trailer park wasn't an option.

That's when she had an epiphany of sorts. Remembering how anxious Talton had been every time he called from jail, she realized that he would be at her mercy once he got locked up again. All she'd have to do was sit back and wait. Get comfortable, kick up her feet and wait for his inevitable call from the county jail. It's not like he had anyone else; Ant was dead and his boys had turned him in.

As she finished cleaning her C-section wound, she ironed out the details of her plan. She would accept his collect calls, play the role of a concerned baby mamma, even set up some visits. Then, after his guard was down, she'd have him sign a Power of Attorney, giving her full rights to all of the toys. After selling everything, she'd live like a Queen for at least six months.

Cita farted before standing up from the toilet. The smell was a nasty mixture of sweat and eggs, making her crinkle her nose as she dropped the last of the dirty gauze in the toilet. Now she felt like she was back in control of her immediate destiny. A house on the beach, shiny cars, leather furniture; all hers.

Today is a good day, she thought to herself. Then she started on the task of cleaning her house, but not before she made sure that the ringer on the house phone was on. She didn't want to Miss Talton's call from the Pinellas County jail.

CHAPTER SIXTY-ONE

The mood at Ze's house was festive. The aroma of expensive marijuana and dark liquor floated throughout the home. Moments after arriving, Talton was inside giving and receiving long overdue hugs and daps. For years he'd been away from the 'hood; now, here he was... in the midst of a pride of killers.

After a while, everyone got situated. K.P. made himself the designated bartender, mixing drinks and passing out shots. Killa Dirt and his brother were stationed in front of the television, competively battling one another in a game of Madden. And Staxx and Snubbz had Brittany on the far side of the living room, whispering things in her ears that was making her blush. While all of this was going on, Talton settled in at the breakfast bar with M.S. The whole time Alize was quietly standing next to Gangsta as if she were afraid he would suddenly disappear.

Mark and Gangsta were both close to a decade older than the rest of the Underworld Zillas. Needless to say, they had a unique history that surpassed their relationships with the others. They used this time to exchange notes on what they had been up to throughout the last several years.

Neither one of them had any regrets. Other than Talton's current situation, they had both played the cards they were dealt. Yes, M.S. was now a millionaire, but they both agreed that if Talton would've been in California when the contract was put out, the bounty would have been split. That's how tight they were.

So, everyone did what they usually did while confined inside of a house. Video games, drinking, smoking, and gambling. Before they knew it, the clock on the microwave read 1:26.

Alize tapped on Talton's shoulder and said, "I'm taking a shower, then I'm going to bed. You wanna shower with me?"

Before Gangsta could answer, M.S. cut in, "Let her go on and get cleaned up, nigga. It's been years since we've had the chance to conversate like this." Then, to Ze he said, "He'll still be here when you get out, ma. We ain't takin' 'em nowhere."

"That's not what I–" began Alize.

"It's OK, Ze. I'll go to bed when you get ready," said Talton.

M.S. watched as Alize reluctantly pulled away from his friend. After she left, he said, "Damn, blood! What you done did to that girl? I ain't never seen Ze like that."

"I'm feeling the same way about her," replied Talton.

"I know you ain't in love, nigga."

"Am I! Blood, I've been looking for someone like her my whole life. I'ma marry that girl... raise a family wit' her."

Leaning closer to Talton so as not to be heard by the others, Mark said, "Gangsta... my nigga, this is me, blood. Ain't no way in hell you're gonna get me to believe you're in love."

Talton looked at his friend. Staring straight into his eyes he said, "I love that girl."

For a moment M.S. didn't know what to say. The Talton of old was a cold-hearted player. Could his friend have gone soft on him? "What about these cases? How you gonna juggle a family while you running from the law?"

"I'll take her with me until shit gets settled. This ain't no different than any other murder charge I've had. In the end, I'ma beat this one too." Talton paused to take a drink from his glass, the liquor burned his throat as it went down. "And, I'm not juggling nothin'. When this shit is over, I'm letting the game go."

"Lettin' it go!? Blood, you're trippin'. Niggas like us don't get out the game!"

"Why not? Who's to say I can't change? I'm getting my son from that punk-ass bitch, and me and Ze are gonna raise 'im."

All of a sudden M.S. started laughing. Then he said, "Gangsta, you playin', blood! Check this out; all you need is some rest and a different piece of ass."

"You sound like Ant," said Talton.

Mark stared at his friend for a moment before making his next statement. "Maybe Ant was right."

"Anthony was trying to make me give up my kid for the game. I already did that and it never got me nowhere. This time, I'ma be a man, homey. I love that girl and that's that."

"Yeah... a'ight," replied Mark, not believing what he was hearing.

Changing the subject Talton said, "Anyways, what's up, nigga?"

"Yeah tho', I was wondering something... I know you sent your brick money with them fuck-niggas. Who was you finna cop from?"

"One of Ant's people from back home. A nigga named Snoop, he's from the town."

"Snoop?"

"Yeah."

"Blood, you know Big Snoop. He grew up on 47th. Blood from the "P", he started that Playboy shit."

"I know, but I never met 'em."

Damn, blood... I didn't know Snoop was pushing them thangs out here."

After that the subject was changed and they continued catching up on old times. Then, someone found a pair of dice and a craps game broke out on the kitchen floor. The whole clique was having a good time when Alize came back wrapped in a bathrobe.

Walking up to Talton she said, "I'm ready to go to bed now. It'd be nice if you'd come with me. It's getting late, and I gotta go to work in the morning."

Before Gangsta had the chance to say anything, Staxx looked up from the dice game and said, "Damn, Ze! You got a job, too? I thought you were out here selling weight."

"I work at a bank," she said. Then to Talton she

said, "So, you coming to bed, or what?"

"Yeah, it's gettin' late. Alright then, y'all. I'm calling it a night."

Alize then took Talton's hand and led him into her bedroom, totally blind to the fact that in that mere exchange, a seed had been planted that promised to bring more violence and larceny into her life.

As soon as they left from within earshot, Staxx looked up towards M.S. and said, "Say, bruh... since we ain't got no bodies to drop, we might as well hit that bank."

The comment was made as a statement yet everyone knew it was really a question. M.S. didn't reply, but that didn't mean he wasn't thinking about it. The idea of robbing Alize's bank came to him the very first time she mentioned the fact that she had gotten the job. He had always been too busy though.

With his drink in his hand, M.S. studied his team. K.P., Killa Dirt, Insane B, Staxx, Snubbz... they all handled themselves well under pressure. They also knew what it was like to be locked away in a cage. Therefore, they could be trusted to do what it takes in order to pull a bank heist and get away with it. And Talton had experience; Mark knew he could trust him. Yeah, M.S. thought to himself, the situation was ripe for a bank job.

After making up his mind, he stood up, stretching out all of his six-foot, five-inch frame. Then he said, "It's time to call it a night, y'all. We can't be in this girl's house partying all night. Time to get some sleep."

Killa Dirt stood up from his crouched position at

the dice game and said, "I see you plottin', Mark. We hittin' that lick, or what?"

That's when Brittany stepped in the kitchen with a stack of plates that needed to go in the dishwasher. "Plottin' on what lick?"

"That bank where your sister works... that's what lick," said Staxx.

M.S. had seen Brittany coming so he managed to make eye contact with Dirt, silently telling him to stop talking. But Staxx didn't notice the exchange and spoke too fast.

Brittany looked at Staxx as if he had just made a joke. "The bank?!" she said. "You guys have got to be cray-cray. I know my sister, and trust me... if I were you, I wouldn't let her hear you talking about robbing that bank."

"Why's that?" cut in Snubbz.

"She's not having it," replied Brittany. "Look... a few years ago, when she first got the job, some dude came in and handed her a note. Throughout her whole training they kept telling her not to argue with a robber, that the money was insured and that she would get fired if she argued with a robber. So, when Ze got the note, she gave him the money, and he left. He got away, but then the FBI came and started grilling her like she had something to do with it. They took her to some office building, downtown, and treated her like a criminal. While they were questioning her, the dude got caught at a hotel in Orlando. The cops killed him and the whole time they acted as if it were her fault. So now, anytime somebody even makes a joke about robbing her bank, she goes ballistic."

"Well," began M.S. "we ain't gotta worry about Ze going 'ballistic' on anybody, cuz nobody's robbing shit. Now that's a dead convo'. Brit, go on and get us some blankets so we can get some sleep. I got the couch, y'all..."

The clique didn't need to hear anything else. They all settled in for the night, knowing there'd be a bank heist the next day.

CHAPTER SIXTY-TWO

In the bedroom, after turning off the lights, Talton climbed into bed next to Alize. As much as he wanted to relax, he knew he couldn't afford to get naked, but that didn't stop Ze from snuggling up to him and resting her head on his chest.

"I thought that was it," she whispered. "I thought I'd never get to lay up with you again." Ze paused for a moment before continuing. "Why'd you leave me like that?"

"I was trying to get your money back."

"Then why were you with your baby mamma?"

Shaking his head, Talton said, "I was trying to do something. I thought if I could just get in her head things would get better. I just need her to take back her statement and I'll be good. But she lied to me. Now I'm fucked."

Alize lifted her head from Talton's chest. Looking at him she said, "Let me get this straight. Are you telling me she's the only thing keeping this case open?"

"If it wasn't for Cita, I wouldn't even be a suspect. Without her, it might drag on for a minute, but they wouldn't have a case.

"So, what's next? Are you leaving again? Now that you got your boys, I guess you'll be going back to Cali, huh?"

"Truthfully, I don't know what I'ma do. I know I can't stay here. My only option is to leave the state. The thing is, I never left any loose ends like this. For some shit like this, these folks ain't gonna let it rest. Ze, I'ma tell you something...

"I don't know what the future will bring. Anything can happen. But, for now, let's just enjoy the moment. Let's forget about the rest of the world; just for tonight." Talton gave Ze a squeeze and she hugged him back. Then he asked, "So, what's up wit' your son? You talk to 'em?"

"What?" she asked, sounding confused. "Oh, yeah. You know, I've been kinda neglecting him since all this messy shit started happening. It's not like I can bring him around while all this is going on."

"Man, I'm sorry 'bout that, Ze. I know how much he means to you. I hate being the cause of the rift."

She didn't reply. For the first time in years, the memory of her baby had finally began to fade. For some reason, she wanted to cry, yet, for the life of her, she couldn't understand why.

CHAPTER SIXTY-THREE

The next morning Alize awoke to a house full of movement. She tried to stay in bed for as long as she could, not wanting to leave Talton, but she had business to handle. She finally got dressed a little after seven a.m. Everyone else, except for Talton and Brittany, had already been up and running for at least an hour before she stepped out of her bedroom.

After getting ready for work, instead of driving herself, Alize asked Mark for a ride. She had decided to go to work without her car so that she would need a ride home. A ploy to get one last meeting with Talton before he left town.

M.S. was more than happy to give her a ride to work. Having her to himself before she went in was perfect. She had a treasure trove of information that he needed to extract and he didn't have much time. During the trip from her house to the bank, he took his time, subtly obtaining the details he would need to pull off an efficient bank robbery. Without her realizing it, he got her to tell him all kinds of useful information. Like the fact that she hated Mondays the most. They were boring because she had to spend the better part of her day in one of the side offices counting money. Mondays were when all the local businesses turned in their weekend deposits; which consisted of dirty bills that mostly came from strip clubs and fast-food restaurants.

If Ze hadn't been so preoccupied with what she had planned for this particular Monday morning, she probably would have censored herself. However, instead, she allowed her brain to get picked by a career criminal who made a living from taking advantage of other people's weaknesses.

Everything she said was instantly internalized by the violent gangster. By the time she was ready to exit his vehicle, he knew that all of the cash registers at her branch had a specific twenty-dollar bill that, when pulled, activated a silent alarm. He also found out the tellers each had a stack of bills that contained a dye pack or GPS device. The quickest way to find out which stacks had them was to try and bend them. If they didn't bend like paper, the stack was bad. By the end of their trip, M.S. had enough information to leave Clearwater with a lot more money than he came with.

Before stepping out of the Navigator, Alize made sure to remind him that she needed a ride home. His reply was, "Don't trip, Ze. If it ain't me, I'll send one of my goons. Somebody will be here by the time you get off from work."

Alize watched M.S. drive away before she turned towards the Checker's fast-food restaurant on the other side of the bank's parking lot. Walking away from the bank, she took out her phone and called her manager to tell him she wouldn't be in until after lunch, she had an emergency dentist appointment and that she'd rush back as soon as she was finished.

Then she called Brittany.

$$\$\$\$\$\$$

Cita's ride pulled in at the hospital where her newborn was waiting to be taken home. Shannon was driving the Delta while she rode in the passenger seat. For the first time since she became pregnant Cita had started thinking of the baby in a maternal fashion. Throughout her pregnancy, she never once looked at the bulge in her stomach as a piece of her that she would come to love and nurture into adulthood. But now, as she headed into the maternity ward to pick up her baby, she was suddenly overcome with a feeling of excitement. Somewhere, deep in her soul, there was an instinct to love this child. And it was now beginning to slide into the forefront of her consciousness.

The second-most decisive moment of Cita's life came when the nurse handed her the small bundle of blankets that held her baby. She took one look into his big brown eyes and suddenly she felt an emotion that she couldn't recognize. Her heart melted as it skipped several beats. For the first time in her life, she knew what it was to truly love someone. She knew from that point on she would no longer be selfish or evil. In that first second, she realized that she was no longer number one in her life. Her baby was.

On the ride home, Cita sat in the back with her

baby. Which surprised her twin sister, but not as much as when she looked in the rear-view mirror and saw tears trailing down Cita's face. Shannon was shocked, but then a smile crept across her face. Maybe, just maybe, her sister had finally met her match.

$$$$$

By the time Mark turned onto the street where his current base of operations were set up, he had already formulated a plan for the bank robbery. He knew that sometimes the best robberies occurred spontaneously. He wanted to utilize that type of mentality so he and the clique could be in and out within the next few hours. Yet, M.S. was the kind of planner who always kept the end game in mind. Therefore, in order for his plan to go smoothly, all loose ends would have to be clipped.

As he pulled into Alize's driveway, he noticed her car was gone. Immediately he was angered. Some heads would roll if anyone had gone anywhere with Brittany. They all knew he had something on his mind. And that meant they should've stayed ready for whatever. Leaving with Brittany was definitely not being ready for whatever.

After parking the Navigator, Mark rushed to the front door.

It was locked. Good, he thought. Security came first. When it finally opened, the first question out of his mouth was, "Where's Ze's car?"

Brittany had taken off. No one knew where to, or

why.

"Good," said M.S., calming down. "I didn't want her around for the planning phase anyway."

The clique lit up. They all knew he was referring to the bank. All of them except for Talton; he looked confused.

"Planning phase?!" he said. "For what? What's brackin'?"

CHAPTER SIXTY-FOUR

When Alize called Brittany and told her to go into her closet for a specific shoe box, it hadn't occurred to Brittany to ask why. She didn't even think twice when Ze told her to take it to the checker's instead of the bank. But now, as she watched her sister approaching the passenger side of the car and not the driver's side, where she could have simply handed her the mysterious box, Brittany was beginning to wonder what was going on.

Alize got inside the car and immediately asked Brittany if she had brought the box.

"Yeah, it's in the back seat," she replied. "What's so important about this box that I had to leave a house full of fine, black Mandigos to bring it to you?"

"Do you remember how to get to the house where Talton's baby mamma is at?"

"Yeah... you already know this. Why? What's up?"

"I need you to take me there." Alize opened the K-Swiss shoe box and took out a black Larson .380. Then, noticing her sister watching her she said, "Hurry up! I gotta be back by the lunch rush or my boss is gonna trip!"

"You know she's fuckin' with that cop, right?" asked Brittany, while putting the car in gear and taking off. "What're you planning on doing?"

Ze popped the clip out from the bottom of the pistol to make sure it was loaded. It was. "Don't worry about all that, just drive. I gotta handle this, Brit. After Rick took Shawn, I've been stressed out of my mind. Then, after I met Talton, I finally felt happy. You saw how I got when I thought I lost him. That wasn't an act, Brit. I'm not about to lose him again. His baby mamma's the only thing standing between me and my happiness. So, I'm fixing it all, once and for all."

For a while the siblings travelled in silence. Brittany knew without a doubt what they were going to do. And she knew her sister good enough not to try to talk her out of it. The last two weeks had been wild; like their teenage years. Nothing had changed, and just like their teenage years, Brittany would forever have her sister's back...

$$$$$

Cita couldn't wait to get her baby home. Her sister had just turned onto their street while Cita was thinking of how she was going to redecorate the extra bedroom in all baby-blue. Then, as Shannon was pulling the car into the driveway, Cita saw Detective Krasinski parked on the curb in his unmarked Impala. Suddenly, her face turned crimson and she said, "Shannon, take Marcus inside!" They had barely come to a halt when Cita opened her door and jumped out of her seat.

Krasinski was resting his head against the headrest with his eyes closed, oblivious to the world around him. He'd been nursing a hangover from the night before. After botching the raid he ended up on the receiving end of an ass chewing of ass chewings by his boss. He had made a spectacle of himself and the whole Sheriff's Department. After having to sit through an extremely vociferous tirade, Krasiriski drank himself into oblivion, eventually falling asleep behind the wheel of his car at a park. He hadn't even made it home yet. He was sipping on a hot cup of gas station coffee when Cita came running across the street.

"Hey! Hey! Motherfucker!" yelled Cita, on her way across the street. "You raped me! You think you can do whatever you want 'cause you've got a badge! I'm calling internal affairs, motherfuckin' rapist!" Cita was being so loud that her neighbors had began looking out their windows. "I'm not testifying against nobody! Deal with that, rapist!"

Krasinski spilled his coffee all over his lap when Cita started pounding on his window. His pants were all wet and she was now kicking the side of his car while calling him a rapist. On top of that he had just heard one of her neighbors yelling something about calling the cops... He was a cop! This was the last thing he needed in his life. Krasinski started his car and drove away.

Shannon watched the whole incident from the doorway of the house. With the baby in her arms, it was impossible for her to run after Cita and stop her from cussing out the detective. She was glad when she saw him finally driving away. However, what she didn't know was that her only chance at surviving the afternoon had just driven away with a crotch full of hot coffee. "Come on, sis," she said. "Forget that pig!"

"Give me my baby..."

CHAPTER SIXTY-FIVE

Meanwhile, back at Ze's house...

"The way I figure it, if we go in there and hit 'em for everything they got, we'll be able to drop a hundred G's on your defense. You're gonna need it, blood. Florida be washin' niggas, and that's without evidence. In your case, they got an eye witness that's laid up with a cop. We can't touch her. But, if we get this money and drop it on a mouthpiece, along with this flick of your bitch with the cop, then we'll have a fighting chance." Talton had seemed hesitant when he first heard of the plan to rob the bank. So, M.S. was making sure he understood the importance of pulling it off. "You need this, blood. And, just so you know, none of us really need to do this. I bet everyone in this room has at least enough money to sit back and not do nothing for the next six months." Looking around the living room, Mark was backed up by a chorus of affirmative statements.

"Don't get me wrong," said Talton. "Anybody can use that type of money, no matter how much you got put up. But you're pushing too fast. We're talking 'bout running up in a bank... today! Why not holla' at Ze and get the logistics?"

Insane B replied, "What's the problem, blood? You ain't even going inside. All you gotta do is let us fuck this pussy, and you enjoy the ride."

Talton said, "First off, all that shit M.S. talking 'bout having me sit in the truck is nonsense. I'll be damned if I sit back while you niggas take a risk to pay for my lawyer money. You already know that's not me. All I'm saying is that we got a bitch on the inside. She can give us all the details we need so we can get the most revenue. Why not take our time to get more info? You niggas talking 'bout running up in that bitch blind."

As M.S. listened to his childhood friend, he realized that Talton had already made up his mind to go along with the plan. He just needed a little more assurance that their crew was prepared for the job. "We ain't going in there blind, homey. I've been plottin' on this lick for months. How you think I know about the alarms and dye packs? Ze's in on it, bruh. I'm the one who took her to work. She's expecting it to go down. If you're 'nervous' cuz you're not going in there to 'supervise', then fuck it; go in then. The main thing is, we do this today. It's gotta be on a Monday, and we gotta get you up outta here, so it might as well go down today."

Talton looked at Mark, then around the room. These were his people. They had all came up in the same world as he. With their long dreads and ominous glares, he knew he would never find a more dangerous crew. "A'ight. But I'm going in with the rest of y'all."

The moment Talton gave his approval, the

energy in the room exploded. K.P. was the next one to speak and said, "Alright, Park Gang, it's on! We'll be using T-shirts for masks; like we used in Y.A. during the riots. There's a Walgreens around the corner from here. That's where we'll get some glue to cover our hands with."

Then Mark spoke up, "That's what's up, K.P. You can take the truck to go get that glue. I want you to find a Walmart, too. We need twelve backpacks. Somebody else needs to raid Ze's dresser for some T-shirts. But first I need you guys to memorize your place in the formation." To Staxx and Snubbz he said, "When we go in, you two look for the room where the tellers are counting the weekend deposits. You won't have to worry about dye packs or GPS devices cuz it'll be fresh money."

"Don't trip, Zilla! We got this," replied Staxx while rubbing the palms of his hands together.

Then Mark continued, "Dirt... Insane, y'all need to hop over the counter and lay down the tellers. Don't let them hand you shit, don't take any loose bills either. Make sure there's nothing in any of the stacks. Talton and K.P., you two are gonna watch the doors. Nobody comes in or out during the lick." Then to everyone, he said, "We all understand what happens to heros, right?"

They all knew the answer to that last question. If anyone even looked like they were thinking of trying something, that person would be shot down in cold-blood. Their livelihoods depended on successfully completing this crime. If anyone dared challenge them in any way, their sin would be met with force, resulting in death.

M.S. continued, "I'll be driving on this lick, and I put that on 21-26, if any K9's pull up during this lick, I'm shooting. If you hear any shots being fired, come out with your thangs blazing. Remember... the number one rule–"

All of a sudden, the whole clique cut Mark off in mid-sentence; in unison they said, "The number one rule of a jux is to get away!"

Talton was loving the energy in the room. At first, he didn't realize that his homey had been planning this robbery for a while, so he wasn't sure about going in, but now he was sure that everything would go down smoothly. This was a crew of demons that he helped raise. He couldn't ask for a better team. He was already making plans for the money he would get when Staxx asked him why there was a room with unopened toys. In reply he said, "Ze's got a son. He only comes over on the weekends though. Her baby daddy pulled a stunt and got the kid."

M.S. was cleaning his Glock 40 when he heard the exchange. Without looking up, he said, "Is that what she told you?"

"Yeah," replied Gangsta. "She calls 'em every night and picks 'em up on the weekends."

This time M.S. looked at his friend. "Blood, I live in Orlando. I've known Ze since she was taking trips to Vegas. Trust me... she ain't got no kids."

Staxx, who was listening to his two big homies, picked up a picture frame from the entertainment center; it was of a small toddler taking his first steps.

Holding it up for them to see he said, "I think you're wrong, M.S. She's got pictures all over. I just barely noticed it."

"See, Mark," said Talton with a smile. "You just never seen 'em cuz he's always with his daddy." Then Gangsta left the room to go find some T-shirts.

"You know... you're probably right," commented M.S. while cleaning his gun. "You're probably right..."

CHAPTER SIXTY-SIX

Brittany slowed the car down as she approached the house. "That's the spot right there... where the blue Suburban is parked."

"I can tell," said Ze. "I recognize the older car with the big rims." Alize scanned the street for any police, but there weren't any. It looked like any other quiet, residential street during the middle of the day. Serene, with no traffic. "This bitch really thinks she's getting away with this. Taking Talton's life away, and for what? A few shiny cars and a house that ain't even paid for?" After passing the house, Brittany was now making a U-turn. "It looks clear, doesn't it?"

"Yeah, but, Ze, what're you gonna do?"

Ignoring her question, Alize said, "Drop me off right here. Go around the block really slow. I'll be out by the time you come back around. If I'm not, do it again until I am."

Brittany stopped the Malibu directly in front of the house. Then, just as Alize reached for the door handle she whispered, "Be careful, sis."

Alize smiled, then leaned in and gave Brittany a kiss on the cheek. After that she got out of the car and headed for the house.

Brittany drove away slowly keeping an eye on her sibling through the rear-view mirror. At the stop sign, on the corner of the street, she grabbed Ze's phone and called her own cell phone. The call went straight to voice mail so she left Talton a message...

$$$$$

Cita was laying on the king-size bed, peacefully watching her tiny baby sleep, softly running her fingers through his dark curls. For the first time in her adult life, Cita understood what it meant to experience tranquility. While watching her infant sleep, she began to wonder what kind of life he would lead. That's about the time she heard the doorbell ring, then her sister called out, "I got it!" If Shannon wouldn't have been there, Cita probably wouldn't have answered the door. She had no reason to; nothing else mattered, only the baby. This tiny little man who she would nurture for the rest of her life.

When Shannon opened the front door she was greeted by the pretty face of a redheaded woman in a business suit. She had a calm air to her that immediately set Shannon at ease.

"Hello, my name is Dezire Patten, I'm your neighbor from up the street. Is your name Cita?"

"No, I'm her sister. She's in the bedroom with her baby. Can I help you with something?"

"Well... actually, I need to speak with the lady of the house, if that's OK. Do you mind if I come inside?"

Shannon opened the door wider and said, "I don't mind, come on in. I'll go get her for you. Have a seat on the couch, I'll be right back."

Just as Shannon turned away to fetch Cita, Alize reached into her waistband for her .380. Gripping it tightly, she quickly raised it above her head then slammed it into the back of Shannon's cranium. Instantly she collapsed to the floor. She was unconscious before she hit the ground, but that didn't stop Alize from smashing the butt of her pistol into her face, splattering blood all over the carpet.

The only sound was a dull, "Thmph! Thmph! Thmph!" everytime Ze's pistol came down. Alize had snatched a handful of Shannon's bloody hair to lift her head up as she beat her face in with her gun. Blood sprayed all over the walls, the carpet, and all over Alize's own face. She swung with such furry that her once perfectly arranged hair was now as wild as her eyes. She must've swung her anvil at least twenty times before realizing she was being sidetracked.

With a bloodlust only known to the most dangerous of predators, Alize let her victim's head drop to the floor and headed deeper into the home. From the hallway she could see into the master bedroom, where Cita was lying on the bed, staring at her child.

Cita was wondering what was taking her sister so long when she looked up and saw a woman standing in her doorway with blood all over her face. Seeing the gun in her hand, Cita immediately sat up and said, "What the hell! What's going on?!"

Alize stepped into the room while pointing the gun at her. Then she said, "So this is the bastard that keeps Talton running back to you, huh?" Her eyes were glazed over, giving them a faraway look that distinctively showed how disconnected from reality she was. "I'm gonna go ahead and put a stop to all that once and for all."

Suddenly realizing what all of this was about, Cita said, "You can tell Talton I'm not testifying against him. I already told the cops I'm not doing it. That's why they left. He doesn't have anything to worry about. Tell 'em I'm not saying shit."

"It's too late for all that. I know you're lying anyway. You probably lie so much you don't know the difference between truth and fiction. So, I'm gonna give you a dose of extreme reality. I'm gonna give you a choice. You get to choose who dies first, you or your baby. You got three seconds to decide, bitch! One... two... –"

"Are you crazy?! I told you I wasn't testifying! Where's Talton?! Call Talton! You don't have to do this!"

"Time's up!" Alize was beginning to squeeze the trigger when Cita slowly stood up.

The third and final most decisive moment in Cita's life took place when she said, "Kill me. Don't kill my baby. You don't have to hurt the baby, take him to Talton."

"Pop! Pop! Pop!" four times, five times, six times, and seven. Cita's body went into convulsions as her nerves reacted to her chest being blown apart.

The baby shrieked!

Cita's body fell against the nightstand.

The baby strained his vocal cords, screaming so loud. Cita's body fell to the floor...

The insistent hollering from the baby is what woke Alize from her frozen state. She let her shooting arm fall to her side. Then she stepped towards the bed where the innocent newborn was in a vociferous mound. However, the baby that Alize saw was asleep in its crib. She reached towards him, still holding her pistol and picked up the sleepy child who had just started to awaken. "Shhh, baby, it's OK. Mamma's gonna make everything right." Marcus was crying out loud but Alize didn't hear the sobbing. The baby in her arms was calm, loving and understanding.

Alize walked out of the bedroom with her redheaded newborn clutched closely against her chest. When she got to the living room, she saw the bloody stump of a woman on the floor to her right and the kitchen to her left. She turned left.

"Shhh, little guy, everything's gonna be alright."

When she entered the kitchen, she went to the microwave, opened its door and put the baby inside. After shutting it, she set the timer for sixty minutes. Then she pressed the cook button and walked away.

Moments later, Alize was outside just in time to see her sister pull up to the house...

$$$$$

Detective Krasinski was still dabbing at his wet crotch with a paper towel when he turned onto Cita's street. He didn't notice the burgundy Chevy with the tinted windows going in the opposite direction. He would sit outside of the house, go home and come back for three days straight before realizing that something had went morbidly wrong.

CHAPTER SIXTY-SEVEN

The troops were preparing for war. Talton had a shirt tied around his neck. When it came time for business, he'd pull it over his face like a ninja mask. He was already feeling the anticipation of the upcoming jux. The same rush of excitement he experienced years earlier, when he hit his first bank.

Gangsta was in his late teens when he and M.S. robbed a bank in North Sacramento. It was the move that firmly established their rank among the upper echelon of Oak Park's underworld. Not because of the actual robbery itself; bank heists were common during that time. It was what they did with the money that set them apart from the rest.

At the time, Oak Park was at war with the Del Paso Heights Bloods. Both sets were equal in power until Gangsta and his cohorts turned the tides. After robbing the bank, they took the proceeds to Arizona. Out there they took advantage of the state's lax gun laws, purchasing hundreds of high-caliber firearms. Then they shipped them back to California. After filing the serial numbers down, they systematically handed over the weapons to the Park's most active gang members. Some as young as twelve were given a pistol. Their only request was that the guns be used against their enemies. That summer ended up being the bloodiest three months in all of Sacramento's history.

Gangsta was lost in thought as he remembered that summer, thinking of how ironic it was that that first bank job was done to bankroll a string of homicides. And now, years later, another bank was being hit to fund the defense against a string of homicides. Sometimes, life was just funny like that.

$$$$$

Alize was rummaging through the glove compartment in search for wet wipes. Her face had splatters of blood across it and her hair was in disarray. "Did anyone come out of their houses?" she asked after finding what she was looking for.

"No. The whole block was quiet," answered Brittany. Clearly acting calmer than she felt.

"I gotta get back to work. Everything's fixed now. Talton doesn't gotta worry about a thing. Now we can get married and leave the game behind us." Still wiping her face with the cleansing tissue, Alize tried Talton again. But just like her other calls, it went to voice mail. "God! I hate when he takes the battery out of the phone!"

"Sis, I need to tell you something—"

"Don't ask me about what just happened! It is what it is. I don't need you getting all paranoid on me. Just get me to work, Brit."

"I wasn't going to ask you anything, bitch! I was

gonna say that I think you need to cut the party short with M.S. and his boys. Especially now that you took care of Talton's situation."

"What're you talking about?" asked Ze, while putting her hair in a bun. "Less than an hour ago you were complaining about having to leave a house full of 'fine, black, Mandingo warriors'. Why the sudden change of heart? I think they're cool. Yeah, they carry guns and all that, but they're no different than us."

"They are though."

"How?"

"They rob people."

"What are you saying?" asked Ze, finally leaning back, content with her appearance.

Brittany stopped at a red light. "Last night I walked in on them when they were talking about robbing your bank."

"That doesn't mean... wait... what?! Why didn't you say something before?"

"Like you gave me a chance! Plus, they dropped it as soon as Mark told them to. But, sis, those guys are crazy. They were 'bout to shoot at the cops yesterday. I can totally see them robbing a bank."

Alize's mind was suddenly going in several different directions at once. If the bank got robbed, the FBI would be all over everyone who worked there. It would only be a matter of time before they connected her to Gangsta and M.S. Then she'd never get a chance to settle down with Talton and start the life she had always wanted. Then something Mark had said to her earlier knocked at the door to her thoughts. Whispering to herself she said, "I bet your bank has a crafty lil' alarm system..."

"What?" asked Brittany, while changing lanes.

"Damn it! Brittany, go to the house!"

"Why? We're almost–"

"I don't care! Go to the house! They're gonna rob the bank! I got so caught up planning on what I was gonna do for Talton I didn't pay attention to M.S. Damn! We gotta catch Talton before they hit the bank!"

$$$$$

The last of the crew was filing out of Alize's house when Talton realized he had forgotten Brittany's phone. "I'll be out there in a minute," he told K.P. before running back to the bedroom.

Staxx and Snubbz were already in the Navigator with M.S. The older gangster orchestrated it that way by signaling for them to meet him outside a few minutes earlier. He had an unique relationship with his two, youngest goons. They had an appetite for violence that was unparalleled to any other duo he had ever come across. And being the master manipulator that he was, M.S. fed their cravings every chance he had.

Today would be no different than any other. Someone would die and it would be one of their own. The call for murder wasn't motivated by pride, nor financial gain; the person hadn't even done anything wrong. Yet one of them was sentenced to death by the hand of Zilla's grim reapers.

Just as he finished prepping his pit bulls on what

he wanted them to do, the rest of the clique started coming out of the house. Everyone got in the Navigator, Talton taking the front passenger seat for himself. As soon as they all got settled in, M.S. pulled away from Alize's house for the last time. At this point, it was established, there was no turning back. They were now officially on U.Z. business.

Seconds later they were on their way. If they would have only taken a minute longer, Brittany and Ze would have caught up with them. Instead, they left on time, and the sisters wound up being too late...

CHAPTER SIXTY-EIGHT

A little while later, when the sisters turned onto their street, they immediately saw the driveway empty. Still, she pulled in, parked, and along with her sister, they ran up to the house. Since Brittany had the keys, Alize had to wait for her to open the door before running through the house in search of Talton.

"Damn! Damn! Damn!" yelled Ze. "They're probably on their way right now!"

Brittany was in the living room when Ze came back in the room, holding her cell phone to her ear. "At least you're not at the bank."

"That makes it worse! All of a sudden the bank gets robbed on the day I have a fake doctor appointment. You already know who they're gonna blame. I gotta do something before Talton fucks up!"

"Just calm down–"

Alize snatched her keys from her sister. Then she ran outside. When she got to her car, she said to Brittany, who was standing in the doorway, "Wait here, in case they come back. If they do, have Talton call me. But don't say nothing about his baby mamma."

Alize got in her car and pulled out of her

driveway just as a group of clouds moved in front of the sun. Suddenly a rainstorm materialized; an ominous sign of what was to come. Meanwhile, Brittany watched in silence as her sister raced away. Alize had put both of their lives on the line to save Talton. She couldn't help but wonder if it was truly worth the trouble...

$$$$$

M.S. was stopped at a light when his phone vibrated for the umpteenth time. He didn't have to check it again to know who it was. The calls were coming from Alize's phone and he had no intentions whatsoever of answering it. Mistakes like that are what gets people convicted of crimes. He wasn't about to create phone records showing him on the phone with Alize right before her bank was robbed.

He wasn't feeling the traffic, either. It seemed as if they were catching every single red light in the city. Nevertheless, he knew better than to run through any of them. Right now wasn't the time to risk getting pulled over. As he sat at the light, he thought about Gangsta. This was the same homey he had grown up with. Sitting next to him was one of his closest friends, yet something about him was different. The Talton of old would have never professed to loving a bitch. He would've never hesitated to hit a lick with the homies, either. He wondered if Talton had lost his edge, if he was no longer the man he used to be. If so, then all of this was for nothing.

"...M.S."

"Yeah."

"The light," said Talton, pointing at the green light.

"Thanks." Mark pulled off. "Alright, y'all. This ain't shit. We in and out, just like any other lick. Just look at it like we're hittin' somebody's trap." Never taking his eyes off the road he said, "Insane, run it by me again. What're you gonna be doin'?"

"Me and Dirt finna hop over the counter, lay down all the tellers. After that, we hit the registers; no loose bills, only wrapped money. And we bend every stack before we put 'em in the bags, making sure there's no GPS or dye packs."

"That's good," remarked M.S. "What about Staxx and Snubbz?"

Staxx spoke up. "Me and Snubbz finna search through the side rooms until we find the tellers counting the weekend takes. Then we'll most graciously 'takes' that!"

"That's what's up, baby." Then Mark turned towards Gangsta, "What about you and K.P.?"

"Me and blood got the doors," replied Talton before turning to the group and saying, "We already know what happens if someone gets stupid, but there's no reason to be trigger happy. There's no security in this bitch. All we doing is going in and out. Y'all got that?"

He looked around and saw affirmative nods, so he turned back around; in his mind, everyone was on one accord. What he didn't know was that Staxx and Snubbz had a whole different set of orders.

Instructions that they were more than happy to fulfill.

$$$$$

Alize was flying through traffic, totally disregarding all the other vehicles in her path. The rain was falling hard; her windshield wipers were going at full speed, yet she ignored the road conditions as she weaved in and out of traffic. All she wanted to do was get to the bank before Talton and his friends did anything stupid. She had to let him know that she had solved all of his problems, and that he had nothing to worry about.

She almost sideswiped a soccer-mom's van as she changed lanes. The streets were getting wetter by the second. And it didn't help that she was only using one hand to drive, and the other on her phone. "God damn it! Answer the phone, you son-of-a-bitch!" She was only three blocks away from the bank. The closer she got, the more anxious she became. She kept imagining Talton being shot down by FBI agents. If that happened, she would only have one option: Suicide. Without Talton, she had no reason to live.

She finally reached 49th Street. From where she was, she could see the Wachovia. But, to her surprise, everything seemed normal. No cops, no paramedics, nothing. It looked just like it had earlier that morning, and every other day for that matter. She took her foot off the gas pedal a little, wondering if she had been overreacting. Maybe there wasn't going to be a robbery. She had taken a shortcut, but still if they would have left her house with the intentions of robbing her bank, they would've gotten there already.

As she pulled into the parking lot and stopped the car, her anxiety began to lift. She stepped out and looked around. There was no sign of M.S.'s Lincoln Navigator. Suddenly the rain stopped. The sun came into view. Feeling better than she had in a long time, Alize told herself, "It'll be alright." Then she went inside.

CHAPTER SIXTY-NINE

The Navigator was three blocks away when Mark saw Alize standing next to her car. Wondering what she was doing, he decided to circle the block a few times to see if anything was out of place. After a couple rounds and nothing looking suspicious, he figured Alize must have called Brittany to come drop off her car. Then she took her home and came back to work. Nothing to worry about, he assured himself before continuing on his mission.

As soon as the others saw the bank in the distance, they started getting ready; pulling their ninja masks over their faces and making sure everything was squared away. Talton took his phone out of his pocket and placed it inside the glove compartment. Everyone else left theirs inside the truck as well.

The second they pulled up to the bank, three of the SUV's four doors opened in unison allowing five demons to escape from its belly, each beast with his own form of tunnel vision. Gangsta was the first one inside. Glad to see there weren't many customers, he ran across the lobby towards the far set of glass doors. The whole time, scanning the bank for Alize, but not finding her.

Insane and Dirt were the loud ones, their booming voices echoed throughout the once calm lobby. "Get-da-fuck-down! Step away from the registers!" Within seconds, they were on the employee side of the counter, stuffing money into a pile of cheap backpacks. "Faces down, people! If you wanna make it home tonight, you'll keep ya' fuckin' faces down!"

During all of this, Talton watched Staxx and Snubbz blitzing the side offices, quickly coming out of each one until they reached the third room. When he saw them go in, he expected them to come back out. But they didn't, and he could've swore he heard Alize yelling at them in the background. Then his attention was diverted; K.P. called him from across the lobby, "Gangsta! Heads up, uz!"

He looked up just in time to catch the backpack that was flying through the air. For a split second he wasn't there with a black T-shirt wrapped around his face. He was at Show Girls and the backpack he just caught wasn't a backpack at all. It was a leather Dominatrix vest. Then came another bag, and two more were tossed to K.P. That's when he heard the shots.

"Pop! Pop! Pop! Pop!"

Then Snubbz came running out of the room where the shots had come from. The same office where Talton heard Alize yelling. Staxx came out next, carrying his share of backpacks, plus several currency bags with Wachovia etched across them.

Killa Dirt came flying over the counter like an

Olympic hurdle jumper, toting two backpacks in each hand. Insane B smashed through the half-doors at the end of the teller's barrier carrying the same amount.

They were almost home free. Talton's job was to cover the rear, and he did this, but as he passed the room from where he heard the gunshots, he had to look in. He had to see for himself. On his way out he looked in through the room's window and saw a woman crouched down in the corner, afraid to look up. Then he noticed a body slumped over an overturned chair. It was impossible to see who it was, but he recognized the shoes. They were Ze's.

Gangsta stopped and reached for the door, but then he heard a familiar voice calling him. "Come on, blood!" It was K.P., the clique was waiting. Talton turned towards the exit and the rest became a blur. He made it to the truck; he opened its door; he got in. They drove away. In the minutes that followed their successful getaway, there were celebratory cheers in which he didn't participate in. Music played, a blunt was passed around. Talton wasn't there, though. He felt weightless, heartbroken, and lost.

As they left Clearwater, the clique went through their own, individual versions of what took place during the jux. But no one mentioned the shooting. It was an unspoken rule amongst thieves; murders were never discussed. By the end of the night, most of them would be on the plane heading back to California, where rumors of a bank heist would be whispered throughout the neighborhood, yet Alize's death would never be spoken of. As if she had never existed.

About an hour into the drive, Talton remembered that Brittany's phone was in the glove compartment. For a second he thought of checking for missed calls, but then he figured it wouldn't matter so he tossed it out the window. If only he would have taken the time to check his messages, he would've heard Brittany's voice...

"Talton, this is Brit-Brit. I've wanted to tell you something really important, but something always comes up. So, I'm just gonna tell you. My sister loves you and I know you love her too. That's why I think you need to know this. Alize doesn't have a son. She did, but he's dead. Four years ago she was committed to a mental hospital for killing him. Ever since, she's been in denial and refuses to admit that he's gone. Then she met you and she's been getting better. I just dropped her off at the house where your baby mamma's at and I think your problems will be over by the time she comes back out. Talton...when the smoke clears, please don't break her heart."

To be continued...

MIKE ENEMIGO PRESENTS

THE CELL BLOCK

MIKE ENEMIGO is the new prison/street art sensation who has written and published several books. He is inspired by emotion; hope; pain; dreams and nightmares. He physically lives somewhere in a California prison cell where he works relentlessly creating his next piece. His mind and soul are elsewhere; seeing, studying, learning, and drawing inspiration to tear down suppressive walls and inspire the culture by pushing artistic boundaries.

THE CELL BLOCK is an independent multimedia company with the objective of accurately conveying the prison/street experience with the credibility and honesty that only one who has lived it can deliver, through literature and other arts, and to entertain and enlighten while doing so. Everything published by The Cell Block has been created by a prisoner, while in a prison cell.

THE BEST RESOURCE DIRECTORY FOR PRISONERS, $17.95 & $5.00 S/H: This book has over 1,450 resources for prisoners! Includes: Pen-Pal Companies! Non-Nude Photo Sellers! Free Books and Other Publications! Legal Assistance! Prisoner Advocates! Prisoner Assistants! Correspondence Education! Money-Making Opportunities! Resources for Prison Writers, Poets, Artists! And much, much more! Anything you can think of doing from your prison cell, this book contains the resources to do it!

A GUIDE TO RELAPSE PREVENTION FOR PRISONERS, $15.00 & $5.00 S/H: This book provides the information and guidance that can make a real difference in the preparation of a comprehensive relapse prevention plan. Discover how to meet the parole board's expectation using these proven and practical principles. Included is a blank template and sample relapse prevention plan to assist in your preparation.

THEE ENEMY OF THE STATE (SPECIAL EDITION), $9.99 & $4.00 S/H: Experience the inspirational journey of a kid who was introduced to the art of rapping in 1993, struggled between his dream of becoming a professional rapper and the reality of the streets, and was finally offered a recording deal in 1999, only to be arrested minutes later and eventually sentenced to life in prison for murder... However, despite his harsh reality, he dedicated himself to hip-hop once again, and with resilience and determination, he sets out to prove he may just be one of the dopest rhyme writers/spitters ever .... At this point, it becomes deeper than rap .... Welcome to a preview of the greatest story you never heard.

LOST ANGELS: $15.00 & $5.00: David Rodrigo was a child who belonged to no world; rejected for his mixed heritage by most of his family and raised by an outcast uncle in the mean streets of East L.A. Chance cast him into a far darker and more devious pit of intrigue that stretched from the barest gutters to the halls of power in the great city. Now, to survive the clash of lethal forces arrayed about him, and to protect those he loves, he has only two allies; his quick wits, and the flashing blade that earned young David the street name, Viper.

LOYALTY AND BETRAYAL DELUXE EDITION, $19.99 & $7.00 S/H: Chunky was an associate of and soldier for the notorious Mexican Mafia – La Eme. That is, of course, until he was betrayed by those, he was most loyal to. Then he vowed to become their worst enemy. And though they've attempted to kill him numerous times, he still to this day is running around making a mockery of their organization .... This is the story of how it all began.

MONEY IZ THE MOTIVE: SPECIAL 2-IN-1 EDITION, $19.99 & $7.00 S/H: Like most kids growing up in the hood, Kano has a dream of going from rags to riches. But when his plan to get fast money by robbing the local "mom and pop" shop goes wrong, he quickly finds himself sentenced to serious prison time. Follow Kano as he is schooled to the ways of the game by some of the most respected OGs whoever did it; then is set free and given the resources to put his schooling into action and build the ultimate hood empire...

DEVILS & DEMONS: PART 1, $15.00 & $5.00 S/H: When Talton leaves the West Coast to set up shop in Florida he meets the female version of himself: A drug dealing murderess with psychological issues. A whirlwind of sex, money and murder inevitably ensues and Talton finds himself on the run from the law with nowhere to turn to. When his team from home finds out he's in trouble, they get on a plane heading south...

DEVILS & DEMONS: PART 2, $15.00 & $5.00 S/H: The Game is bitter-sweet for Talton, aka Gangsta. The same West Coast Clique who came to his aid ended up putting bullets into the chest of the woman he had fallen in love with. After leaving his ride or die in a puddle of her own blood, Talton finds himself on a flight back to Oak Park, the neighborhood where it all started...

DEVILS & DEMONS: PART 3, $15.00 & $5.00 S/H: Talton is on the road to retribution for the murder of the love of his life. Dante and his crew of killers are on a path of no return. This urban classic is based on real-life West Coast underworld politics. See what happens when a group of YG's find themselves in the midst of real underworld demons...

DEVILS & DEMONS: PART 4, $15.00 & $5.00 S/H: After waking up from a coma, Alize has locked herself away from the rest of the world. When her sister Brittany and their friend finally take her on a girl's night out, she meets Luck – a drug dealing womanizer.

FREAKY TALES, $15.00 & $5.00 S/H: Freaky Tales is the first book in a brand-new erotic series. King Guru, author of the *Devils & Demons* books, has put together a collection of sexy short stories and memoirs. In true TCB fashion, all of the erotic tales included in this book have been loosely based on true accounts told to, or experienced by the author.

THE ART & POWER OF LETTER WRITING FOR PRISONERS: DELUXE EDITION $19.99 & $7.00 S/H: When locked inside a prison cell, being able to write well is the most powerful skill you can have! Learn how to increase your power by writing high-quality personal and formal letters! Includes letter templates, pen-pal website strategies, punctuation guide and more!

THE PRISON MANUAL: $24.99 & $7.00 S/H: *The Prison Manual* is your all-in-one book on how to not only survive the rough terrain of the American prison system, but use it to your advantage so you can THRIVE from it! How to Use Your Prison Time to YOUR Advantage; How to Write Letters that Will Give You Maximum Effectiveness; Workout and Physical Health Secrets that Will Keep You as FIT as Possible; The Psychological impact of incarceration and How to Maintain Your MAXIMUM Level of Mental Health; Prison Art Techniques; Fulfilling Food Recipes; Parole Preparation Strategies and much, MUCH more!

GET OUT, STAY OUT!, $16.95 & $5.00 S/H: This book should be in the hands of everyone in a prison cell. It reveals a challenging but clear course for overcoming the obstacles that stand between prisoners and their freedom. For those behind bars, one goal outshines all others: GETTING OUT! After being released, that goal then shifts to STAYING OUT! This book will help prisoners do both. It has been masterfully constructed into five parts that will help prisoners maximize focus while they strive to accomplish whichever goal is at hand.

MOB$TAR MONEY, $12.00 & $4.00 S/H: After Trey's mother is sent to prison for 75 years to life, he and his little brother are moved from their home in Sacramento, California, to his grandmother's house in Stockton, California where he is forced to find his way in life and become a man on his own in the city's grimy streets. One day, on his way home from the local corner store, Trey has a rough encounter with the neighborhood bully. Luckily, that's when Tyson, a member of the MOBTAR, a local "get money" gang comes to his aid. The two kids quickly become friends, and it doesn't take long before Trey is embraced into the notorious MOB$TAR money gang, which opens the door to an adventure full of sex, money, murder and mayhem that will change his life forever... You will never guess how this story ends!

BLOCK MONEY, $12.00 & $4.00 S/H: Beast, a young thug from the grimy streets of central Stockton, California lives The Block; breathes The Block; and has committed himself to bleed The Block for all it's worth until his very last breath. Then, one day, he meets Nadia; a stripper at the local club who piques his curiosity with her beauty, quick-witted intellect and rider qualities. The problem? She has a man – Esco – a local kingpin with money and power. It doesn't take long, however, before a devious plot is hatched to pull off a heist worth an indeterminable amount of money. Following the acts of treachery, deception and betrayal are twists and turns and a bloody war that will leave you speechless!

HOW TO HUSTLE AND WIN: SEX, MONEY, MURDER EDITION $15.00 & $5.00 S/H: *How To Hu$tle and Win: Sex, Money, Murder Edition* is the grittiest, underground self-help manual for the 21st century street entrepreneur in print. Never has there been such a book written for today's gangsters, goons and go-getters. This self-help handbook is an absolute must-have for anyone who is actively connected to the streets.

RAW LAW: YOUR RIGHTS, & HOW TO SUE WHEN THEY ARE VIOLATED! $15.00 & $5.00 S/H: *Raw Law For Prisoners* is a clear and concise guide for prisoners and their advocates to understanding civil rights laws guaranteed to prisoners under the US Constitution, and how to successfully file a lawsuit when those rights have been violated! From initial complaint to trial, this book will take you through the entire process, step by step, in simple, easy-to-understand terms. Also included are several examples where prisoners have sued prison officials successfully, resulting in changes of unjust rules and regulations and recourse for rights violations, oftentimes resulting in rewards of thousands, even millions of dollars in damages! If you feel your rights have been violated, don't lash out at guards, which is usually ineffective and only makes matters worse. Instead, defend yourself successfully by using the legal system, and getting the power of the courts on your side!

HOW TO WRITE URBAN BOOKS FOR

MONEY & FAME: $16.95 & $5.00 S/H: Inside this book you will learn the true story of how Mike Enemigo and King Guru have received money and fame from inside their prison cells by writing urban books; the secrets to writing hood classics so you, too, can be caked up and famous; proper punctuation using hood examples; and resources you can use to achieve your money motivated ambitions! If you're a prisoner who want to write urban novels for money and fame, this must-have manual will give you all the game!

PRETTY GIRLS LOVE BAD BOYS: AN INMATE'S GUIDE TO GETTING GIRLS: $15.00 & $5.00 S/H: Tired of the same, boring, cliché pen pal books that don't tell you what you really need to know? If so, this book is for you! Anything you need to know on the art of long and short distance seduction is included within these pages! Not only does it give you the science of attracting pen pals from websites, it also includes psychological profiles and instructions on how to seduce any woman you set your sights on! Includes interviews of women who have fallen in love with prisoners, bios for pen pal ads, pre-written love letters, romantic poems, love-song lyrics, jokes and much, much more! This book is the ultimate guide – a must-have for any prisoner who refuses to let prison walls affect their MAC'n.

THE LADIES WHO LOVE PRISONERS, $15.00 & $5.00 S/H: New Special Report reveals the secrets of real women who have fallen in love with prisoners, regardless of crime, sentence, or location. This info will give you a HUGE advantage in getting girls from prison.

THE MILLIONAIRE PRISONER: PART 1, $16.95 & $5.00 S/H

THE MILLIONAIRE PRISONER: PART 2, $16.95 & $5.00 S/H

THE MILLIONAIRE PRISONER: SPECIAL 2-IN-1 EDITION, $24.99 & $7.00 S/H: Why wait until you get out of prison to achieve your dreams? Here's a blueprint that you can use to become successful! *The Millionaire Prisoner* is your complete reference to overcoming any obstacle in prison. You won't be able to put it down! With this book you will discover the secrets to: Making money from your cell! Obtain FREE money for correspondence courses! Become an expert on any topic! Develop the habits of the rich! Network with celebrities! Set up your own website! Market your products, ideas and services! Successfully use prison pen pal websites! All of this and much, much more! This book has enabled thousands of prisoners to succeed and it will show you the way also!

THE MILLIONAIRE PRISONER 3: SUCCESS UNIVERSITY, $16.95 & $5 S/H: Why wait until you get out of prison to achieve your dreams? Here's a new-look blueprint that you can use to be successful! *The Millionaire Prisoner 3* contains advanced strategies to overcoming any obstacle in prison. You won't be able to put it down!

THE MILLIONAIRE PRISONER 4: PEN PAL MASTERY, $16.95 & $5.00 S/H: Tired of subpar results? Here's a master blueprint that you can use to get tons of pen pals! *TMP 4: Pen Pal Mastery* is your complete roadmap to finding your one true love. You won't be able to put it down! With this book you'll DISCOVER the SECRETS to: Get FREE pen pals & which sites are best to use; Successful tactics female prisoners can win with; Use astrology to find love; friendship & more; Build a winning social media presence; Playing phone tag & successful sex talk; Hidden benefits of foreign pen pals; Find your success mentors; Turning "hits" into friendships; Learn how to write letters/emails that get results. All of this and much more!

GET OUT, GET RICH: HOW TO GET PAID LEGALLY WHEN YOU GET OUT OF PRISON!, $16.95 & $5.00 S/H: Many of you are incarcerated for a money-motivated crime. But w/ today's tech & opportunities, not only is the crime-for-money risk/reward ratio not strategically wise, it's not even necessary. You can earn much more money by partaking in any one of the easy, legal hustles explained in this book, regardless of your record. Help yourself earn an honest income so you can not only make a lot of money, but say good-bye to penitentiary chances and prison forever! (Note: Many things in this book can even he done from inside prison.) (ALSO PUBLISHED AS *HOOD MILLIONAIRE: HOW TO HUSTLE AND WIN LEGALLY!*)

THE CEO MANUAL: HOW TO START A BUSINESS WHEN YOU GET OUT OF PRISON, $16.95 & $5.00 S/H: $16.95 & $5 S/H: This new book will teach you the simplest way to start your own business when you get out of prison. Includes: Start-up Steps! The Secrets to Pulling Money from

Investors! How to Manage People Effectively! How To Legally Protect Your Assets from "them"! Hundreds of resources to get you started, including a list of "loan friendly" banks! (ALSO PUBLISHED AS *CEO MANUAL: START A BUSINESS, BE A BOSS!*)

THE MONEY MANUAL: UNDERGROUND CASH SECRETS EXPOSED! 16.95 & $5.00 S/H: Becoming a millionaire is equal parts what you make, and what you don't spend – AKA save. All Millionaires and Billionaires have mastered the art of not only making money, but keeping the money they make (remember Donald Trump's tax maneuvers?), as well as establishing credit so that they are loaned money by banks and trusted with money from investors: AKA OPM – other people's money. And did you know there are millionaires and billionaires just waiting to GIVE money away? It's true! These are all very-little known secrets "they" don't want YOU to know about, but that I'm exposing in my new book!

HOOD MILLIONAIRE; HOW TO HUSTLE & WIN LEGALLY, $16.95 & $5.00 S/H: Hustlin' is a way of life in the hood. We all have money motivated ambitions, not only because we gotta eat, but because status is oftentimes determined by one's own salary. To achieve what we consider financial success, we often invest our efforts into illicit activities – we take penitentiary chances. This leads to a life in and out of prison, sometimes death – both of which are counterproductive to gettin' money. But there's a solution to this, and I have it...

CEO MANUAL: START A BUSINESS BE A BOSS, $16.95 & $5.00 S/H: After the success of the urban-entrepreneur classic *Hood Millionaire: How To Hustle & Win Legally!*, self-made millionaires Mike Enemigo and Sav Hustle team back up to bring you the latest edition of the Hood Millionaire series – *CEO Manual: Start A Business, Be A Boss!* In this latest collection of game laying down the art of "hoodpreneurship", you will learn such things as: 5 Core Steps to Starting Your Own Business! 5 Common Launch Errors You Must Avoid! How To Write a Business Plan! How To Legally Protect Your Assets From "Them"! How To Make Your Business Fundable, Where to Get Money for Your Start-up Business, and even How to Start a Business With No Money! You will learn How to Drive Customers to Your Website, How to Maximize Marketing Dollars, Contract Secrets for the savvy boss, and much, much more! And as an added bonus, we have included over 200 Business Resources, from government agencies and small business development centers, to a secret list of small-business friendly banks that will help you get started!

PAID IN FULL: WELCOME TO DA GAME, $15.00 & $5.00 S/H. In 1983, the movie *Scarface* inspired many kids growing up in America's inner cities to turn their rags into riches by becoming cocaine kingpins. Harlem's Azie Faison was one of them. Faison would ultimately connect with Harlem's Rich Porter and Alpo Martinez, and the trio would go on to become certified street legends of the '80s and early '90s. Years later, Dame Dash and Roc-A-Fella

Films would tell their story in the based-on-actual-events movie, *Paid in Full*. But now, we are telling the story our way – The Cell Block way – where you will get a perspective of the story that the movie did not show, ultimately learning an outcome that you did not expect. Book one of our series, *Paid in Full: Welcome to da Game*, will give you an inside look at a key player in this story, one that is not often talked about – Lulu, the Columbian cocaine kingpin with direct ties to Pablo Escobar, who plugged Azie in with an unlimited amount of top-tier cocaine at dirt-cheap prices that helped boost the trio to neighborhood superstars and certified kingpin status... until greed, betrayal, and murder destroyed everything....

OJ'S LIFE BEHIND BARS, $15.00 & $5 S/H: In 1994, Heisman Trophy winner and NFL superstar OJ Simpson was arrested for the brutal murder of his ex-wife Nicole Brown-Simpson and her friend Ron Goldman. In 1995, after the "trial of the century," he was acquitted of both murders, though most of the world believes he did it. In 2007 OJ was again arrested, but this time in Las Vegas, for armed robbery and kidnapping. On October 3, 2008 he was found guilty sentenced to 33 years and was sent to Lovelock Correctional Facility, in Lovelock, Nevada. There he met inmate-author Vernon Nelson. Vernon was granted a true, insider's perspective into the mind and life of one of the country's most notorious men; one that has never been provided…until now.

BLINDED BY BETRAYAL, $15.00 & $5.00 S/H. Khalil wanted nothing more than to chase his rap dream when he got out of prison. After all, a fellow inmate had connected him with a major record producer that could help him take his career to unimaginable heights, and his girl is in full support of his desire to trade in his gun for a mic. Problem is, Khalil's crew, the notorious Blood Money Squad, awaited him with open arms, unaware of his desire to leave the game alone, and expected him to jump head first into the life of fast money and murder. Will Khalil be able to balance his desire to get out of the game with the expectations of his gang to participate in it? Will he be able to pull away before it's too late? Or, will the streets pull him right back in, ultimately causing his demise? One thing for sure, the streets are loyal to no one, and blood money comes with bloody consequences....

THE MOB, $16.99 & $5 S/H. PaperBoy is a Bay Area boss who has invested blood, sweat, and years into building The Mob – a network of Bay Area Street legends, block bleeders, and underground rappers who collaborate nationwide in the interest of pushing a multi-million-dollar criminal enterprise of sex, drugs, and murder.

AOB, $15.00 & $5 S/H. Growing up in the Bay Area, Manny Fresh the Best had a front-row seat to some of the coldest players to ever do it. And you already know, A.O.B. is the name of the Game! So, When Manny Fresh slides through Stockton one day and sees Rosa, a stupid-bad Mexican chick with a whole lotta 'talent' behind her walking down the street tryna get some money, he knew immediately what he had to do: Put it In My Pocket!

AOB 2, $15.00 & $5 S/H.

AOB 3, $15.00 & $5 S/H

PIMPOLOGY: THE 7 ISMS OF THE GAME, $15.00 & $5 S/H: It's been said that if you knew better, you'd do better. So, in the spirit of dropping jewels upon the rare few who truly want to know how to win, this collection of exclusive Game has been compiled. And though a lot of so-called players claim to know how the Pimp Game is supposed to go, none have revealed the real. . . Until now!

JAILHOUSE PUBLISHING FOR MONEY, POWER & FAME: $24.99 & $7 S/H: In 2010, after flirting with the idea for two years, Mike Enemigo started writing his first book. In 2014, he officially launched his publishing company, The Cell Block, with the release of five books. Of course, with no mentor(s), how-to guides, or any real resources, he was met with failure after failure as he tried to navigate the treacherous goal of publishing books from his prison cell. However, he was determined to make it. He was determined to figure it out and he refused to quit. In Mike's new book, *Jailhouse Publishing for Money, Power, and Fame,* he breaks down all his jailhouse publishing secrets and strategies, so you can do all he's done, but without the trials and tribulations he's had to go through...

KITTY KAT, ADULT ENTERTAINMENT RESOURCE BOOK, $24.99 & $7.00 S/H: This book is jam packed with hundreds of sexy non nude photos including photo spreads. The book contains the complete info on sexy photo sellers, hot magazines, page turning bookstore, sections on strip clubs, porn stars, alluring models, thought provoking stories and must-see movies.

PRISON LEGAL GUIDE, $24.99 & $7.00 S/H: The laws of the U.S. Judicial system are complex, complicated, and always growing and changing. Many prisoners spend days on end digging through its intricacies. Pile on top of the legal code the rules and regulations of a correctional facility, and you can see how high the deck is being stacked against you. Correct legal information is the key to your survival when you have run afoul of the system (or it is running afoul of you). Whether you are an accomplished jailhouse lawyer helping newbies learn the ropes, an old head fighting bare-knuckle for your rights in the courts, or a hustler just looking to beat the latest write-up – this book has something for you!

PRISON HEALTH HANDBOOK, $19.99 & $7.00 S/H: The Prison Health Handbook is your one-stop go-to source for information on how to maintain your best health while inside the American prison system. Filled with information, tips, and secrets from doctors, gurus, and other experts, this book will educate you on such things as proper workout and exercise regimens; yoga benefits for prisoners; how to meditate effectively; pain management tips; sensible dieting solutions; nutritional knowledge; an understanding of various cancers, diabetes, hepatitis, and other diseases all too common in prison; how to effectively deal with mental health issues such as stress, PTSD, anxiety, and depression; a list of things your doctors DON'T want YOU to know; and much, much more!

All books are available on thecellblock.net.

You can also order by sending a money order or institutional check to:

The Cell Block; PO Box 1025; Rancho Cordova, CA 95741